H50 12

D0518563

Hertfordshire

Please renew/return this item by the last date shown.

So that your telephone call is charged at local rate, please call the numbers as set out below:

	From Area codes 01923 or 020:	From the rest of Herts:
Renewals:	01923 471373	01438 737373
Enquiries:	01923 471333	01438 737333
Textphone:	01923 471599	01438 737599

L32   www.hertsdirect.org/librarycatalogue

SCHOLARS AND SOLDIERS

Other books by Mary Gentle:

A HAWK IN SILVER
GOLDEN WITCHBREED
ANCIENT LIGHT

SCHOLARS AND SOLDIERS

A Story Collection

MARY GENTLE

Macdonald

A Macdonald Book

First published in Great Britain in 1989
by Macdonald & Co (Publishers) Ltd
London & Sydney

British Library Cataloguing in Publication Data

Gentle, Mary, 1956-
Scholars and soldiers.
I. Title
823'.914 [F]

ISBN 0-356-17893-5

Typeset by Leaper & Gard Ltd, Bristol, England
Printed in Great Britain by
Richard Clay Ltd, Bungay, Suffolk
Macdonald & Co (Publishers) Ltd
66-73 Shoe Lane
London EC4P 4AB
A member of Maxwell Pergamon Publishing Corporation plc

Contents

Acknowledgements

To George Hay, for telling me I ought to read Frances Yates'
The Art of Memory and thus getting me hooked on Early
Modern Science and things Hermetic. Thanks, George . . .

To Jaime and Beto Hernandez, for *Love and Rockets*. Because
these are great comix. Because they taught me things about
story-pacing. Not least because of the immortal Hopey. Thank
you.

And to
BEN JONSON (1572–1637)

Introduction

by

NEIL GAIMAN

Scene: A fairground. Persons of anachronistic but stylish demeanour and dress walk back and forth, juggling fire, elegant cats, faster than light drives and extremely sharp blades. Dancing bears tread lumbering pavanes, and hawkers sell candied plums and overspiced cuts of roast lizard.

In the centre of the fair is a brightly coloured tent, and in front of that, a raised platform. From the tent steps a Prologue, in black motley, carrying a scroll. He unrolls it, and commences to read:

'The author bade me come to introduce her tales —' he pauses. Pulls out a quill pen, scritches out a word or two, begins again, 'Now, Mistress Gentle bade me come to introduce her tales (which follow this) to all of you . . .'

A soldier in the crowd, her fancy-boy on one arm, waves at him, and shouts, 'This Mistress Gentle. She's an *author*, then?'

The Prologue nods.

'I always thought that authors were fabulous beasts,' says the soldier with the air of someone misquoting deliberately (proving herself, perhaps, something of a scholar).

'Some of us are, some of us aren't,' says the Prologue, preening slightly.

The soldier frowns. 'So. This author of yours, Mistress, um . . .'

'Gentle.'

'Right. Mistress Gentle. What kind of an author is *she*?'

The Prologue lays down his scroll regretfully, and sighs. 'The better sort. Like all the very best authors she dresses in black, reads comics — *Love and Rockets*, for preference,

7

devoured an unhealthy amount of science fiction (and everything else), as a kid, knows her way around Croydon . . .'

'Is that important?' asks the Soldier.

'Essential.' The Prologue takes up his scroll, and is about to
begin once more, when the soldier asks,

'But what *kind* of author is she?'

The Prologue hesitates.

Another member of the audience (fat, huge as Chesterton or
Aquinas, with globs of lizard-fat still adhering to his chin) chips
in, 'The way *I* see it, she's part of the late twentieth century
cultural fusion. The melting pot (in its true meaning as
crucible) that brings forth, occasionally, gold from dross. In the
stories that follow we can see her gradually assimilating her
influences; from glittery SF to Restoration Drama, from Low
Tragedy to High Comedy, from punk comic-books to Hermetic
philosophy, from courtly fantasy to uncouth horror (and, given
her cultural parameters, vice versa), finally producing something distinctly, uniquely her own.'

'Yeah. What he said,' agrees with Prologue, picking up his
scroll, and clearing his throat. 'Ahem! Mistress Gentle bade me
come this day to introduce her stories to you all. For here are
knights and gallants, and alarums, and here are fantasies and
flights historical, futurities (the fair, the dark, the lost), and —'

'Look, that's quite enough of that,' interrupts the soldier,
her hand on her sword hilt. 'What kind of an author *is* she?'

The Prologue puts his scroll inside his battered black leather
jacket, asks testily. 'What exactly are you asking?'

'Just what I said.'

He sighs. 'Okay. Her hair is currently reddish . . .' An idea
strikes him. He reaches back into his jacket pocket, pulls out a
first folio of *Antony and Cleopatra*, leafs through it, cracked,
yellowed paper falling like confetti, and reads:

Lepidus: *What manner of thing is your crocodile?*

Antony: *It is shaped, sir, just like itself, and it is as broad as it
hath breadth; it is just so high as it is, and moves with its own
organs; it lives by that which nourisheth it; and the elements once
out of it, it transmigrates.*

Lepidus: *What colour is it of?*

Antony: *Of its own colour too.*

Lepidus: *'Tis a strange serpent.*

Antony: *'Tis so; and the tears of it are wet.*

He puts the script away, adjusts his shades. 'There.'

The soldier sighs, tiring of this discussion, eager to be off. 'So Mistress Gentle . . .?'

'Is a strange serpent, yes.'

She turns on her heel, pauses, turns her head, and says, 'There's still one question you haven't answered.'

'And that is?'

'What kind of an author is she?'

The prologue grins. 'Prologues never tell you *that.* For that you gotta read the stories.'

The Soldier nods, curtly, and leaves.

The Prologue walks back into his tent, and he too is gone.

Outside the hawkers offer passers-by sweetmeats and roasted lizards, the tumblers continue to tumble, the small animals, coloured balls, asteroids and dice follow each other through the air, the courtesans (of all sexes) continue to ply their trade, and the bears still dance; and the soldiers and the scholars walk together and in the gathering dusk it is increasingly difficult to tell them apart . . .

Neil Gaiman
May 1989

Beggars in Satin

A Scholar-Soldier got down from the steam train, outside the City gate.

Chancellor Scaris called, 'Master-Captain!'

Yellow dust settled down.

She shifted the strap off her shoulder, setting her bundle down at her feet – a satchel holding scrolls. Her sword-hanger was plain. The sword-hilt was wrapped with leather, stained with sweat.

As she bent to adjust the buckles that held scabbard and sword, a braid fell forward. There was grey in her cinnamon-tawny hair, and at her temples it was growing out white. But when she straightened up and squinted against the sun, there were few lines about her eyes: she looked no more than thirty.

Scaris called again. His words were lost in the noise of the train: the steam, the pistons, and the whine of the siren as it pulled away from the city gate in haste. Nevertheless, she looked directly at him.

He walked across the gate-place to where she waited.

'You're the Chancellor?' she said. 'Scaris?'

'And you the Scholar-Soldier Valentine.'

'Why am I not received as that deserves?'

The hard smell of coal and steam was still in his mouth. Sunlight gleamed on the iron rails, and the clanking of the cars faded. The woman's head tilted, listening.

'Why is there no one here?'

Chancellor Scaris looked at the sandstone walls, now un-patrolled; at the gates that stood unguarded. Grass grew in small golden tufts on the street. No market-stalls, no carts from the provinces; no distant fall (felt through the soles of the feet) of the piledrivers on the building-ground.

'Would he send for you,' Scaris said, 'the Lord-Architect Casaubon, would he send for you if he didn't need you?'

Walking the lanes beside the little man, Valentine trod the earth easily. Some few citizens stared out of shutters as they went by, faces hooded. Most of the leaning two- and three-storey buildings were daubed across the windows with silver paint, that glittered in the sun.

The satchel weighed heavier on her back than its load of scrawled paper would seem to justify.

She glanced down at Scaris.

'My business is to know and to fight,' she said. 'The sooner you tell me what you have here, the sooner I'll get rid of it.'

'Master-Captain, wait –'

'Call me Valentine,' she said, 'and tell me why your Lord-Architect needs a Scholar-Soldier?'

He blinked up at her through white hair that the wind blew across his eyes. Dust stained his embroidered black satin robe; heavy in the summer heat. She saw it was cut to disguise a slightly-humped shoulder.

'You're very sure of yourself,' he said.

'Oh, see you, I've fought a dozen of these matters out in the last year; I was at Karsethra, with the Master-Captain Lindsay, and at Baynard with Tobias Frith, and I assure you, there's not a Scholar-Soldier better for your contest than Valentine . . .'

Scaris's eyes narrowed.

'And for finding out your causes, first and secondary, your sources and origins, and many methods of discovery –'

'There is none better than your Valentine?' he completed, drily.

The lanes became wider. They had to detour round an aban-

doned carriage, the ox dead in the shafts and buzzing with
flies. Valentine saw a figure scuttle across the road ahead, too
far away to tell if it were child or man.

'Master-Captain,' Scaris said.

'Well, sir?'

'Whatever we have,' he said softly, 'it is no shame to be
afraid of it.'

Valentine's boots clacked on stone. Cracked paving sprouted
goldenrod and wild roses. She sneezed, abruptly, hit by pollen;
and then hitched her sword-belt over her shoulder with one
hand, and swung the satchel by its strap with the other.

'I don't know the meaning of the word "fear",' she said.
'Terror, yes; blind panic, yes; but fear? Me?'

Scaris laughed. It was an unfamiliar emotion. He looked the
woman up and down: her cinnamon hair escaping from its six
Scholar's braids; her tanned hands; her rough cotton shirt and
breeches. She was still talking:

'– at Mildenhall I was the only one not to run, when Master-
Captain Eliade fainted dead away on the spot, and then in
Hurot, but you wouldn't know the university barracks there – '

Chuckling, Scaris held up a hand to stem her chatter, and a
swiftness passed him, swift as a bird's flight, or a bee, and a
bead of blood grew in his palm, drawn out by its passing. He
yelled. Pain, bright as metal, stabbed him.

Valentine, ceasing the deliberate flow of inanity, drew her
sword left-handed, and swung the bulging satchel into her
assailant's stomach. He doubled over with a *Whoof!* and the
flat of her sword slammed into his temple.

'Captain!'

Warned, she ducked. Scaris pressed himself back against the
wall of the nearest house, feet scrabbling, seeking a doorway to
hide in. He yelled again. Valentine parried the other assailant's
blow, and – as easily as if the man had consented to it – lifted
his blade with hers and spun it away across the street in a great
flashing cartwheel of metal and sun. She was caught wrong-
footed for a thrust, and by the time she recovered, the man was
running.

'Leave him!' Scaris said, as out of breath as if he had been
the one fighting.

The Scholar-Soldier lifted her blade in a brief salute. Then

she sheathed it, and knelt down to roll over her unconscious assailant. A man, dark haired and with a reddish-dark
beard, he was of middle years. There was a smear of some
semi-transparent substance across his forehead. She touched it:
brought away fingers blotched with silver paint. She looked up
at Scaris:

'Now is this a common cut-purse, or sent for you, or sent for
me, do you think?'

Scaris's blood hammered in his ears. The man was sprawled
on his back on the paving-stones, beard thrust up towards the
sky. The silver paint on his brow caught the sunlight.

'My guards have shut themselves away, for fear,' he said.
'And no one knew that you were coming here, Master-
Captain.'

Valentine sucked a grazed knuckle. She knelt again, to pack
the scattered papers from her satchel. Scaris watched her walk
past him and pick up the thrown dart, inspect the tip, and toss
it away.

'No venom,' she said. She tugged out her kerchief and took
his hand, wrapping the cloth round the cut on his palm. Scaris
shuddered. Then, thinking how that must seem, looked up, and
met her eyes (that were almost more red than brown) and said:

'Thanks, Valentine.'

She hesitated before she smiled.

'We must *hurry*,' Scaris said.

The Lord-Architect Casaubon saw them arrive.

So deep and so blue a summer's sky shone over the city that
it made the marble of the buildings dazzle. The great fretted
facades held angular pieces of sky trapped, in their interstices:
blue on white.

Floridly carved white columns, and rows of pillars, and
covered walks, stretched away around all four sides of the
square. Beyond the towering blocks that were the marble-faced
palaces of the City, Casaubon saw domes, curtain walls, house
facades with niches and statues. But it was the square itself
that dwarfed the man and the woman.

They came through the great Sea Gate, whose marble
breakers reared up fifty feet, ready to crash down in stony surf.
A little man in black robes, his head at this distance no bigger

than the head of a pin; and walking with him a figure in brown, equally ant-like . . .

Casaubon shrugged to himself, dug his fingers into the aspic-jar and pulled out another White Gull, ripped the wing from the body, and began to gnaw it. Spots of gelatine spattered his blue coat, unbuttoned to the waist. He stopped chewing for a moment, his eye caught by the proportions of the half-built wall in front of him – he dropped the cooked meat, scrabbled with filthy hands across his plan-table, and began to draw a succession of swift pencil-lines.

A minute of this, and then he ceased. He rubbed thoughtfully at the inadvertent marks of grease on the paper. Suddenly, he ripped it in two, threw it upwards, and let the wind bowl it across the wide acreage of the square, towards the approaching man and woman.

The woman loped five strides out of her way to snare the blowing paper: by that, Casaubon knew that she must be the Scholar-Soldier. He snorted to himself, knocked the neck off a bottle by rapping it on his drawing easel, and began – with delicate care – to drink from it.

And to wonder what he would say.

Valentine scrolled up the torn paper between her calloused hands. She paused, once, to look at a particular mark. Her curiously-coloured eyes blinked. Scaris, out of breath, grabbed her arm for support; and found his triceps caught in the strong fingers.

'No, no – unneccessary –'

White hair was sweat-plastered to his forehead.

'– the Lord-Architect –'

Valentine, amused, pushed the old man towards a low wall, saying, 'Sit down before you fall down!' Then she dropped her satchel at Scaris's feet, and turned to make her bow to the Lord-Architect Casaubon.

She stood at the foot of a shallow, walled flight of steps. A table and a metal easel stood on the first landing. Above that, the steps went up to end at a rough brick wall, and a stretch of cleared ground, two half-built walls of marble blocks, and a tower smothered in wooden-pole scaffolding.

The Lord-Architect sat on the top step, his belly spreading

over his thighs, the top two buttons of his breeches undone. He seemed about to burst the seams of his yellowed shirt and filthy blue satin coat. The sun gleamed on his tarnished brass buttons, and buckles, and on the bottle in his hand. Valentine judged him to be forty, perhaps forty-five. His fair skin was freckled, his red hair straggled down past his collar, and his hands were stained pitch-black with charcoal.

Casaubon ripped a mouthful from the capon in his free hand, half-saluted her with the bottle, and, spitting out fragments of food, said, 'Master-Captain! *Welcome.* Scaris, you fool, who frighted you? You're white as a headstone.'

'Noble Lord –'

'May the Great Architect rot your soul, you piddling little puppy! I've eaten better Chancellors than you for breakfast.'

Casaubon wiped his mouth with a filthy hand. He slammed the bottle down on the step beside him, and beckoned to Valentine.

'You took your time getting here,' he said, suddenly ungracious. 'How much are we paying you? You should have been here a week since!'

'If not for my – I won't say, valour, but take it how you will – neither of us would be here, noble Lord.'

Valentine stood with her fists on her hips, chin raised, staring up the flight of steps. And then she ran lightly up past the noble Lord-Architect, to the cleared building-ground and the half built walls. She squatted on her haunches, and put a hand to the earth.

Without turning, and in another tone altogether, she said, 'You're building a Miracle Garden. I congratulate you, noble Lord. True, Vitruvius authorizes a more westerly aspect, but I think you'll find Palladio differs in that, claims the northerly frontage no less efficient –'

The Lord-Architect Casaubon put his podgy fingers in his mouth and whistled. After a pause (and, by his frown, too long a pause) the square began to fill with running people: officers, guards, cellarers, stewards.

'Very like,' he answered Valentine, and then broke off to gesture to the officers. They set about dismantling the easel, removing the table, and replacing empty wine-bottles.

'Very like,' he repeated, 'if it weren't for this: that I have enemies. Master-Captain, have you heard of the Invisible College?'

Chancellor Scaris limped up the steps, resting every so often on the marble balustrade. He caught Valentine's eye, as she glanced over her shoulder.

'The noble Lord Casaubon has heard of the emnity between the Scholar-Soldiers and the reputed Invisible College. Tell me, Valentine, is there truth in that?'

The woman stood up. She tucked one of her loose braids back behind her ear; and Scaris saw again how white she was at the temples, and how young she was to be so. Behind her, earth and broken marble shimmered in the midday heat. The noise of the people in the square seemed oddly muffled. Where he stood, beside Casaubon, Scaris's nostrils wrinkled at the smell of old grease and cooking, and unwashed linen.

Valentine, with that new seriousness, said, 'Before I tell the noble Lord what I know of the Invisible College, the noble Lord must tell me why he's building a Garden, and what Garden it is, and what this Garden is for.'

'Rot you,' Casaubon said. 'I suppose I must.'

As she walked a few paces to the east, sighting on another half-built structure, Valentine saw the building-ground open up before her, and all but gaped at the extent of it. A tract of earth some two or three miles square had been slashed into the very heart of the City. Part showed traces of formal gardening. Most was overgrown: goldenrod, bramble, vine, and ivy tendrilling up towards the sun. She hid her amazement; stood looking, with condescension, one hand on the sand-abraded hilt of her sword.

'I'll show you the part of the Garden that I've succeeded – for the time being – in building,' Casaubon said. 'Scaris, stay here. You know it. No need to wrack your old bones for this. Master-Captain, this way.'

Scaris eased himself down onto the balustrade. He watched the fat man, and the woman, as they walked out onto the cleared building-ground. Heat made him sweat in his black robes. When they were a distance away, he made a sudden grab for the aspic-jar and, like a cormorant, pulled out a fragment of meat and began to munch it greedily.

Before he'd finished, a voice hailed him. He looked up, hurriedly wiping his mouth. The Scholar-Soldier beckoned, pointing back towards him; and he realised that her satchel still rested at his feet.

He picked it up to carry it to her. And was shocked at how little it weighed – as if the scrolls were friable wafers, for all their bulk.

When he reached them, they had walked back as far as the wide marble cup of a dry fountain. Valentine stood with her back to the sun, her shadow falling across the statue that, holding a vase, should give forth water. The noble Lord-Architect stomped irritably up and down. Valentine said something that Scaris didn't hear.

Casaubon spat into the fountain, and wiped his mouth with a lice-ridden sleeve. 'I know – I don't look the man to be searching for *spiritual* food. Do I? Forty years ago I didn't look like this. It's been a long fight. How old are you?' he demanded.

'Eighteen,' the woman said.

Scaris nearly dropped her pack.

'And how did you come by this?' Casaubon's fat finger touched the silver-white hair at her temple.

'It's been a long fight,' Valentine echoed.

Casaubon grunted. 'Come this way. Down here. I'll show you – a year's work, ruined.'

Valentine walked down wide steps into a sunken garden. A patch of order, surrounded by towering weeds. But now, on the cropped yellow grass, among the shaped dells and hummocks and hedges, the disorder could be forgotten – could it?

She reached behind her, without looking, and felt Chancellor Scaris put the strap of her pack into her hand.

A path was paved with square stones; into each square a pattern of interlocking circles was incised. The sun burned on her head. There was the rank smell of Casaubon's clothes. She squatted down, sorted through her satchel, and took out a bent and thumbed copy of a pamphlet. Then she straightened up, and walked on seven more steps.

The path went through a golden hedge, that was cropped into an arch over it, and on one side of the arch was a bronze statue of a child, and on the other a silver statue of an old man.

Valentine stepped onto an incised paving-stone.

Metal whined. A hollow voice, seeming to come from the bronze child, said, '*All bright youth ends soon in age!*'

She took the next step, onto a plain paving-stone, and a different voice sounded, apparently from the silver-metal statue of the ancient man:

'*All reverend age doth to corruption tend!*'

And as she passed under the hedge's arch, the two voices together said:

'*All things decay to the same end!*'

'Is that how you directed them to speak?' Valentine called back to Casaubon. He shook his head. She walked back, treading carefully, this time avoiding certain paving-stones. But when she was seven steps from the path, a hissing metal voice whispered, '*Hasten, hasten, even now your flesh rots on your bones!*'

'That's an ill trick,' she said, 'and a lesser person might be offended by it, noble Lord-Architect; your good fortune is to have me. How long have these automata been like this?'

'The pneumatic mechanisms were perfect,' Casaubon said soberly. 'I have had executed craftsmen who made me inferior work. These people know, now, to work well. This was to be a device to introduce visitors into the Miracle Garden. They were to speak common pleasantries, *Seize the Hour*, and *Love While Ye May*, to put one in mind of the pleasures of the flesh. Great Architect! Who knows what we're put in mind of now!'

A hiss of steam escaped the child-statue. It was almost like laughter.

'I swear, no hand has altered the mechanisms,' Casaubon added. 'They've been well guarded. And afterwards taken apart, and there is no mechanical reason for them to speak so! It must be the Invisible College. Who else?'

Valentine said nothing. Chancellor Scaris moved to her elbow, with a brief side-glance attempting to see what pamphlet it was that she thumbed through. *Pneumatithmie* and *Menadrie* caught his eye, and *Perspective*, *Stratarithmetrie*, and *Zographie*.

'See you,' Valentine invited, offering him the open page. 'There is your art of mechanical devices using air or water, that's your singing fountain or your speaking statue – *pneuma-*

tithmie. And your mathematical art used in moving with weights or pulleys, *menadrie*; and – but you know this, I'm sure.'

Scaris said, 'If you were to come this way, Master-Captain, I would show you what part of the Miracle Garden is of my own devising. Although I fear it is in as great a disarray as the Lord-Architect's statues.'

Valentine followed the noble Lord-Architect, who swore foully under his breath, and Scaris, past the speaking statues and into the hedged garden. Here, many metal and stone figures stood on plinths, or in niches. A slow mutter began to grow in the air around, of mockery, and oaths as foul as Casaubon's. The sun gleamed on the golden hedges, on complex topiary, and on the bindweed and ivy that ran riot across fountain, grotto, and fish-pool.

'It's my design to build a Memory Garden,' Scaris said.

Valentine blinked. 'The same as a memory-palace?'

'It would have the same locations, in which to place images,' Scaris said. 'Here.'

Passing under another topiary arch brought Valentine into a maze. The close-leafed hedges were trimmed smooth, with a marble pillar and plinth let into them at intervals of five or so yards, and larger topiary niches at the junctions of each maze-alley. Valentine walked down one alley, turned left and then right, right again, left . . .

Silence clung to the garden.

The tawny-gold leaves breathed out a heavy perfume. She rested a calloused hand on the nearest marble pillar, and the stone was hot in the sun. Then, as she turned her head, she jerked her hand away. On the flat-topped pillar, level with her shoulder, stood the painted stone carving of a lion's paw. From its claws, dripping, hung eyes ripped from their sockets.

Five yards on stood another pillar; on it, something from which Valentine swiftly turned away.

Scaris's voice at her shoulder made her spin round:

'This was to be an image to remind me of canon law; it was a cannon, upon it a shield to mind me of how Law shields the community; on that shield five stars, to call to mind the five branches of civil law. You perceive how it works; the rebus is placed here, immediately I see the image, it calls knowledge out of my memory, that would not have come without the causal image.'

The Chancellor shuddered.

'The images *change*. None of my guards have caught the persons responsible. They ... change in such ways. I think *that*, now, is *lex tallonis*; the law of –'

'An eye for an eye.'

Valentine abruptly turned and walked back out of the maze (unhesitatingly taking the correct turns), her pace too fast for the old man to keep up with her. Out in the open again, she found the Lord-Architect waiting.

'Turns your guts, don't it?' he observed. 'You should have seen what the Erotic Garden became.'

Valentine said sharply, 'The man's a fool. A memory palace or memory garden isn't to be *built*, it's to keep knowledge here, in the mind! If I'd to carry all the written down Scholar-Soldiers' knowledge with me, I'd never walk!'

She rubbed her hand across her eyes as if erasing images. More calmly, she said, 'Pictures are more easily remembered than written words, and carry a whole web of associated knowledge. I've a palace memorized – one of Palladio's – and in every palace room a curious image, that leads me to further volumes of memory, so that I only have to walk through the palace in my mind.'

Casaubon shrugged. 'Some of my marble-pillar-of-rectitude Councillors would say we ought to confine that to images of Justice, in an Interior Temple. But Scaris and I thought it a pleasant conceit, to have a material Memory Garden. You see what becomes of it!'

Valentine pushed the tendrils of white and cinnamon hair back from her face with her palms. She squinted up at the sky. Then she turned her tawny-reddish eyes on the Lord-Architect.

'You ripped out the guts of the City to make this,' she observed.

'Geometry is the culmination of the city. The temple garden must stand in the heart of the city, as the Interior Temple is built in the heart of man.' The Lord-Architect Casaubon broke off, shrugged. 'So, you know this as well as I, Master-Captain. I don't need telling how to construct a building, nor what it's for, nor how to lay out a garden, nor what I may put in it and where. All I need to know is where this corruption comes from!'

Chancellor Scaris appeared at the exit from the hedge-maze. His face was red, sweaty; and he appeared more than somewhat embarrassed. The Lord-Architect broke out into a laugh that sent his reeking breath clear to where Valentine stood:

'Lost in your own Garden, master Chancellor? Great Architect, what next!'

Valentine sat beside the Lord-Architect, on the wide marble rim of a fountain. She put her satchel down between her feet, and rummaged, putting one scroll back, taking out another. Casaubon rested his ham-hands between his fat legs and watched her. The fountain began suddenly to play an ordered, formal tune; but so off-key that Casaubon, Scaris, and Valentine, by common unspoken consent, got up and walked away.

'Now I know what kind of a Garden,' Master-Captain Valentine said, 'I need to know why.'

Scaris said, 'Salomon de Caus built such a Garden, once, four thousand years ago. Why not we, ourselves?'

She nodded. 'But why exactly this, and why now?'

Casaubon's deliberate stomp carried the Lord-Architect at a slow walk; Scaris himself was old enough to move carefully. He saw the young Scholar-Soldier slack her pace. Finally she stopped. Brambles here grew in barbed golden arcs over a disc of polished black stone, laid into the earth, in whose centre was an onyx sundial. Their reflections stared up at them, blinded by weeds.

'It's the oldest Art,' Chancellor Scaris said. 'To build. Our Archemasters laid the City out according to just proportion; therefore Justice exists in us. As above, so below. Our Fathers builded high, according to the principles of universal harmony, therefore we were able to build an Empire.'

Casaubon snorted. He wiped at his nose, leaving a glistening trail on one blue satin sleeve.

'Listen to the orthodox mind! Young Valentine, come here. See that? Past the trees, down the slope – *there*. That's the lower city. There's no more justice in there than in my arsehole. Scaris is an old fool. If we don't do something soon, I wouldn't give you a farting farthing for an Archemaster on the open market! That's what the Garden's for.'

Coming in at the gate, Valentine had only seen a few of the City Lanes. Now, on top of this slope, she could look out over mile after mile of them; brick blockhouses, squat foundry-chimneys spouting steam and dirt. They lay under the midday sun like a scab on the earth. But when Valentine looked over her shoulder, she saw that, even so, the lower city was dwarfed by the extent of the City proper: that dream of white marble.

'What will the Garden do?' She shoved the last pamphlet back under the satchel-flap, and lifted reddish-brown eyes to Casaubon's face. He wiped his sweating forehead and left black charcoal smears across it, over the freckles, and the yellow scurf at the hairline. After some searching in his pockets, he brought out a dubiously-coloured kerchief and wiped his face and hands.

'You're the Scholar, tell me about the first Archemaster,' he invited.

'They write that the first Archemaster builded a Tower, and that when it fell, the One Language fell into babble. And that he retired, and wrote how your Interior Temple of the soul might be builded, which,' Valentine said, 'I suppose if I were such a failure, I might do too.'

Scaris was watching her when she said it; he saw the glint of provocation in her eye.

'Oh, his principles are no failure, witness *that.*' Casaubon's fat arm swung in an arc that took in marble palaces, galleries, temples, domes, and the City wall. 'Don't play the fool, Master-Captain. Where *we* err is in building less than we might. We need to raze the lesser city, burn the warrens down, build again from the ground up. Let the paupers live well, as our servants do, not fester down there in those plague-stricken hovels.'

He stuffed the brown kerchief back in an inner pocket.

'Still, that's not to the point. Except that until the Garden's built, I see no way of convincing my Council that we need to rebuild the lower city . . .'

Scaris said, 'It's a Garden in which to learn.'

'Learn?'

It was Casaubon, finally, who answered the Scholar-Soldier. 'It's a Garden that will teach wisdom. The One Language, even. Teach us the knowledge that the ancient rulers of this Earth had, before all fell in fire. When those of the lower city come here, it will teach them temperance – and respect. Great Architect! *Now* do you see why the Invisible College sabotages me at every turn? They're known seditious!'

The Scholar-Soldier said, 'It wasn't the Invisible College that tried to kill your Chancellor, and myself, an hour ago. They're called "invisible" for their secrecy, and that attack was hardly secret!'

Casaubon grinned at her waspishness. 'Well, Master-Captain, what now?'

'I'll do something here,' she said. 'First.'

Scaris, beginning to limp and favour one hip now, followed the Lord-Architect and the young woman back through the corrupted Miracle Garden. At almost every plinth, statue, and dry fountain, the Scholar-Soldier paused to affix a paper strip or scroll, pulled from her bulging satchel. Some she weighted down with rocks. Others she tucked into crevices in the stonework. When they arrived back at the steps leading down to the great square, she unrolled a long thin paper streamer, written over with obscure characters, and fixed it from top to bottom of the stairs.

Then she stood, a hand on her sword-hilt, and absently swung the scabbard up and rested it behind her elbows, and watched the Lord-Architect Casaubon wheeze his way down the steps behind her. She frowned.

Still smarting from her earlier insult, Scaris said, 'I would have thought a Scholar with her own memory-palace would have little use for written records.'

'The papers? See you, they're not for me to read. They're for others. Other . . . readers. They're warnings.'

A warm wind blew tendrils of hair, brown and silver, round her plain oval face. Her lashes and brows were reddish-brown. They gave her a look, Scaris thought, like a she-fox.

'Give me the rest of today,' she asked Casaubon, as he stepped heavily down into the square.

He coughed, gobbed on the marble, squinted up at the sun that was passing noon, and then glanced back at the building-ground.

'I can see no way to end the corruption – but pulling down

what I've built, ' he wheezed. 'And to construct something that won't turn into – abomination – I confess to you, Master-Captain, *I don't know how*! Would I have consented to – you coming here, if I could?'

When she looked enquiringly at Scaris, the Chancellor nodded.

'I suggested a Scholar-Soldier might help us. If not . . . if not, Valentine, we have razed the centre of the City for nothing. We can build nothing new on the site, because nothing is built that does not immediately rot.' Scaris tugged the black satin robe away from his neck, suddenly breathless. 'What do you need?'

She said, 'If you're fool enough to build a material Memory Garden here, Chancellor, then I'd wager that this City has somewhere in it a Library. I'll begin there.'

The Lord-Architect demanded thickly, 'Can you do anything in six hours?'

'That's all the time we have,' Valentine said. 'Noble Lord, I've seen this before – once. You don't have long. See you, *I* don't have long; I must be about it. Something is growing in that Garden that you won't like if it fruits. All you've seen yet are buds and shoots. If you let it come to flower, I think corruption will spread out from here into the City itself.'

The interiors of the Library's domes echoed to a faint whispering, the turning of leaves of parchment. Valentine's boots clicked loudly on the tiles as she walked. Heads lifted. When they saw the swagger in her walk, and the deftly-slung swordblade, they bent immediately to their parchments again. Valentine grinned.

And then, by a stack so tall that the higher scrolls must be reached by a metal causeway, she stopped, and stared down past the crimson-and-blue painted shelves. She squinted in the hot, gold twilight. Then she walked down and stood behind one of the students.

'I need a book and can't find it.'

The student wore a long dark robe, with a cowl pulled up, half-shadowing her face. She looked up from the scroll she held. Valentine knew the sharp, pale young features, her long lashes, and slightly-snaggled teeth.

'Tell me what theosophist book you need,' the young girl asked ritually.

'*Under the Shadow of Bright Wings –*'

'*– In the Heart of The Womb.*' She finished the recognition-code in a whisper, and laughed.

'Janou, I thought it was you!' Valentine glanced round the vast hall.

'How are things in the Garden?'

'Much as we thought they would be. We must not speak with each other here. Where can we go?'

Janou looked up with clear, irreverent eyes. 'You need to see the other half of it, don't you? Come with me. I know just the place.'

The sky over the city was skimmed with cloud now, and a drizzle fell as they walked, turning the yellow dust to mud that clogged on Valentine's boots and Janou's bare feet. The cowled girl led Valentine a swift way out of the marble avenues, into the lower city.

'I thought I'd have no hard time making contact with you,' Valentine boasted. 'Well, we have a friend in the Garden, although he knows it not; and we have an enemy, also, although he thinks I don't know him. They're a strange pair, and like each other indifferent badly. As for the rest . . . I left warnings. And, to say true, I was never so glad to leave a place in my life. That Garden's deadly.'

Janou pushed the cowl back, and scrubbed her fingers through her baby-short hair. It fluffed up fine-blonde in the warm wind. She strutted beside Valentine, with an occasional skip to keep up with the Scholar-Soldier's longer stride.

'I've not been idle, me. Things are happening here that your Architect-Lords don't credit. 'Wait,' Janou said, 'and you'll see.'

Now, three-storey buildings pressed close together, leaning over the narrow lane, blocking out the tawny-yellow sky. Valentine's neck prickled. There would be a storm soon. She hefted her satchel on its fraying strap, and plodded on after Janou.

The lane opened into a marketplace.

Dirty straw had been thrown down, to make walking over the yellow mud possible. Market stalls offered bruised fruit, meat stinking in the summer heat, and steaming pies. Further

over, beasts squealed in pens. A great crowd of people pushed
to and fro. Their voices rang off the plaster-and-daub walls of
the inns that surrounded the market square: here a herder,
playing Three-Cup with a shabby gallant; there women
auctioning for egg-money; a tailor spreading out bales of
cotton cloth, and swearing when an end trailed in the mud; a
company of players setting up on the back of a baker's cart.

'Down this way!' Janou dug her fists in the pockets of her
long robe, hitching up the front of it, walking with a kick-heeled
strut that Valentine remembered from way back.

She led the Scholar-Soldier down one of the ranks of stalls.
By the time Valentine had pushed through the people to catch
up with her, Janou had halted. She stood on bare tiptoes, peer-
ing up at a man who, in the shelter of the inn-wall, turned the
handle of a hurdy-gurdy.

'*Him,*' Janou said.

He had a trimmed beard, and dark hair growing to his
collar; and that was all that was visible – his high-crowned hat
had a wide brim, pulled down. A broken feather was tucked
into his hatband. His broad hand turned the organ-handle, and
a bright tune fell into the air, and two or three of the young
children in the crowd jigged up and down at his feet.

Spidering across the ground, in a red velvet jacket, a beast
with the gold eyes of a snake, and the spindly limbs of a lizard,
danced on its hind legs. Some of the men and women who had
turned to look threw coins.

Valentine threw down a silver angel. When the man looked
up at her, she said, 'I'll buy you a drink for a song, master.'

There was no trace of the silver paint that had smeared his
forehead; there was, however, a purple-and-yellow bruise on
his left temple.

Janou said, 'He's my singing-bird, this one. Yes, let's drink.'

Valentine grinned at the man. 'We've met, sir, if you recall;
but I'd be glad to know your name.'

Feliche sat with his back to the inn-room's wall. His eyes
were never still as he talked to Janou, they sought low door and
bottle-paned window and cellar-door in rapid succession.
Valentine sat with her satchel between her feet, and her knife
unsheathed and held out of sight under the table.

The rest of the conspirators sat round the table – two or three men indistinguishable from the hurdy-gurdy man Feliche except by the colour of their beards; a woman in grey cotton with washer-woman's red hands; two younger women, and a boy. They merged into the market-day crowd drinking in the inn.

'I hold to the original plan.' Feliche's deep voice was pitched not to carry beyond their table. 'Kill the Lord-Architect and the Chancellor, and any other of the Archemasters we can reach.'

Valentine, under the table's edge, picked her nails with her dagger. She watched the lizard-ape squatting on the hurdy-gurdy. From time to time it reached down a scaly hand to touch Feliche's shoulder, and the man put a finger up for it to grasp. He was a big man, a head taller than anyone in the inn-room; with a high gleaming forehead and intense dark eyes. He fixed those eyes on Valentine now:

'I had thought we could take powder from the foundries, and blow their marble Council-chamber to fragments, they with it. Then the city's ours, and can stay as it is. We'll have their riches, besides, then.'

One of the younger women put in, 'Keep the halls. Then we can make our own Council. There's people in my Ward, I'd like them to see me a Councillor, and then wouldn't I make them sweat!'

'I, also!'

'And me!'

Under cover of the general agreement, Feliche bent towards Valentine, laying his big hands flat on the rough wooden table.

'Janou told us a Master-Captain would come here. But why were you with that whoremaster Scaris this morning? And Casaubon – I'm told you spoke for over an hour with the Lord-Architect. What were you telling them?'

Valentine studied the bruise on his forehead, where she had struck him with the flat of her sword.

'At least now you stop to ask questions.'

He coloured. 'Then answer me this, Master-Captain – why is a Scholar-Soldier seen in company with one of the Invisible College?'

Another of the men asked, 'Are you and they allies, or

enemies as we've always been told?'

Janou, bouncing up and down on the bench, said, 'Oh, see you, we can trust these people, Valentine! Yes, allies and more than allies. Did you not know, the Scholar-Soldiers are only the College made visible? And we, only they disguised.'

'Janou!'

'We need their help,' the girl said stubbornly. She slicked down her fluffy hair irritably, but the heat made it stick up in cat-fur tufts. She pushed the robe's sleeves up to her elbows. 'Valentine, explain the matter to them; we can never act without allies, and these are mine. Whose are yours? The Chancellor and the Lord-Architect?'

When Valentine turned back to Feliche, she saw him hide a smile. She sighed. She saw him smile at that, too.

'What she says is true, Master Feliche. It's put about that we and the Invisible College are enemies, and opposites, for then, no matter of what faction people be, they are bound to employ either the Scholar-Soldiers or the College in these matters – and so we're safe.'

'Safe?' he echoed.

'Oh, see you, there are matters that only we can deal with.'

Feliche nodded at the inn-room's back window. Through it, Valentine saw a rider in cherry-coloured satin; cursing as he pulled his gelding up, waiting for a butcher's cart to pass through the lane. The noise of his oaths came through the open window, with flies and the stink of slaughtered carcases.

'The Architect-Lords would tear our district down,' the big man said softly. 'In these lanes, even a rider has to stop and wait for a cart or an old man to get out of the way. Up in the City, in their avenues, they force us up onto pavements, and leave us nothing to do but watch them ride by in their carriages. It's fair, Master-Captain, if we seek to bring down their palaces.'

The heat made Valentine sweat. She pushed her braids back and up from her neck, for a moment, leaving her knife in her lap.

The light was an odd colour now, almost saffron. The pressure of the approaching storm made horses shy in the lane, and sparked and crackled on Janou's hand when she stroked the inn's cat.

'Did you tell them about the Garden?' Valentine asked.

'We know about the Garden. It's a teaching garden. We've no great wish to see it completed. What's amiss with it?' the washerwoman asked.

Valentine looked round at their faces. Faded skin, with broken veins in the cheeks; blear eyes and silvering hair; even the young boy seemed a little old man. She put her hands under the table again, sought her knife, and dug the sharp tip of it into her forearm. Pain focused her sight. Their faces regained some life.

Janou said, 'What was *that*?'

Feliche, half up off his bench, sat down again, and stared at Valentine. 'She said it – what *was* that?'

'Something beginning to flower.' Valentine sheathed her knife at her belt. She reached down to her satchel, almost as if that comforted her. 'Now hear what I say to you. Janou's right. We need help. The Architect-Lords of this City have stumbled on something that is found, once in a hundred years, perhaps, and when it's found . . . oh, see you, it was because of the first time this happened that the Invisible College was founded. Our grandsires put an end to it then. Now it's up to us.'

The storm-pressure was building; bad-tempered quarrels broke out in the inn-room. Valentine spoke under their noise:

'*As above, so below.* That's the Archemaster's law, and it's true. Someone said to me in the Garden that if a city's buildings are built in just proportion, and its streets laid out in the laws of universal harmony, then Justice herself is compelled to come down and dwell on earth, there.'

Feliche laughed sardonically. Valentine continued:

'As for Justice, I don't know. But the Invisible College learned long since, that if a thing is built according to certain laws, then it becomes a dwelling-place, and a thing of its nature is compelled to come and inhabit it.'

Feliche rumbled, 'What thing? Built how?'

'Say, a Miracle Garden. There are patterns in number, universal patterns. The Architect-Lords are building according to those patterns, and,' Valentine said, 'I think, truly, they may not know why corruption is happening. But they've constructed a place in which Corruption is compelled to dwell –'

The young boy protested. 'But houses are for people to live

in, and gardens are places for people to go. I don't understand.'

Valentine didn't look at the livid sky outside the inn's window.

'We need your help. We need it now,' she said. 'One man in that Garden has begun to love what it holds. I told you things might be drawn down from the rim of the heavens, to us, but did I say that they would be things that human minds could comprehend? If the Architect-Lords razed the lower city, they could only make a wasteland of it. If what is growing in the Garden spreads here, then you'll think that wasteland would have been paradise!'

In the quiet, they turned each one to look at one another.

'I can't believe it,' one man said.

'It's tales, only tales!' another of the men burst out.

'What does she know?' a woman demanded, 'she's only a mendicant lecturer; what does a beggarly scholar know!'

'She just wants to protect the Architect-Lords!'

Janou shook her head, and vigorously rubbed sweat from her upper lip with the back of her hand. Feliche glanced down at the scarred, carved surface of the table. When he looked up and met the reddish-tawny eyes of the Master-Captain, he smiled wryly.

'I don't doubt you seek to fright us into helping you,' he said. 'That would be easily dismissed, except that I believe, also, you're telling the truth.'

Valentine opened her mouth to reply, and was forestalled by another person entering the inn. A man in a dark robe, who pushed the cowl back from his head as he sighted Janou, shoved his way through the crowd to her, and leaned down between her and the washerwoman to whisper.

Janou's face fell.

'They want you,' she turned to Valentine. 'Someone has died. In the Miracle Garden. The Architect-Lords are turning the City upside down for you.'

The cinnamon-haired woman stood up.

'That doesn't give me long here. Master Feliche, will you come with us? Janou, we'll have to arrange things now, and act at once.'

The body lay on the circle of black marble paving that was

set into the lawn, with its arms outstretched, as if to embrace the onyx sundial that stood in the centre. In the livid storm-light, the gnomon cast no shadow. A great streak of drying blood dulled the reflective paving.

'Rot him!' Casaubon said, 'I need the old fool for a while longer. Well, Master-Captain, how did he come by his death?'

Valentine, who knelt by the body of Chancellor Scaris, not touching it yet, said, 'Turn this thing over.'

The Lord-Architect Casaubon grunted in surprise. He scratched at his red hair, inspected the scurf under his finger-nails, and then made a shrug with his massive shoulders that strained the blue satin coat almost to bursting, and stepped forward. He planted a heavy foot either side of the Chancel-lor's head, bent down –

'No!' Valentine grabbed his sleeve. She pulled him back several paces from the sundial.

'I'd give an angel's fart to know what game you're playing!' Casaubon swore. 'Bid a Lord-Architect do your errand, then stop him; I don't understand you! And who in the name of the Great Architect are those two?'

Valentine glanced back at Janou. She was leaning up against the hurdy-gurdy man, a fluffhaired child barely level with his collarbone, as if his physical nearness comforted her. Feliche himself was staring fixedly at the entrance to the hedge-maze.

'We should leave this Garden before we talk about it, noble Lord. No – leave Scaris. He's not about to walk away. See you, *there.*'

Grunting, Casaubon bent into a half-crouch, looking where the tawny-haired woman pointed. It seemed to him as if the dead Chancellor lay in a pool of black water. Then he saw how that impression came about: the old man's head and shoulder looked half-submerged in the shining onyx. But the body was resting on the surface of the stone. It was glued to the stone by blood, and half the face and shoulder were – missing.

'Great Architect, that's foul!' Casaubon straightened, with an effort, looking pale under the dirt; and turned his head aside to heave. After wiping his mouth, he said, 'You don't cast, Master-Captain? You're used to this?'

'Your fortune to have an iron-stomached Scholar-Soldier,' the woman said greenly, adding, 'We should remove ourselves from here, noble Lord, these people and I would speak with you urgently.'

As they crossed a wide avenue, Casaubon caught his foot on a crack and stumbled. He recovered himself, looked back, and saw that there was a split in the marble paving. A faint, ominous creaking sounded.

'Master-Captain –'

'I see it,' the woman said. She knelt briefly, pulled a strip of character-marked paper from her pack, and gummed it across the split. There was a sense of groaning strain in the air itself. She stood, tossed her sword to Janou (the girl rapidly slipped the hanger over her head and shoulders), and turned, waiting for the hurdy-gurdy man to catch up.

'By the Great Architect's Symmetrical Balls!' Casaubon swore. 'Will you tell me what's happening to my city!'

They were among people now, officers and guards and stewards, who passed them at a jog-trot, urgently on the way to somewhere else. Anywhere else, Casaubon guessed. He panted, breath quite gone, and rested a hand against the balustrade of a palace that fronted the avenue.

There were leprous marks on the marble, blackish and greenish stains. When he dabbed at one with his sleeve, the stone itself liquified and ran down the carved ornamentation.

A crack in the palace facade split, with a noise like a cannon, and opened wide enough to put a hand in. Casaubon heard screams.

'If you're planning something, Master-Captain, now would seem to be a good time to do it.'

'No. We have time yet. Come inside and talk.'

Casaubon limped heavily toward the steps of the Belvedere, with the woman all but treading on his heels. The girl, Janou, picked up the skirts of her cowled robe and ran towards them, sword-blade jouncing on her back.

'Where's Feliche?' Valentine called.

'He has something yet to do. He'll come!'

The last thing the Lord-Architect saw before he went inside was the sky above the City. It hung over the marble avenues, filthy and black, and a grimy rain began to fall, streaking the stone, and eating into it with the ferocity of acid.

★

The Scholar-Soldier Valentine sat on the window-ledge, her back to the City beyond.

'What we must do is destroy the Miracle Garden. If the pattern that it makes no longer exists, then those entities that are . . . growing through into this world . . . will no longer have a guide here. It's the only way. As for how it's to be done –'

Janou hoisted herself up on the sill beside the Master-Captain and leaned out of the window at a dizzy angle.

'Here's Feliche!' she yelled. 'He's brought the wagon!'

'Now see you,' Casaubon scowled thunderously. 'That's five acres, there, in the heart of the City, and –'

'Powder.' Janou slid round, her legs bare to the thighs for a moment, and slipped down to the tesselated marble floor.

'Powder from the foundries,' Master-Captain Valentine confirmed. 'We'll use the cannon you have here; bombard that earth into patternless ruin.'

'*You will not!*'

'Lord-Architect –'

'*That is my Miracle Garden that took me a year to build and by the Great Architect's Womb I will not have it subjected to cannonade!*'

Valentine stood up. 'You will if I say so.'

'I will not!' Casaubon shouted. 'What gives you and your pox-rotted College the right to take my Garden away? Poor dead Scaris and I, we dirtied our hands for a year creating it. Whatever it is now, we made it with love. You and that little girl playing Providence, with the hand of the Invisible College behind you, when did you ever *make* anything?'

She stared at him, wordless.

Janou skipped to the high doorway, and peered down the stairs. 'Feliche! Have you got cannoneers with you?'

'Who fights the Architect-Lords' wars?' the big man asked, rhetorically, taking off his broken-plumed hat as he entered the palatial chamber. 'Every alley in this city has a master-bombardier or cannoneer in it. Greetings, noble Lord.'

'You're all mad,' the Lord-Architect Casaubon said. 'Now hear *me*. I have still men enough and power enough to keep order in this City. Whether it be powder conspiracies (yes, master Feliche, I know you and your plague-sign fraternity), or links between the Scholar-Soldiers and the Invisible College (which I did not know), no matter, there are dungeons deep enough for all of you.

'However,' he added, as another ominous creak sounded, and the storm-light darkened through the grimy rain, 'we stand in some danger, I truly believe it. Master-Captain, you are Scholar as well as Soldier. Find me some way to save my Miracle Garden. Or else I care not if the City falls, no, not every building in it.'

Valentine opened her mouth to speak, and Feliche interrupted her.

'I think I could ask this, Master-Captain Valentine: how are you different from the noble Lords, who send us out to fight their wars for them? It's we who'll use the cannon. And, if what you say is true, against nothing human.'

He smoothed the broken feather of his hat with one hand, looking remarkably uneasy for a big man. He continued:

'Well then, see you, you cannot tell how Corruption might fight back. And we'll be in the way of it if it does. I hate to speak with the noble Lord's tongue, but I agree with him. Find some way to save the Garden.'

'*It can't be done!*' Valentine shouted. 'I was at Mildenhall, and Karsethra, the first to stand against that enemy and the last to fly from it, and I *know* –'

'That's a pox-rotted shame,' Casaubon said. 'Because I think the slave's right. I've seen the Archemasters' records. What you call Corruption feeds on disorder, and so breaking the Garden-patterns by cannonade will only help it to spread.'

And Valentine shook her head. 'Then . . . I don't know what to do.'

'You're never too old for a new sensation,' the noble Lord-Architect observed. 'Although it may shock you to discover that you're not infallible. I know it would shock me.'

Valentine broke out in a great surprised laugh. Casaubon guffawed. Janou and Feliche looked blankly at both of them.

Janou, puzzling, said, 'See you, there *might* just be a way.'

'We've run out of time.' Valentine pointed outside.

Beyond the window, Casaubon saw the bright disc of the sun bitten into. Over the City spread the crepuscular light of an eclipse.

★

They ran across the square towards the building ground and
the Miracle Garden, dodging the stinging black rain.

Feliche paused, hearing the chittering of the lizard-ape. It
danced on the powder-wagon, scarlet coat stark against the
black sky. The big man bent down and scooped up the hurdy-
gurdy, slung it over his shoulder, and the lizard-ape made a
leap and clung to it, gold eyes bright with fear. Valentine heard
him call to the men and women who crouched for shelter under
the other wagons, before he ran on.

They ran – Janou pulling up her cowl to shield herself from
the acid storm, kilting her robe up to sprint; even the Lord-
Architect Casaubon managing a jog-trot. He wheezed and
panted, and at last fell, belly up against the marble balustrade
of the Garden steps, clutching it for support.

It was a while before he realised no rain scalded him.

Casaubon raised his head. He still wheezed. His pulse
pounded deafeningly, so that he could see the Scholar-Soldier
Valentine speaking, but not hear her. The woman stood on the
top step, cinnamon-braids flying loose in the gale. Janou and
Feliche stood back to back, staring up at the sky.

Above his head, the Lord-Architect saw a sky of boiling
blackness. Spiked lightening walked a circle around the
horizon – no, around the *Garden*. Now that he could get his
breath, he found the air here was sweet, no rain falling; and
when he turned to look up the steps at the building-ground, he
saw sunlight.

The mellow light and clear air of a summer afternoon lay
over the Miracle Garden.

Casaubon leaned forward on the balustrade and heaved.
Only a little bile came up. He spat. He looked up at Valentine,
where the Master-Captain gazed into the Garden. 'Great
Architect! perhaps you *are* fearless. That turns my guts more
than back there.'

He jerked a pudgy thumb at the blackened, decaying marble
of the City.

Then he saw that the Scholar-Soldier's face was white;
white enough that her freckles appeared dark as moles.

'We must go in,' she said, 'as I think, we can't get out.'

They walked in a close group up the steps and into the half-
built Miracle Garden. The Master-Captain Valentine went

first, carrying her drawn sword in her left hand, and, with her right, thumbed the scrolls in her pack. Janou, being relieved of the sword, let the lizard-ape ride chittering on her shoulder and pick at her cropped fair hair. She held Feliche's hand. The big man went warily, looking at every bramble-clump and over-grown hedge and statue as if it might bite.

Casaubon brought up the rear. The noble Lord-Architect glared, and muttered under his breath. At one point he stopped, bent down, and picked up an abandoned bottle of wine, and knocked the neck of it off against the marble thigh of a nymph. He drank, and belched.

When they passed the sundial, Chancellor Scaris's body was gone.

'Did you order that moved, noble Lord?'

Casaubon met the Scholar-Soldier's fox-red eyes. 'I did not.'

'No, I thought as much.'

Casaubon snorted. It was much too loud a noise in that silent, sunlit garden. 'Then, if you know so much, tell me what our aim is in coming here!'

Valentine looked to Janou but the girl remained silent.

Feliche spoke. His bass voice had a shake in it.

'Why don't you ask our guide?'

Valentine and Casaubon both turned around. In the topiary arch, between the speaking statues, stood a figure. A fold of its black silk robe cowled its face.

The bronze statue of the child said, '*Time is.*'

The silver statue of the old man said, '*Time was.*'

The cowled figure between them said, 'But, *Time will not be.* Not now. We have taken that for our own.'

The voice was Scaris's, something muffled.

Janou kicked the golden grass with her bare heel. In a high squeak, she said, 'I don't want to see him – not its face.'

It turned away. The fold of black silk fell, as it turned, and Valentine saw fine white hair: the back of Chancellor Scaris's head. When it held up a hand and beckoned them to follow, she stepped forward immediately.

'For fear he should turn round again?' Casaubon needled, but when Valentine didn't answer, only walked on under the topiary arch, he muttered, 'I've had no such nightmares as this since I was breeched,' and followed her.

'I smell spices,' Feliche said wonderingly, as they walked. He
looked down at Janou. 'As strong as they were in my mother's
shop, when I was a child.'

'Ordure,' Valentine said, overhearing, as they caught up.
'Great Architect knows, I've smelled enough of that since I
walked on the highways for the Invisible College!'

'Master-Captain –'

She cut the Lord-Architect's protest off with a gesture.

'If a chance should come, we may only have a minute in
which to act. See you, we should not miss it.'

The tufted golden grass gave out a heavy scent. The over-
grown garden had no insects, no birds; only the towering
masses of bramble and thorn that spidered into the blue sky.
Ahead, the clean-cut lines of the topiary maze formed the
horizon. Valentine could see the marble niches at the entrance
– they were empty.

Janou stumbled. She seized Feliche's arm, rubbing her
bruised foot, and the lizard-ape abandoned her shoulder for
his. When she looked down, she saw what she had fallen over.
Dry bones were half-buried in the golden grass. Skull, femur,
vertebrae like a scatter of dice.

The figure of the Chancellor vanished into the maze, without turning round to see if they followed.

'Listen,' Feliche said. He hefted the hurdy-gurdy that
weighed down his shoulder. The lizard-ape growled. Feliche
said, 'I hear – music?'

It grew stronger as they listened. Valentine shifted uneasily,
feeling the vibrations through the ground itself.

'That's – *foul.* It makes me feel dirty just to hear it,' Janou
said.

Valentine saw Casaubon, silhouetted in his blue satin
against the golden hedge. The fat man had his head cocked,
listening. He said, 'You spoke of patterns. I've spent my life in
stone, patterning out the order of the universe in City streets. I
know others who made that order out of numbers, or out of
strings stretched to the just proportion for each note – you
follow me, out of music.'

'As above, so below,' Valentine said.

His fingers were wrapped round a bottle, almost hiding the
glass from view. Now he lifted the bottle and drank, and

added, 'If I were to build a City in *that* pattern, it would be a chancre on the earth.'

Janou said, 'It's a summons.'

'If order and harmony call up Justice,' Casaubon said, over the increasing discordance, 'then what does this music summon? Well and so. Valentine, do we enter the maze?'

Before Valentine could answer him, Janou gave a short choked-off scream. She held her hands out, and Valentine saw that her palms were oozing red; blood dripping down into the grass.

'We're close enough for it to touch us,' Valentine said. She reached out and took the girl's hands, heedless of the stigmata, and hugged Janou close for a minute, and then let her go.

'This will spread out to the city?' Feliche asked. When the Scholar-Soldier nodded, he shrugged broad shoulders, and stepped towards the entrance of the maze. Janou followed; Valentine walked at his side. The Lord-Architect Casaubon drained the wine-bottle and set it neatly upright on the grass before going after them.

As she walked under the topiary entrance, Valentine felt something brush her face.

She put up a hand, and took it away stained black. The close-cut leaves dripped an oily substance onto her rough-cotton shirt. A change in temperature made her stop, stand for a second, while the breath from her mouth clouded the suddenly-frosted air. She couldn't see Scaris, or whatever wore Scaris's shape. This twilight –

Valentine looked up to see the sun a copper disc, edged with fire. The shadow of eclipse lay on the maze.

With a little soft hiss, the hedge in front of her deliquesced. It fell into a black mess of leaves, with a sound like snow thrown onto a fire, and then spread out in sludge over the golden grass. And the grass itself began to blacken like paper held too close to a fire.

She looked, once, at what lay in front of her, and then spun round to face away from it, catching Janou's shoulder as she turned, and pulling the girl with her.

'Filth,' the Lord-Architect whispered, gazing ahead, 'filth, forever. No order, no shape, no *pattern* –'

Feliche rubbed his eyes with his hand, and said, 'It goes down forever – the Pit –'

The discordant sounds grew louder: less music than anti-music. Valentine fumbled with the buckles on her pack. A wind began to gust, seizing each strip of patterned characters and numerals before she could use them, sucking them away into whatever lay behind her. She clutched at them in panic.

Close at her ear, Scaris's voice whispered, '*Time will not be.*'

She felt the earth crumbling under her heels.

A flare of scarlet crossed her vision. Bright in that twilight, glittering with gold embroidery: the lizard-ape's scarlet coat. The beast growled, leaping up and down on the grass, and jumped up at Feliche's hand, where he stood transfixed, gazing ahead. One scaly paw caught the hurdy-gurdy's handle.

A raw, jingling tune jabbed the air, and then died.

Feliche looked down. Almost in spite of himself, he pushed the handle round once more. The cheap tune echoed.

It roused Casaubon: he pulled his gaze away from what had been the maze, and was now patternless Chaos.

'Again!' he said. 'You, beggar, you play for pennies. Now play for silver angels. For our lives!'

'For *you*?' Feliche said.

Janou laughed. 'For us!'

In Valentine's ear, Scaris's voice cried out in pain.

Spurred by the hurdy-gurdy's jangling tune, the lizard-ape began to dance. Valentine slipped to one knee, pushed herself away from the edge – *the edge?* – behind her, and got up from the grass. She seized Janou's hand.

'Dance!' she cried.

'*Dance?*'

Casaubon suddenly lumbered forward. 'Patterns!' he said. 'Oh, this is not your musico-magic, this is not your high Art, but Great Architect! what does it matter? Old tunes, old patterns – dance!'

Feliche turned a switch. The mechanical hurdy-gurdy began to play a country dance.

'When I was a child –' Valentine began to step, curtsey, step, bow; and Janou, laughing so hard that she could barely stand, began to copy her. With all the airs of a City lady, she took Casaubon's hand and drew him into the figure.

The lizard-ape leaped at their side, bowing, skipping forward, skipping back.

'I cannot –' Casaubon began to wheeze.

'Oh, see you, sir, you must!' Valentine seized his hands. Janou, like a hoyden, waltzed around Feliche where he played. Valentine shouted above the music: 'We're so close to the heart of it now. We can *hurt* it. This is a better way than we could ever have planned. Oh, sir, dance!'

They dance a pavane on the golden grass, to nursery tunes ground out by a hurdy-gurdy.

The crop-haired girl skipping the measure, heels kicking the earth, eyes half-shut, lost in the pleasure of knowing each turn, each move, each step.

The fox-haired woman and the fat man, touch hands and part, turn, touch and part; gliding over the sun-warmed grass, their shadows following them in neat measure.

Ape and player moving also, in gentle steps that go back and forth, back and forth, tapping out the rhythm for the other dancers.

And now there is another shadow on the earth.

The clanking hurdy-gurdy drowns out birdsong and the buzz of insects, playing dances that were old before stone was laid upon stone of the City, playing lullaby rhymes and temple-bell chimes, each note slotting into the next like dovetailed joints or unmortared stone.

The Scholar-Soldier, dancing, pack and sword forgotten, seizes in the dance a stranger's hand, and sees, pink with exertion, the familiar lined face of Scaris.

They dance a pavane, they dance the pattern of the microcosm, number and particle and force; they dance the dance of the world above: stars, suns, galaxies.

The hurdy-gurdy grinds on, tireless, and they dance a pavane on golden grass, circling a sundial that stands at the centre of a maze.

'Rot you!' says the noble Lord-Architect Casaubon, 'Time *will* be!'

The automata have no answer to make.

Sun slants in through the clerestory windows of the Belvedere, falling sixty feet to the tesselated marble floor. As the Scholar-Soldier Valentine crossed the Belvedere's presence-chamber, alternate sun and shade made her now a drab brown, now a vixen-red figure. The others turned as she entered.

'He's agreed to see you?' Janou asked.

Janou had abandoned the black robe of the Library. Now she wore a gown of sapphire that shaded in the flowing skirt to rich indigo. The hem, where her bare feet peeped out, was already stained with mud.

Valentine shrugged lithe shoulders. 'Finally, yes.'

Feliche stood with Scaris. At their feet was the hurdy-gurdy, the lizard-ape curled up on top of it, asleep in the sun. Its scarlet coat gleamed.

The big man, having pulled the broken feather from his hatband, picked at his teeth with the quill-end. He said, 'Does he not remember the Garden?'

Scaris fingered the collar of his black satin robe. 'He may remember it too well, I think, for me.'

Valentine smiled at Scaris. 'He'll say *Rot you, I've only just got my Chancellor back, I don't want to lose him again!* But are you determined?'

The white-haired man seemed frailer, and aware, too, of how Janou and Feliche shrank back from him, sometimes, without any conscious intention.

'That evil in the Garden – it took me so easily,' Scaris said, 'that it frightens me still. I cannot be Chancellor, knowing that. What I will do, Master-Captain, is what you mocked me for: I'll care for the Library, and books that are written down.'

He smiled, looking at the lizard-ape asleep on the hurdy-gurdy.

'And on bright days, when I have been too long indoors, I shall shed my satin coat for cotton, and go into the square and play music for pennies.'

The Scholar-Soldier impulsively handed him her satchel, that bulged with scrolls still.

'Choose some of these, to care for in your Library? I can get more when the Invisible College convenes again. They're sovereign against bad dreams. Against things that stray out of bad dreams into waking.'

Scaris took the pack by its worn leather strap, and the

weight of it surprised him until he realized it was his, now.

Valentine glanced at Feliche.

'Shall I say, you and yours, in the lower city —'

The big man interrupted her. With a look at Chancellor Scaris, he said, 'When those in satin turn beggars, then beggars take up satin — I plan to travel. Maybe the Invisible College can show me how to solve the City's troubles. For I've seen nothing in the lower city, and, surely, nothing *here* to help us.'

'He's coming with me!' Janou picked up her skirts, strutting back to where they stood. 'Tell the Lord-Architect, the Invisible College will be present in his City from now on — I've had word: they're sending others to replace us, whose faces aren't known.'

Feliche put his hands on Janou's bare shoulders, and the fluffhaired girl leaned back as if he were a wall to support her.

'But tell him, Valentine, there must be something done about the Garden — then we can leave!'

With a brief nod, the Scholar-Soldier Valentine walked on into the marble halls and galleries beyond the ante-chamber.

The same sun shone in through the interior windows of the Belvedere. It gleamed on marble, white and pink and lapis-lazuli-blue, and glinted off ornamental silver taps, and was made hazy by the coils of steam rising up and filling the vast bath-house.

Valentine found Casaubon there.

'Noble Lord,' she said. She put one booted foot up on the rim of the marble bath, rested her arms across her raised knee, and then rested her chin on her arms. She looked down at him.

Casaubon ducked his head for the fifth or sixth time, came up spluttering, and squeezing water out of his copper-red hair. Steam and boiling water made him pink as a new-washed baby; and he rested back in the stepped bath, arms spreading over the wet marble, like some leviathan come to land. Newly-clean, he was found to be freckled, and otherwise of pale complexion.

'Well, young Valentine?'

'Nothing's changed in the Garden.' She spoke without moving her chin off her arms. 'That is a fair three days, and so time, I'd think, for anything lingering to show itself. Still, it's an uncanny place. Time will scab over the wound eventually. but . . .'

'Oh, see you,' Casaubon said, 'I have my thoughts on that matter also.'

He lowered his head, nestling his chin in three several layers of flesh, and looked up at Valentine with pale-blue eyes. When he rolled over, a wave of hot water splashed the marble surround of the baths. He sat down on the lowest submerged step again, and shook water from his eyes.

'You may hand me the towel,' he said. 'I have master Feliche to see in a short while, which I anticipate to be difficult. I think your colleague will stay here with him for a time. The little Janou.'

'Janou stays nowhere long.' Valentine straightened up, glancing round for the towel.

'As for the Miracle Garden,' the noble Lord-Architect continued, 'it seems to me that it would be dangerous to destroy it, not knowing what patterns we might uncover while so doing.'

'Yes, I'd say that also.'

'And rather than leave it to overgrow, a better manner of proceeding would be to rebuild it as a true Miracle Garden.'

'I agree.'

'You,' the noble Lord Casaubon pronounced, 'are not happy.'

Valentine looked at him in some surprise. She came back to stand by the bath, careful of her boots on the wet marble.

'That has nothing to do with anything, noble Lord.'

He heaved himself up to the next submerged marble step. A lap of water splashed up over Valentine's boots. She didn't move back; only watched his pink, clean bulk.

'Well then,' Casaubon said, 'stay here.'

'Stay here? Why would I do that?'

'Valentine, you're eighteen,' he said as he wiped sweat and hot water from his face, 'eighteen, and you look thirty-five. In a very few years you'll look sixty. Life on the road for the Invisible College I take not to be an easy life. Much better to settle down here in the City and advise me how to build my next garden.'

'Advice?' Valentine said incredulously. '*You*?'

'I would take advice from you,' the Lord-Architect said, 'on that.'

Steam coiled round the woman, shot through with the sun's gold as it fell in through the Belvedere's high windows. It pearled on her tawny-white braids.

'On that. And on much besides,' Casaubon said.

The woman scratched absently at her rough-cotton shirt. There was a scent of bath-oils in the air, sharp herbs and woodsmoke. She opened her mouth, shut it again, looked at Casaubon, and the corner of her mouth twitched up.

He said, 'Stay here. Be my Lady.'

There was silence in the Belvedere's bath-house.

Valentine tucked a braid behind her ear, and began to walk thoughtfully around the sunken marble bath. Casaubon watched, only his head turning. The cinnamon-haired woman absently tugged at one of the buckles of her sword-belt. Then, with a little exclamation, she pounced, and came up with a vast white towel in her hands.

She held it up, outspread.

The Lord-Architect stood up, and water sucked back into the bath with a splash. He trod lightly up the steps and let her wrap the towel around his body.

' *Well?*' he demanded.

'Well enough,' Valentine said, grinning. 'See you, I'll help you build your new garden. Take, oh, four to five years.'

Casaubon clutched the towel round his bulk toga-fashion, with what dignity he could manage. 'And the rest?'

'Why, yes,' Valentine said. 'The rest, too.'

The Harvest of Wolves

Flix sat in the old sagging armchair, leaning forward, and tore another page from the *Encyclopaedia Brittanica*. The fire took it, flickering in the grate.

'What the –' the boy, closing the door as he entered, strode across the room and slapped the book out of her hand. 'What's the matter with you? You could *sell* that for –'

'For money to buy fuel?' Flix suggested. Adrenalin made her dizzy. She looked down at her liver-spotted hands, where the veins stood up with age; they were shaking. 'Thank you, I prefer to cut out the middle man. Self-sufficiency.'

He glared; she doubted he recognized irony.

'You're crazy, you know that?'

'If you know it, that ought to be enough. Have you put in your report yet?' She shot the question at him.

He was still young enough to blush. Angry because of it, he snarled, 'You keep your mouth shut, citizen. You hear me?'

'I hear you.' Age makes you afraid, Flix thought. Pacifying him, she said, 'Well, what have you brought me?'

'Bread. Milk's out. Can't deliver, there's no transport. I got you some water, though. It's clean.'

You wouldn't know clean water if it bit you, Flix thought

bitterly. She watched the boy unpacking the plastic bag he carried, throwing the goods into the nearest cupboard. He was growing taller by the week, this one; broad-shouldered with close-cropped black hair, and the changing voice of adolescence.

'Marlow,' she said, 'what makes you choose community service?'

'Didn't choose it, did I? Got given it, didn't I?'

He straightened, stuffed the bag in the pocket of his uniform jacket, and came over to squat beside the open fire. Though he never admitted it, it attracted him. Probably because he'd never before been in a house old enough to have a grate, she thought.

' "Community service",' she repeated, unable to keep the edge out of her voice. 'Snooping under cover of charity; you call that service? Bringing Welfare rations, weighing me up . . . and all the time new laws, and cutting it closer every time, eh? If they've got as far as these slums, Marlow boy, then pretty soon we'll all be gone.'

Resentment glared out of him. 'Think I want to come here? Crazy old house, crazy old bitch –'

'That's "citizen" to you, if you can't manage "Flix".' She offered him a crumpled pack of cigarettes, forcing a smile. 'Only tobacco, I'm afraid.'

The Pavlovian response: 'Filthy things'll give you cancer.'

'Ah, who'll get me first, then: lung cancer, hypothermia, starvation – or you and your bloody Youth Corps?'

'You got no room to talk – it was your lot got us in this mess in the first place.' He stood up. 'You think we want to live like this, no jobs, nothing? You got no idea. If it weren't for the Corps I'd be –'

'You'd be waiting out your time on Welfare,' Flix said, very carefully. 'Seeing the deadline come up. You'd be being tested – like I am now – to see how fit you are to survive. To qualify for government food. To get government water, so you don't die of cholera. Government housing, so you don't die of cold. Instead you're here, waiting for me to –'

'That's the way it is,' Marlow said. He lowered his head, glaring at her from dark, hollowed eyes. (Why, she thought, he's been losing sleep.) 'You got to produce. You got to work.

You got to be worth keeping on Welfare. Or else – and don't tell me it ain't fair. I know it ain't fair, but that's the way it is.'

'Ah,' she said, on a rising inflection, 'is that the way it is.'

'*Look* at you!' He swung his arm round, taking in the single-room flat. The wallpaper was covered by old posters, garish with the slogans of the halcyon '90s (that final, brief economic flowering) when protest was easy. Planks propped up on bricks served as shelves for old books and pamphlets and magazines. Some had sat so long in the same place that the damp had made of them an inseparable mass. A long-disconnected computer terminal gathered dust, ancient access codes scratched on the casing. Cracking china lay side by side on the drainer with incongruously new plastic dishes, and a saucepan full of something brown and long-burned sat on the stove. A thin film of plaster from the ceiling had drifted down onto the expanse of worn linoleum, left empty by the clustering of table, chair, and bed round the open fire.

Flix poked the ashes with a burnt slat, and glanced up at the windows. Beyond the wire-mesh, the sky was grey.

'You could fix those boards,' she said. 'There's a wind whips through there that could take the barnacles off a ship's hull, since your friends left me with no glass in the windows. . . . What, no reaction?'

'You can't blame them.' The boy sounded tired, and very adult. 'Thinking of you in here. Eating, sleeping. Doing nothing to earn it.'

'Christ!' Flix exploded, and saw him flinch at the word as he always did. But now she wasn't goading him for her amusement. 'There was a time you didn't have to *earn* the right to live! You had it – as a human being!'

'Yeah,' he said wearily. 'I know. I heard about that. I hear about it all the time from my old man. Free this, free that, free the other; holidays in the sun, cars for everybody, everybody working – yeah, I heard. And what happens? What do you leave for *us*? You let the niggers come here and steal your jobs, you let the Yanks put their missiles here! You let kids grow up wild 'cause their mothers were never home; you sell us out to the Reds –'

'Oh, spare me. If you're going to be bigoted, at least be original!'

'Citizen,' Marlow said, 'shut up.'

Not quite under her breath she said, 'Ignorant pig.'

He yelled. 'Why don't you clean this place up? *You* live like a pig!'

'I was never one for housework – and besides, I've got you to do it for me, haven't I? Courtesy of the Welfare state. Until such time as the state decides I'm not worth keeping alive.'

His would not be the first report made on her (though the first under this name), but time and purges had culled the number of officials willing to turn a blind eye on changes of code, name, and location.

I am, Flix thought, too old for this fugitive life.

'Pig,' Marlow repeated absently. He rummaged around in the toolbox by the window, and began nailing the slats back over the lower windowsill.

'There's coffee in the cupboard.' Flix made a peace-offering of it. 'Have some if you want it. You'll have to boil the kettle. I think the power's still on.'

'Where'd you get *coffee?*'

'I still have friends,' Flix observed sententiously. 'They can't do much, being as they're old like me; but what they can do, they will. The old network's still there.'

'Subversive,' he accused.

Lord Brahma! I can't seem to keep off it today, Flix thought. What is it with me – do I *want* to die? Well, maybe. But not to suit their convenience.

'Do you ever listen to anything except what they tell you?'

Marlow whacked the last nail in viciously, threw down the hammer, and stalked over to the sink. Filling the kettle, his back to her, he said, 'I know what's right. I know what's true.'

'I am sick to death of people who *know*. I want people who aren't sure. I want people who're willing to admit there's another side to the argument – or even that there is an argument, for Christ's sake! Marlow, will you bloody look at me!'

He plugged the kettle in. Turning, and leaning back against the chipped unit: 'What?'

'You don't believe all that bullshit.' Again, he flinched. They are abnormally sensitive, she thought. 'You can't believe it, you're not the age. Sixteen's when you go round questioning everything.'

'Maybe in your day. It's different now. We got to grow up quick or not at all.' He shrugged. 'Listen, I'm looking back at it, what it was like – I can see what you can't. While you sat round talking, the commies were taking over the unions; and if it hadn't been for Foster we'd be a satellite state today –'

Flix groaned. 'Jesus. Marlow, tell me all the shit you like, tell me we were all commie pinko perverts, tell me we were capitalist running dogs who brought the world to ruin –' she was laughing, an old woman's high cackle '– but in the name of God, don't tell me about your precious Foster! I knew all I needed to know about dictators before you were born!'

His mouth twisted. She could see him lose patience with her.

'You don't know what it's like,' Marlow said. 'Five of us in a two-room flat, and the power not on, and never enough food, and for why? Because there's no work, and if there was, there's nothing to buy with the money! At least he's making it better. At least there's less of that!'

'Where do you go when there's nowhere to go?' Flix asked rhetorically. 'I'd OD if you could get the stuff, but that's another thing banned in your bloody utopia. Fetch us the coffee, Marlow, and hand me that half-bottle in the top cupboard.'

He was as disapproving as any Youth Cadet, but he did what she asked. Whiskey, and coffee (the last now, the very last) bit into her gut. I am fighting, she reminded herself sourly, I am fighting – God knows why – for my life.

'I suppose it's no good offering you a drink? No, I thought not. Hell, Marlow, loosen up, will you?'

She had, over the weeks, gained some small amusement from tormenting him. Like all of Foster's New Puritans, the Corps strongly disapproved of drugs, blasphemy, lechery – and there, she thought, is a fine old-fashioned word. Not that I've quite got round to that . . . but wouldn't he react beautifully! Or is it that I'm afraid of him laughing? Or afraid of him? For all his 'community service', he's still a thug.

She tore a few more pages from the thick book, crumpled them, and poked them into the fire where they flared briefly. 'What about coal, Marlow?'

'Reconstituted.'

'Christ, that stuff doesn't burn. Still, what the hell. Come and sit down.' She watched him kneel by the flames. In the dim cold room, the light made lines on his face; he looked older.

'In the nineties,' she said speculatively, 'there were, for example, parties without supervisors – supervisors! – and music without propaganda –'

'Without whose propaganda?'

'Bravo, Marlow!' She clapped gently. 'Without theirs, of course. With ours. Now it's the other way round. Do you realize, I wouldn't *mind* if he had the grace to be original? But it's the same old thing; no free press, no free speech, no unions; food shortages, rabid patriotic nationalism –'

'You were traitors! Was that any better?'

No way out, she thought, no way in; God preserve us from the voice of invincible ignorance.

'One thing we didn't do,' she said. 'We didn't weigh people up as to how useful they were to the state – and let them die when they got sick and old.'

He was quiet. 'Didn't you?'

'We didn't *plan* it.'

'There's less poverty now. Less misery. It's a hard world,' he said. 'They're starving in Asia. Dying. That's not going to happen here. You used it up, this world. So you got yourselves to blame if you don't like what's happening now.'

'Marlow,' Flix said, 'what are you going to say in your report?'

Now there was no evading the question. He looked up with clear puzzled eyes. 'I don't want to do it.'

'I know, or it wouldn't be nearly a month overdue, would it? No, don't ask me how I know. Like I said, the old grapevine's still there. When are they going to start wondering, Marlow? When are they going to start making reports on *you?*'

He stared into the fire. She got up slowly, taking her weight on her wrists, and went across to pull on her old (now much cracked) leather jacket. The cold got into her bones. Now would I be so weak if there was proper food? she thought. Christ, my mother lived to be eighty, and I'm not within twenty years of that!

'I've got family,' Marlow said. 'The old man, Macy and the baby. We got to eat.'

She could see herself reflected in the speckled wall mirror, lost in sepia depths. An old woman, lean and straight, with spiky cropped hair that needed washing from grey to silver. Marlow, out of focus, was a dark uniform and the glint of insignia.

Flix looked straight at him, solemnly; and when his eyes were fixed on her, she smiled. She had always had one of those faces, naturally sombre and sardonic, that are transformed when they smile. Vanity doesn't go with age, she thought, savouring the boy's unwilling responsive grin.

'I could have shown you so much – so much. You haven't got the guts to run wild,' she said, 'you haven't got the guts to *question*.'

The implication of promise was there. He watched her. The light dimmed, scummy and cold; and the fire glowed down to red embers. The ever-present smell of the room, overlain for a while by coffee and spirits, reasserted itself.

'You're a drunk,' Marlow said. 'D'you think I haven't seen the bottles you throw out – and the ones you hide? Yeah, your friends keep you supplied, all right! I've come in here when you were dead drunk on the bed, place stinking of shit; I've listened to you maundering on about the old days – I don't want to know! If this is where it leaves you, I don't want to know!'

'Is that right?' Tears stung behind her eyes, her voice thinned. 'You'll never live the life I lived, and you'll never know how I regret its passing – ah, Jesus, it tears you up, to know it's gone and gone for good. *You* were the people we wanted to help. I mean you, Marlow! And when it came to actually thinking – God knows how difficult that is – you don't want to know. You'd sooner march with your mobs. You'd sooner smash places up on your witch-hunts. You'd sooner cheer the tanks when they roll by. And God help you, that's not enough, you've got to think you're *right*!'

The boy crossed the room and pushed her. She fell back on the bed with an ugly sound. He stamped back and forth, sweeping the cracked cups crashing to the floor. Violently he kicked at the piles of old books and pamphlets. They scattered in soggy lumps.

'This!' he shouted. 'You preach about your precious books and you burn them to keep warm! You talk about your "subversive network" but what is it really? Old men and women hoarding food and drink, keeping it from us who need it!'

She, breathing heavily and conscious of pain, didn't answer. His first energy spent, he came back and helped her into the chair; and made up the fire until it blazed. The cold wind blew belches of grey smoke back into the room.

Flix felt down into the side of the chair for the hidden bottle there; fist knotted about it, letting the alcohol sting her back to life. When she looked up again he was putting on his coat.

As if nothing had happened, she said, 'Books aren't sacred. Ideas are, and I've got those up here.' She touched her lank hair. 'Whatever else we are, we subversives, I'll tell you this – we care about each other. That's more than your Corps will do for you when you're old.'

'I'll come in again tomorrow.' He was all boy now, gangling, uncertain, sullen.

'I don't care if you don't agree with me! Just think about what you're doing – for once, *think* about it!'

At the door he turned back and said, ' *Will* they look after you?'

After she heard the door slam, she plugged the power outlet into the antique stereo equipment, and played old and much-mended '90s revival-rock cassettes, blasting the small room full of sound. It served to stop the treadmill-turning of her mind.

'You've got a letter!' Taz yelled down the stairs after her the next morning. She grunted, not taking any notice; the old man (occupier of the building's only other inhabitable room) was given to delusions, to happenings that were years after their time.

But when she crossed the hallway it lay there in the crepuscular light: a thin rough-paper envelope folded and addressed to Citizen Felicity Vance. Flix picked it up, wincing at the pain in her back. An immature hand, the letters mostly printed. So she knew.

She took it into her room, closing the door and resting her old bones on the bed.

Where is there anyone I can tell? she thought. That's another one of the boy's taunts – 'if you had a husband, citizen.' Ah, but I could never live in anyone's company but my own.

Now it came to it she was afraid. Shaking, sweating; the old cold symptoms. She opened the letter.

'Citizen –

'I have to tell the truth. They check up on me too. It is the truth. You drink too much and your alone and cant take care. I have to live. If your friends are good friends you better tell them I sent my report in. Its not your fault things are like this. Im sorry I said it was. Sometimes I wisht I lived in the old days it might have been good. But I dont think so not for most of us.

'Peter Marlow'

She dressed slowly; fashions once adopted from a mythical past and previous revolutions: old jeans and sweater and the ancient leather jacket – the smell took her back, with the abruptness of illusion, to boys and bikes and books; to bright libraries, computer networks; to Xerox and duplicators, to faxsheets in brilliant colours that had been going to change the world.

He believes I'm a drunken old woman, alone, friends no more than geriatrics; he has to report me or be reported himself – and does he hope that it's more than an illusion, that some secret subversive organization still exists to whisk me off to – what? Safety? Where?

Things are bad all over, kid.

But at least he's sent in the report.

She left, locking the door behind her. It was a long time and a long walk to where she could borrow a working telephone. When she called the number, it was a while before it was answered; and a while before he remembered her name.

'Well,' Flix said, 'you'll have had the report by now.'

'You're a fool,' the man said. 'You won't last a week in the Welfare camps! Flix –'

'I'll last long enough to tell what I know,' Flix said. 'About you – and who your father was – and what "societies" you used to belong to. I'll do it, Simon. Maybe it won't make much difference, maybe it won't even lose you your job. But you won't have much of a career afterwards.'

After a pause he said, 'What do you want?'

'I want somewhere decent to live. I want to be warm. I want enough to eat, I want to play my music and read my books in peace. That's all. I'm tired of living like a pig! I want a place like the one you've got put by for yourself when *you* get old. No Welfare camps for Foster's boys, right? Now they'll put me in one – they can't ignore that report – and when they do, you know what I'm going to say!'

She could feel his uncertainty over the line, knew she had to weight things in her favour.

'Would it help,' she said, 'if you could turn in a few of the old subversive cells, by way of a sweetener? Those that didn't know you, those that can't give us away?'

'"Us".' His tone reluctantly agreed complicity, barely masked contempt. 'Names?'

'Names after, not before.'

And he agreed.

Flix grinned to herself, a fox-grin full of teeth and no humour. You and me both, Marlow, she thought; you and me both . . .

'Like someone once told me,' she said, 'I have to live.'

The Crystal Sunlight, The Bright Air

Paul Broderick came to Orthe a haunted man.

You'll have no trouble, the Intendant who briefed him promised. Orthe's a regained world. There were Earth settlements on it before the Insurrection. The natives are used to humans.

Go down, Broderick. Find out if this world needs the Interdict.

Carrick's Star scorched down on Orthe, on Kasabaarde's narrow streets, reflecting back from the white domes and ankle-deep dust. The acid light bit into his eyes, even behind the face mask's protective glass. Dust irritated his skin. He quickened his pace towards the wall separating trade district from inner city. If there was cause for the Interdict, it had to be there. Nothing outside the wall was unusual – after the Insurrection. An agricultural society living in the ruins of a high-technology past . . .

Wind brought the smell of marine life from the harbour, close by the gate. Sunlight fractured off the sea like broken glass. Broderick approached the Ortheans at the gateway.

'You wish to enter the inner city?'

His hypno-trained mind translated the breathy sounds and sharp clicks. He answered as well as he could.

The Orthean who spoke was a head shorter than Broderick. Bleached skin under the city's dust showed a hint of scale-pattern. Masked – as all Ortheans were outdoors – there was only a glimpse of eyes set widely apart under a broad forehead. Under the mask's edge, thin lips curved in a reptilian smile.

'Wait,' the humanoid said. Pale hair was caught up in complex braids; as she turned to consult the others he saw the mane was rooted down her spine to the small of her back. A length of cloth wrapped her narrow hips. Thin ribs were prominent. Small breasts were set higher than in the human norm, and a second pair of rudimentary nipples were visible on her lower ribs. He noted the seamed belly. Oviparous.

'It is permitted.' She faced him again. 'Touch the earth.'

He knelt and touched the dry ground, and when he stood she took a bowl of water from another Orthean and offered it to him. He drank, indifferent to infection.

'If you have weapons you must leave them with us. They will be returned to you when you go.'

He carried a knife for just such occasions, and gave it to her. The weapons he carried wouldn't be recognized on a world like this.

'Is there somewhere I can stay in there?' he asked, as they registered his name and possessions in the gatehouse. 'Somewhere cheap?'

'Anywhere.' Her six-fingered hand flicked out, a gesture including all the streets and domes beyond the wall. 'All the Order houses are open to you, Outlander. Open and free. There is no gold in the inner city, not for strangers, nor for us.'

'"Free"?' Broderick said, appalled; and when they had translated it several ways so that there was no mistake: '*free?*'

And then:

What are you doing here, Paul?

No, he thought. No! Not again. Don't think about it –

What right does the Holy Dominion have over this world, what justification for the Interdict? Why, Paul, why?

His haunt was a woman-shaped emptiness visible on the air, distorting the pale sky and squat buildings. Grief and doubt threatened to overwhelm him. He stifled the remembered voice.

Broderick entered the inner city of Kasabaarde.

When Clare Felix died the whole world grieved.

They told Paul Broderick she was dead and he didn't believe it. He heard and smiled: it was a fiction, like the games he and Clare played. A world couldn't exist in which she could be dead.

They thought they made him understand. He understood. The shock blinded and deafened him, but not for long. News of that death would have touched him, he thought mechanically, if he had been dead himself.

He went out blindly into the streets of the megalopolis, into the dust and fumes of a wholly inappropriate summer day. In the crystal sunlight, the bright air, he stood trying to realize it: Clare is dead. Is dead. Clare is dead but the world's still whole, I still exist, and Clare –

– is dead.

He walked past familiar crowded shops. The news was out by then, satellite-broadcast to the world. On the faces of people he passed, he saw a shadow of that raging grief.

He didn't notice when it began, but after a time he knew that in every shop he passed the tapes of Clare Felix's songs were being played. The music and the words that she had sweated over, snarled at him for interrupting, hummed when they loved – those songs were coming out into the dusty grieving city.

He might have run. He found himself, gasping for breath, in front of a public news screen. The dead woman's voice sang out under the noise of traffic, the rumble of the distant starport. People slowed, hesitated, listened; a girl cried. Lines of type formed beside her picture on-screen. Her kind of death would have attracted attention on Parmiter's World in any case: they tended to long lives, not massive coronaries at twenty-seven. Being who she was . . .

Broderick read the customary closing line with a new razor-edged attention. '*She lives in the union of the Holy Dominion; her spirit is with us forever.*'

He waited for the comfort that always brought him. It didn't come. When the weeks turned to months, he realized it would never come.

Wider streets opened here, still with the cloth awnings stretched from dome to dome. The shade was welcome. Sweat tracked down between his shoulders. Few Ortheans moved in the noon heat; they sprawled on the steps that led up to the domes, or sat with their backs against the dome walls and stared into space.

Broderick walked for some time down the avenues. At last, having no better guide, he chose a door at random; pushing through the bead curtain and entering the bright room beyond.

'Welcome to Thelmithar.' A male Orthean paused at the head of a flight of spiral steps. He was darker-skinned than many, his mane receding from his brow until there was only a white crest left. His movements had the carefulness of age.

'Is there somewhere I can eat?' Broderick asked.

'Of course. Will you stay here?'

It was as good a place as any, he thought. 'Yes.'

'Come with me. I'm Surinc,' the old male said. 'Ask for me if you need anything.'

Broderick followed him down the spiral stairs and came into a bright underground hall. Silver light reflected diffusely from mirrors set in the vaulted roof: sunlight directed down from above. A young Orthean played the twin-flute in a corner. The tables round the still pool were mostly empty. Children scuttled past, sparing him curious glances.

He ate what time in the trade district had proved unlikely to cause allergic reaction: breadfungus, *brennior*-meat, and *arniac*-herb tea. When he left the table, he called the old Orthean.

'I'll pay for a room now,' he said, testing.

The thin lips curved. Surinc weighed the cord of metal beads that passed for money in the trade district and handed them back to Broderick.

'You will be an Outlander, then, not to know there is no payment in the Order houses. Here at Thelmithar – and Geth-firle, Cir-nanth, all the others – they'll feed you, house you, clothe you if you desire it. Freely.'

'For how long?'

'As long as you wish to stay.'

His mind protested, *nothing's free!* 'If not money, then what? Labour? Information?'

The old Orthean unmasked. Broderick saw his whiteless animal eyes, and the nictitating membrane that slid slowly across the slit pupil. Those hooded eyes held indefinable amusement.

'We're fortunate,' he said. 'All who travel up the Desert

Coast to trade must pass through Kasabaarde, and also all who come down from the north and the islands. All who pass us pay. The Order houses have tolls and taxes, Outlander. They can afford the inner city.'

Broderick shook his head. 'Why give anything away?'

'If you have to ask, why have you come?' The tawny eyes veiled. 'We give only one thing – time. Come here and we free you, feed and house you; but what we give away is time.'

This, Broderick thought. *If anyone can come here, and not have to work – this is why we're considering the Interdict.*

'Time for what?'

' "Idleness breeds violence and vision," the Orders say. There are other values besides what you wear on your back and put in your belly, Outlander. Thelmithar can give you time – what you do with it depends on what you are.'

'Violent or visionary?' It was an involuntary, cynical remark.

Surinc's six fingers linked in a complex gesture. 'I can't tell you what you'll find here. If I could, it wouldn't be the true illumination.'

Reduced to simplicity, Broderick protested, 'People can't just do nothing!'

'No, indeed. Most can't. But those who can . . .'

Left alone, Broderick sat for a while, then felt driven to go back up into the open air. Under the awning's shade, many Ortheans sat on Thelmithar's steps. Come from both continents? Brockerick wondered. The concept of the inner city stunned him. It was dangerous.

And will you bring the Interdict down on this city of philosophers?

He shook his head to clear it, but couldn't rid himself of the caustic, loving voice of the dead woman.

Broderick left Parmiter's World a scant few weeks after Clare's death. Her face stared down from news screens, her voice followed him in the streets. He left because he knew he'd never hear her songs offworld, never hear her name.

Clare Felix's songs and music were under Interdict.

'How can they do it?' she'd raged. 'I'm good, Paul. All over this planet –'

'Too good,' he admitted. 'Too strong, if you like, for the

average mind.'

'Intendant!' She snarled it like a curse. 'What's the Dominion afraid of? Think there'll be another Insurrection if Felix sells offworld, that it?'

She was acid, dismissing his explanations. She didn't want explanations, only justice.

'How can I communicate? I know I can reach them on other worlds – they're different from us, yes, but I can touch them – feel the way they feel, make them listen to me when I sing!'

'How do you think the Insurrection started?' Broderick asked. 'Something in the mind responds, philosophy and religion spread from world to world, psychic epidemics – man tends to chaos. If the Dominion didn't keep the Interdict on that –' that –'

'So you interdict religion, politics, art, music . . .' She sat hugging her knees, knuckles white. Tension drew the brown skin taut over her high cheekbones, sharpened the line of her mouth. 'You've put me in a cage.'

And so he left that cage, Parmiter's World. His fear and hope was that passing under Interdict might wipe out his feeling for her, and the doubt that gnawed him. It did not; it left him more hollow than before.

He went out by way of the Dominion orbital station, traveling on a Dominion ship – there was no other way to travel. The Interdict – a combination of hypnosis and aversion therapy – didn't destroy memory. It implanted a strong disinclination to communicate the Interdicted subject. Perhaps what it did, Broderick thought, was kill the belief in a thing; so that after he left Parmiter's World, Clare glowed bright in his mind, but her music was only noise.

Something with terrifying potential, the Interdict, and so only to be trusted to the highest power: the Holy Dominion . . .

But that was when I believed in the Dominion, Broderick thought. Now who do I trust?

You came here to judge. So judge.

Broderick knew he was hallucinating. Nevertheless Clare Felix followed him from Thelmithar to Cir-nanth, from Cir-nanth to Gethfirle, and from Gethfirle to the Order house Durietch.

The curved wall of Durietch was hot against his back. The scent of *kasziz*-creeper filled the air. In the past week Broderick had heard any number of philosophies, many varieties of mysticism. Any Intendant would recognize at once how dangerous Kasabaarde's inner city was, breeding such things.

'Outlander,' said a young Orthean near him, 'what do your people believe in?'

The creed came to Broderick's mind: 'I believe in the Dominion, in our immortality in the union of spirit; I believe in the Peace of Mankind, and in the holy instrumentality of the Intendants –'

I believe Clare Felix is dead.

'I don't know,' he said.

'I left the Islands for much the same reason.' The Orthean's skin shimmered, crystalline. 'I thought I might find the answer here.'

'Have you?'

'I don't know. Perhaps.'

Dangerous, Broderick thought. If the inner city's principle spreads. An epidemic of fads, philosophies, cults, heresies. No Intendant should hesitate. *Interdict!*

He missed one ship's pick-up date, and the next one too.

A fight began without reason, and finished as rapidly; a brief scuffle. No one moved to stop it. Broderick, caught in the fringes, rubbed skinned knuckles. Few of the crazies would tackle the Outlander, as a rule. He left Durietch all the same, walking back through dry alleys to Thelmithar. The egg-basket domes of the inner city blazed white against the pale sky.

When are you going back, Paul?

Now it was movement out of the corner of his eye, creeper fronds that mocked the line of her throat, the turn of her head.

You had no business sending me here! This needs an Intendant with faith, not a man who doubts everything!

Clare, Clare, Clare is dead. Known for so long, so familiar; lived with so close (Broderick thought) that you couldn't say I loved her, you'd have to say we were part of each other. So that death is amputation. Without reason. No, no reason. All the Intendant principles: peace, power, and love . . . all of them hollow. Measure it up against her death and what answer's left? Nothing.

Self-pity, Clare jeered. *And selfishness. How many times have you thought of suicide? Paul, Paul, and you always told me you believed in the unity!*

He sat on Thelmithar's steps, among the tranced Ortheans.

Work, Paul – are you going to waste your life?

He retained a lunatic hope that it was a real experience. That it was Clare in communication from the unity. But however hard he begged her, she wouldn't sing. Then he resigned himself to the fact that it was his own mute mind producing her image.

Clare, I miss you. All our lives together wouldn't have been long enough. I miss your touch, your smell, your love. There are so many questions I wanted to ask you.

The last pickup date was close. Broderick, restless, went from Order house to Order house, questioning those who thought they'd found some illumination, some revelation in the inner city. To any who would listen, he spoke of Clare Felix.

'We're not so intense,' one elderly Orthean woman said. 'We love many times. But you . . . better to have had her a short time than not at all.'

Another, so young he couldn't tell if it were male or female, said, 'The earth is. The stars are. The wind blows and the land grows. What more should there be, Outlander?'

Passionately, he said, 'It doesn't answer her death!'

'I'll die,' the young one said. 'So will you. Does that thought disturb you?'

Broderick laughed at the irony. 'No.'

'If you can forgive the universe for your death, then forgive it for hers. Her death is her own, not yours.'

He left them, unanswered. The ever present dust worked under his mask as he wandered the streets, irritating his sore eyes. Fury possessed him. Sometimes he shouted aloud. No one took notice of that. He was not unique to the inner city. The short twilight passed, and the fierce stars of the Core blazed in the night sky. Heat radiated back from the stone walls. Broderick kept walking. He crossed and recrossed the inner city, ignoring fatigue. The stars turned in the moonless night.

Dawn found him on the steps of Cir-nanth, dully watching

the sunrise. Fatigue blurred his mind. His body ached; he had walked all the long dark hours. Light flooded the face of the dome. A dawn wind blew off the sea. Broderick eased himself down to sit by the bead-curtained door.

It happened then. Between one heartbeat and the next, welling up in him. His eyes stung, wet. He reached out and touched the mortar crumbling between the curved stone blocks, the dead leaves in the dust beside him. He saw the flaring light of the sun and the pale glory of the sky, felt the salt-laden breeze. Felt the breath in his lungs, the beat of his heart, the blood in his body. The pulse, the rhythm . . .

Nothing was changed: Clare was dead. Everything was changed: he was alive.

Broderick drew breath, shook his head in amazement; looking at her death as if it were a thousand years ago, and at her life as if it were a miracle. All the people she had reached out to –!

The inner city said to him: The world is. You are. I am. This is all there is.

And if this is all there is, Broderick slowly pieced together his conclusion, then all that's important is communication. To know ourselves and to know others. Reach out, touch: love. The past and the future don't exist. What matters is us, alive, now.

In Orthe's dawn was a pinprick of falling light, no morning star. The ship. If he didn't leave willingly, they would take him. And take it as further proof that the Interdict was necessary.

'You're our litmus paper,' an Intendant once said to him. 'We drop you in, stir you round, and pull you out, see how you've changed. How else can we judge the really powerful effects on the human psyche?'

On Orthe there are two populated continents where a man might vanish. On Orthe there are remnants of a high-tech civilization, a star-travelling people. Broderick watched the star fall. If a man should build his own ships . . .?

It would not be the first time someone had gone up against the Dominion. He would most likely fail. Even if there were – as he thought there might be, later – others to carry the word, failure was still probable.

Will you put music in a cage? Clare Felix had asked.

Broderick put on his mask, and walked on into the long morning shadows of that alien city.

The Tarot Dice

It begins with a rose. A white rose, its embroidery old and stained so that it is closer to yellow, to the colour of old bone. That rose-badge has been on the breast of his jacket for years now. He has caught his reflection in the glass window that faces the night, stands for a moment transfixed – face almost as worn and old as the badge – and then he takes up shoulder-slung gun and descends through the Levels. Others acknowledge him as he passes by, with the genuflection of the White Rose, of whose orders and degrees he is (with but one exception) the highest.

Walking down towards the river-dock: the naphtha flares bleach all colour from his lined face, from the hair like frayed hemp-rope and pale, sparse beard. Now that you can see him, he seems younger than his thoughts or his walk; he could be under forty-five, even under forty.

Mist coils in the silver gloom.

Between the buildings runs the river.

Flat mud stretches out, bubbling and stinking, to the rotten brickwork on one side and the black moss-covered masonry on the other. Acres of mud, but here the deep channel of the river runs close by the dock; the water glinting with blue, platignum, purple, green. The colours of poison. It runs, both visibly and by underground sewers, towards the Edge.

He walks along the dock, keeping to the shadows. The White Rose is used to concealment: like the iceberg, only a tenth of his Church is visible at any one time.

There, in the circle of light, a flare of white naphtha, men are crouched on the cobbles of the quay. See now what they are doing:

Playing dice – but these dice have no number-spots. Each die on its six faces carries one image of the Thirty Cards of the Major Arcana. These Tarot images are enamelled, small and very precise; and in the light they tumble like icons spilt on the pavement. The men who play dice are squatting in a circle, sheltered from the night wind by boxes and piled crates; and shadows fall on their faces, black in eyes that seem only sockets now, so that they sit in a circle of skulls.

He sees a boat nearing the river-steps, the dip and plop of each oar, the scattering trail of metallic water-drops. There is a figure, so still, in the prow. Again, all kinds of premonitions touch him: all legends of chosen ones that will come to this city by way of the river . . .

The river is never silent, the river flows: the bank a constant and the waters always new. He has spat in this river, passing over the city's many bridges, is there (he wonders) some small part of him now that is part of the sea?

The boat docks, the passenger steps ashore. The men look up as a woman enters the light. A thin young woman in man's clothing: dark jacket and trousers and boots; and with startling hair. She nods a greeting, speaks one in a thick, almost-unintelligible accent. They make a place for her. She squats down on her haunches, and as she reaches out to take the five dice – there are Minor Arcana dice, but few can afford the whole set – he steps from the cover of a warehouse entrance.

'Sanzia?' he says.

Look at her now: she gives us such a penetrating look. Her eyes in that pale, sharp face (malnourished, certainly, and for some time by the look of it) are a brilliant pale blue. Her hair is silver-white, thick and coarse and long; not an old woman's hair that is yellowed because she is no more than nineteen – or is that a trick of shadow? Is she twenty-five? Thirty-five?

As he moves forward, she looks up; that pale gaze is something he cannot easily look away from. He sees it register the badge of the Rose, and his fingers stray automatically to feel the bulk of ancient embroidery: the nine-petalled rose, the rose whose serrated petals could so easily be teeth.

She (as if hours and yards separated them, not years and continents) says 'Hainzell.' And throws the dice that she has gathered:

The Phoenix. The Weaver. The Rose. Death. Flight.

These are well-made dice. Though the space for the image is no larger than a thumbnail, they are there and clear:

The eagle that burns and is not consumed, forked white fire issuing from its own body: *The Phoenix,*

The spider whose back, looked at carefully, becomes the image of an old woman's face: *The Weaver,*

A skull in whose eye-sockets are set tiny periwinkle-blue flowers: *Death,*

And then *The Rose,* whose petals are toothed and cogged, are interlocking clockwork. And *Flight,* sky-blue, with one Icarus-feather falling. . . . or is it rising?

One of the men, reading casually as Tarot gamblers do, says 'Intrigue, well-made plans. Immortality and re-birth. Death and great change: the fall of a mighty house. . . .'

'Content,' Sanzia observes, her accent more obtrusive than ever. She reaches out a hand, rests one finger on a die. There is a callous on that middle finger of her left hand, which only comes from long use of a pen. She touches *The Weaver:*

'Read me that one.'

Hainzell steps forward, bends and scoops up the dice in one rough movement. He meets her startled gaze.

'Empty the pouch – show me!'

The men playing dice are dock-workers, soldiers, a smith, a boy who has the look of an armourer's apprentice. While they mutter and stare, they as yet make no move.

The rage that creeps into his voice is response to her stillness:

'Show me!'

She takes her pouch from her shoulder. It is large, thick,

full; from it she draws sheets of paper. All are inked. All are in large ill-set type, all are identical. He snatches one, reads it, sneers.

'Pamphlets! Heresy and revelation – is that why you've come here?'

And in disgust or anger he throws down the handful of dice, that rattle on the cobblestones, gleam in the spitting naphtha glare:

The Rose. Flight. Death. The Phoenix. The Weaver.

An indrawn breath, in that circle. There are thirty faces that can fall – too many for the fall of these same five to be coincidence.

It is, surprisingly, the apprentice who reads: fingers touching the Icarus-feather of *Flight,* not quite daring to touch *The Rose*:

'Knowledge through suffering; intrigue and death; the passing away of a great power.'

Hainzell stares down at the dice, then turns and strides away; confusion and anger in him contending with something else.

Sanzia stands up, looking after him; takes a pace or two after him, and then pauses indecisively. The group of men remain squatting in a circle, the Tarot dice spilling onto the flat cobbles. The armourer's boy suddenly picks them up, seizes her hand in his cold fingers, and presses the bone-and-enamel dice into her left hand:

'Take them!'

She might have said much, but Hainzell is gone, the sound of his footsteps diminishing, so with only a nod (thanks, or merely acknowledgement?) she tightens her fist round the dice and hurries off after the man.

'Why?' This from an elderly dock-worker.

'Oh, she might – need?' The boy hesitates. 'She's a stranger, a foreigner, she might. . . . things are bad in the city now.'

The men rise and stand looking into the dark.

'We can't trust her,' one of the older soldiers says.

The apprentice nods. 'She can't betray what she doesn't know. She's not from here. She knows the Church of the White Rose, but not as we do. But it's the man of the Rose that I'm sorry for.'

'Well, I am sorry for all of them,' another dock-worker says. He flicks a match from his fingers into the river, and the red spark arcs down. 'Sorry for all of them who take no notice of us because they can't see us. Well, they will see us soon enough.'

A fifth man (they are all men here, you will notice – or perhaps you will not notice – although some of them have wives, and some have children; the former not a necessity for the latter; and I don't know where the women are), he says 'They don't matter to us at all.'

The armourer's apprentice says, 'What about the Bridge-builder? What about the Visconti?'

The group remains together for some few minutes, talking, but with the dice gone, some of the spirit is gone from them, and they soon disperse, each going separately back into the alleys that open onto the dock.

Hainzell is passing shells of buildings so tall that clouds can float in through the broken windows. And cellars where fungus grows tall as a man: inkcaps and puffballs, stinkworts, creeping veined mats of white fungus-flesh, slatted layers and shelves of it, spores like a fine mist in the air.

He walks quickly to begin with. Then, aware of the inevitable, slows his steps; not quite willing to admit he is waiting for her to catch up. He has reached the river-bridge before a footstep behind him makes him turn.

'You shouldn't run,' Sanzia says.

'You shouldn't be here –!'

Sanzia wants to touch him, the way that the hair is rough just at the nape of his neck is too much for her, she puts the flat of her hand against the skin of his neck, soft, sweet-smelling; and he knocks her hand aside and turns to face her, his back to the parapet of the bridge.

Her voice, somewhere between resignation and anger:

'You are *not* my brother!'

As if it were the continuation of a long dialogue (and it is, over some years) Hainzell says, 'I feel my blood in you sometimes. I've washed you, seen you naked, sung you to sleep, bandaged your cuts and scrapes, listened to the first words you could speak –'

'I am not your sister!'

'I raised you so.' Hainzell, a little ironically, adds 'The White Rose would have you now, if that wasn't so. I knew of your arrival.'

'I want you,' Sanzia tells him. 'I want no one else.'

They stand on the bridge, unobserved, but for how long?

'Do you still wear that?' She touches the raised embroidery of the Rose. 'I don't understand you. We began together. You came here to bring them down, not join them!'

When Hainzell speaks again, there is the trace of an accent that he lost years ago: her accent. 'Go home. The Church will take you into the Levels. They would do it now if not for the death –' And then he hesitates.

'The Rose made a promise. People have forgotten, or fear to remember. There was a promise to lead us into the Heartland,' Sanzia says, as if thinking of something quite other; and her hand reaches out to his, as if the desire moved it and not her; the same desire that makes the fingers tremble, and he steps back.

Hainzell, touching the Rose again, thinks: Has it been the sweet rose for so long, and is it now to be the devourer? Instantly, as my flesh answers to hers when it should not: sister, sister . . .

He at last looks her in the face, that thin, malnourished face that is framed by coarse silver hair. 'I have had to settle for the possible,' he says, 'and I won't help you, except in this one thing: if you leave the city tonight you will be able to leave, because of what is happening now, but if you stay until tomorrow you will not be able to leave. And that,' he finishes, 'I would tell to my sister but not to my lover, Sanzia.'

She watches him leave, and still she carries the two words that have been together in his mouth: *Sanzia, lover.*

The snow falls on the great square, and on the stone mausoleum, and on the open coffin and the exposed face of the dead man where he lies in state.

Oddly, there is only one thought in the old woman's mind: *Now there is no one left to call me Luce. . . .*

You're cold, Visconti, Luce thinks. And has an impulse, surprisingly strong, to reach forward and wipe away the snow congealing on dead flesh. She suppresses the impulse with a too-easy facility.

She is alone and moving painfully, she who in her youth was a fighter, Luce; could run fast enough to throw molotov-cock-tails into the cabins of tanks (not fast enough to escape the screaming) and now she moves achingly slow, arms bound in the metal grips of crutches. She has been tall and is now stooped, has been fat but is now worn down, like sea-polished wood, to sparse flesh on spare bone. They have slowed the cortège so she can follow it these last few steps to the mausoleum.

Hainzell, beside her, is troubled.

The yellow sky is flecked with falling blackness. Below the city's roofline the snow turns white, softening cornices and cupolas, whitening the shoulders of men (and some women) who stand in drab coats, motionless, their heads for the most part bowed, as the loudspeakers play funeral marches and a requiem mass.

Luce looks down at the coffin, that seems too small to contain that body – too narrow a space for the Visconti, the Bridge-builder, that they have called 'a living force of history', and were well-advised to call him (while he lived and heard).

The cortège stops. The music ceases. A kind of concerted movement goes through the crowd in the square, like wind across a cornfield. The white discs of their faces dip in and out of vision, as they turn and speak with each other.

Luce brought a microphone on the mausoleum steps, and leaning heavily on her crutches, says:

'Brethren and citizens, I speak with you in sorrow. The father of our Church has been taken from us, the Heartland has him, and we are left alone. We know how great a debt we owe to him, through all those years of poverty. There is not a man among you who cannot say: life in the city would be different today had the Bridgebuilder not lived.'

A sudden disturbance in the crowd resolves itself into an eddy of movement, and protesting figures with banners and pamphlets: against squalor, want, disease, hardship. Luce signals to Hainzell and he to his men: voices are silenced with a quiet and brutal efficiency.

'The whole city will mourn our father Visconti's death,' Luce concludes. Her gaze falls on the embalmed body as offi-cers of the Church lift the coffin, to place it in the mausoleum, upon a glass panel of which are engraved the words of the philosopher-magicians of the White Rose: *Between the Heart-*

land and the Edge is only the space of a breath. Luce looks at that dead white face.

Now you bastard – now we're rid of you, and your stultifying grip on us; now there's only me, and maybe we can turn this Church into what we meant it to be, in the revolution – and I hope you can watch what I'm going to do!

To Hainzell, she says, 'That's the old bastard buried at last.'

Hainzell glances at his superior of the White Rose. 'You wouldn't have dared to say that while he was living.'

'There wouldn't have been the necessity.' Luce is acidic, but his words shake her, in the way that truth does. She thinks: One day we may know why we were so afraid of Visconti –

Or is it: Why we loved him for doing what we couldn't and dared not?

Hainzell says, 'Sanzia is in the city.'

This shabby man, who knows (who better) exactly what sedition and heresy pass under the eyes of the White Rose.

'What do you want to do about it?' Luce says. 'If I send her away, she'll return. Shall I have her killed?'

'*No.*'

There is an expression on his face that she cannot identify, and that – after some fifty years experience of the human race – worries her.

'She's dangerous.'

Hainzell, with a cynical humour, says, 'I think she won't give us time to reform. Seeing no further than the Visconti, and expecting us to be the same. And –'

'And who's to say we won't be?' Luce completes his thought for him, seeing his startled look. 'I know. Believe that I know. I have lived fifty years doing what's possible. With these people and this city, the Heartland is a dream and a prayer and a vision, and nothing more. What action will she take?'

Because he is who he is and what he is, he asks, 'Do we *wait* for her to act?'

'No,' Luce says at last. 'When this flummery's done with and the bastard buried, find me a way to speak with this Sanzia of yours.'

Hainzell, much too quickly (and even he can tell that) protests, 'Not *my* Sanzia.'

★

Later they will say, or she will claim, that Sanzia brought these instruments of heresy, but the truth is that they were in the city and in use long before she arrived. Gamblers' dice, children's toys – that use closer to their nature than the use she found for them.

'They are not unknown to the Church of the White Rose,' says a man one night, a little later, when there are many of them gathered in the Tunnels below the city. The tunnel is an iron pipe a dozen yards in diameter. Rivets as big as a child's head weep rust, fanning down in orange-gold runnels. Icicles hang down, two yards long. Light from braziers glows orange on the walls.

Sanzia sits on her outspread jacket. Her head is bowed. The Tarot dice lay before her, unstable on the cloth, and she turns them almost absently in her fingers, laying die-faces upright:

Plague, whose tiny illustration is the knot with which, in this city, they tie the head of a corpse's shroud –

Twig and leaf of *The World-Tree*, a star caught in it; no room on it for the larger images of the Card, the Tree and what rests under its roots and branches –

The Triune Goddess, which is here depicted as a drop of blood upon a surface of stone –

The man interrupts her, indicating the last die-face, protesting, 'That is an old heresy, the White Rose would burn you for bringing it here, what use is it to us?'

Sanzia continues to turn the dice so that in time they will have seen all. The dance of their succession: *Hermit, Lovers, Chariot, Weaver*. . .

As one grows old, one grows careless with the flesh; but still, she thinks, to be burned –!

. . . *The Lightning-Struck Tower, The Fool, The Star, Justice* . . .

'I bring you keys,' she says, 'and you ask me what use it is to go through an opened door.'

It is the kind of saying that may well be recalled and re-quoted – to really fix it in people's minds she should die a martyr's death. And that comment wouldn't have occurred to me, she thinks, if I hadn't met and spoken with him again. Hainzell, brother and not-brother. What do I care about these belly-brained citizens?

There are two or three dozen gathered round her now, hugging close to the warmth of the brazier. They may be waiting for morning to come, and they may be working towards some realization of their own: who can say?

The same man asks, '*Is* there a Heartland?'

Thinking of the Heartland, the light grows brighter, one dreams of older buildings, small and homely, and white courtyards under an everlasting noon.

A child no more than ten says, 'There are houses there full of gold and diamonds, and food, and you can fly.'

'Lovers,' says an old man, 'and children and those we have long forgotten who knew us once, they are waiting for us in the Heartland.'

'No,' says a third voice, lost in crowd and shadow, 'for each of us there is one thing we can do best, one thing we must become. Heartland is where we find out what we are for.'

The dice turn: *Wheel of Fortune, Phoenix, The Players, Fortitude. . . .*

Sanzia says, 'The White Rose tells you what you must do. These show you what you might do. The White Rose tells you what was in the past and what is in the future; these show you Now. I don't know if there's a Heartland or not, or if it's an inner or an outer place. These . . . are a guide but you don't know where they will take you, or when you have reached it, or if the journey continues. There is always a part of us that we don't know, and it speaks to us here.'

They are only words, she thinks, and frail against the grey high walls of the Church of the Rose, and the Rose's servants, and the unreachable Bridgebuilder, who was called Visconti and is now named Luce. What use a handful of bright images that are only children's and gamblers' toys?

A young man as palely fanatical as she says, 'There are ways, We can bring them down. There are ways, but put the dice away now and help us.'

She has pamphlets of heresy and sedition and doubt, but it comes to her now, she has more trust (with these child-brained people) in the toys of children. If used properly. . . . (Does she hear that she now says *must* instead of *might*?)

Sanzia says, 'I know what we must do.'

It begins now with rusted rails, between which the grass

grows tall and brown. To pick a way across these is difficult, to cross them hindered with crutches almost impossible, and it is Hainzell who at the last, diffidently, offers to have her carried; and for his trouble gets what he expects, a vicious refusal.

The sun is a white disc behind mist. Pale blue and milky sky, and the shadows cast by the rails are fuzzy-edged. Luce pauses, wipes her forehead that is running with salt sweat. The quilted black tabard is too hot, she wears it only because, sewn into the quilting, are hard thin plates of metal.

'Here?'

A rusty brazier stands by a broken wall, that may once have been part of a shed. The skeleton of a steam-engine hulks in the background. She is aware of movement as they approach, of how people slide away into distant dips and hollows of the ground, into distant buildings, as a school of fish disperse when water is disturbed. One person remains. A young woman – or is she older? the misty light is kind to her skin – with firewhite hair, who squats on her haunches by the brazier, throwing dice left hand against right.

Hainzell stops a short distance away, gun settled easily under his arm, enough protection here in the Yards. And Luce inches her way forward, weight on metal crutches, not on wasted muscle; until she can stand over the young woman who must be

'Sanzia.'

The young woman ignores her, speaks to Hainzell:

'Brother. I'll call you brother, if it helps. Why are you here with her? Why have you brought so many of your own people?'

Luce looks around. There is no apparent sign of any guard, and that is as it should be: the White Rose are trained well. Luce doesn't speak, and this prompts Sanzie to ask, 'What do you want?'

Luce thinks of the Visconti, buried now, the snow freezing on that mausoleum; how many ages of death now he has to think of the years of power, how many long ages to grow sick of the taste of them.

'I can't do it differently,' she says, 'I must act with what I have, with people as they are and not as they ought to be.'

There is a look in Sanzia's eyes, pale and brilliant and feral, the look of those who search for the Heartland – or the Edge.

Luce says, 'I want you to help me be seated, child. And then I

wish to see you throw and read the dice, as I hear so many now
in my city see you throw and read dice.'

The old woman is helped to sit on the warm earth, her metal
crutches laid down beside her. Hainzell stands at her back. His
eyes are not on her, they move from Sanzia to the Yards and
back again: there is sweat clear on his upper lip.

The woman who is white-haired and may be young gathers
up her handful of five dice, upon which are the faces of the
Thirty Major Trumps: which can be thrown in sequence to
ensure all faces have a chance of coming up in combination
with all others – or who can, as now, be merely cast once.

Sanzia kneels down on the earth, facing the old woman. She
is in shabby black, still, in trousers and shirt; and wears a neck-
lace half-hidden by the cloth, that may be made out of yellow
bone. The dice rattle in her hand. Her fingers are long, sallow,
supple. Luce stares at the earth-stained fingers, at the dice that
are clotted with dust. Then the casual flick:

The Weaver. The Rose. Death. The Phoenix. Flight.

And Luce, before Sanzia can act, reaches down and turns
over a die: the image of enamel bright, as clearly limned as
dreams of fire and silver, as images reflected in black water:

'These are the dice *I* will read for *you* –'

She has turned *The Players* instead of *The Phoenix*: an
androgynous mask, half-comic and half-tragic, across which is
laid a flute.

Luce says, '*Flight* is your presumption in coming here; you
would aspire to my role – *The Players. The Rose* is your nem-
esis, and that's linked with *Death*; and *The Weaver,* that old
spider, entoils you deeper and deeper, girl. . . . Now cast
again.'

Sanzia kneels for a minute, feeling the warm earth under
the palms of her hands, and the sun on her head.

'Madam, you hold the city in your grip, but I will lead them
to the Heartland . . . The dice *I* cast were clear. *The Rose* is
closest to you –'

Set into the die-face is a rosette of petals that are toothed
cogwheels. Above the two women, Hainzell moves one hand to
touch that yellow badge, the serrated petals.

'– you trust him and he will betray you; there are those who
work righteously for your downfall, that's I; and the Church

will fall and you be forced into flight –'

Hainzell interrupts, 'We're not puppets for these!' and in sudden anger flicks the Tarot dice with the toe of his boot and sends them spinning. None of the three of them can help bending forward to see what faces show now:

The Rose. The Phoenix. Flight. Death. The Weaver.

Luce's hand reaches out, quicker than Sanzia's to grab the five dice and cast them a third time:

The Weaver. The Phoenix. Flight. Death. The Rose.

At this the old woman laughs, laughs and cannot be stopped for long minutes, until she coughs herself into silence. The sunlight falls silently on the old deserted sidings of the Yards.

'Now that I admire,' Luce says. 'That I *do* admire – loaded dice! What intelligence. Child, you do him credit.'

Sanzia, prompted, must ask, 'Who?'

'Your lover-brother who would like to see me excommunicated,' Luce says, 'but I am not so easily taken, not after so many years of working at the right hand of the Visconti. *Guards!*'

Luce is still seated, cannot rise without help. She sees the White Rose emerge from nearby shelter, from distant buildings. Hainzell turns his head to gaze at them. And even as she wonders how he feels now, having been their commander for so long, to know they no longer move at his bidding; even as she commands 'Arrest them,' Luce feels for a moment as if she moves in a stylized puppet-masque of Judas-betrayals, almost knows what will come next.

Hainzell and Sanzia exchange glances of complicity.

'Arrest the Bridgebuilder,' Hainzell gives a pre-arranged signal. 'We cannot, any of us, take the chance of having a Visconti back; Madam, you were with him for too long.'

But:

'And you've been with her for too long,' says one of the guards. As it happens, this guard has a brother who works down on the docks. Among the crowd now are the armourer's apprentice, the armourer, the smith (you will notice there are still no wives or unmarried women with them, or perhaps you will not notice), and all, citizen-brethren and White Rose both, wear ragged white cloth tied about their arms as a badge of identification: white that is the colour of the Heartland.

'You are a priest-tyrant, and you her chief of police, and you a fanatic,' says this anonymous guard (to whom, in the traditional manner of dealing with the proletariat in fiction, we will not award a name): 'The city doesn't need any of you and is a dangerous place with you here – go!'

One moment of their unity: then Luce calls to her old supporters, Hainzell to the men he has commanded, Sanzia to the people who have heard her read the dice –

The dice, scattered in uproar and fighting, after all their tumbling fall again to show *The Weaver*, *The Phoenix*, *The Rose*, *Flight*, and *Death*.

There is a great square in the city, and a mausoleum, and on its steps is set a heavy iron cage.

'Do what your predecessor would have done, execute me!' Sanzia insists. Her face is all eyes, brilliant with light. And then that fades. 'Where is my brother?'

Luce says, 'You love him.'

Sanzia grips the bars of the cage. She looks out at the old woman. There is dirt ingrained into Sanzia's skin, and her hair hangs down in grey strings.

'If I could get him away from you –'

'That isn't what you came to the city to do.'

'No,' Sanzia says, 'I came to do what you claimed once that you would do, lead the brethren into the Heartland. He came here with that in his heart, and you took him away from that, and you broke him; but if he was with me I'd heal him.'

Luce says, 'You're free. And I give you a choice. Stay here, use your dice, show these people the Heartland inside or outside of them; try and take them there. You won't do it. They're lazy, and won't think or feel, and if their bellies are full they don't care about anything else. But I give you free leave to try.'

Sanzia tries to stand but the cage is too small. All she can do is hunch over and grip the bars and keep herself in this simian-upright position. The snow beats across the square, and feathers the collar of Luce, and of those brethren still curious enough to gaze on this captive heretic.

'And the other choice?' Sanzia is insistent.

'I set your lover-brother free,' Luce says. 'He could have

stayed here with me, the Church of the Rose is merciful. He could have stayed here with you. Instead, he has gone where he always longed to go, and from which journey the Visconti and I only delayed him. He has gone towards the Edge.'

Luce, reaching for the great iron key, adds, 'I have been called cruel, and perhaps I am. I don't give you the third choice – martyrs are a nuisance, and we not strong enough now to suffer one – the third chance: to stay here in the cage.'

Sanzia, hearing the lock click and slide, says, 'If you had given me that choice I would have taken it.'

It is never a long journey, although the distance is far.

Down at the Edge, the Feral infest the sewers. Down at the Edge there are loners, toilers at solitary machines. This is how it is, where you can look out of filthy half-paned windows and, beyond spiderwebs and dirt, look down upon the stars. The deeps are full with light. The cliffs go down forever.

This is how it is: the morning makes a gold glory of the windows dazzling from the depths. Frost snaps in the dawn. No birds fly on that high wind. Do not let yourself be tricked into thinking it an illusion: this is the Edge.

And time passes.

Sanzia learns as the light grows brighter to draw her strength from it, hardly needing to eat. There is a cold wind that all the time now blows into her face. When she speaks to herself, or calls ahead to him, the sound echoes off glittering ice curtains, in white vapour on frozen air.

Up on either side now rise walls, acres of blackening brickwork that diminishes up to a thread of sky. The crepuscular light shows a metal-floored alley that she can span with outstretched hands. Frost gleams on the walls. A high, almost-inaudible thrumming rings in the ears. She touches her palm to the metal paving, it is faintly warm.

Ahead, the alley widens.

When fog sweeps in and douses the light she feels weakened, having so long taken nourishment from its radiance.

'You!' she calls, not loudly.

And for the first time is answered: 'Leave me to go on.'

'I need you,' Sanzia says.

'No.'

'I came to find you.'

'No.'

'*Yes –*'

He walks out of the mist, a man to all appearances human; the same Hainzell, with frayed-hemp hair and beard, in a worn, patched jacket and trousers; still (she is determined to think) the same Hainzell.

Perhaps it is the force of her will that snaps the world back into focus for him, the Edge drawn a way back off. Hainzell sees that she is shivering.

'Are you cold?'

'*No.*'

Now the mist has encircled them, cut them off from city and Heartland and Edge: a sea-fog, bone-chilling, that blurs the edges of reality.

Hainzell sits down beside her in the shelter of the wall. Her hair gleams, the lashes fringing her eyes are pale, and are those lines, crows'-feet, at the corners of her eyes? The thought of that is strange: Sanzia to show the signs of age . . .

He puts his arm round those thin shoulders, amazed at how clearly he can feel the bone. She is shivering. He reaches down to unfasten her jacket and – as she lies limp and unresisting – fumbles to put his arms round her body. Her skin is warm: her heart beats.

'No harm in it,' he says.

'No harm?'

'I've done this often, when you were a child, when we were travelling and you were cold. It means nothing more.'

Sanzia, bitterly, says, 'And you call that "no harm"?'

So close, the bones of her ribs distinguishable under his hands. He feels her own hand move to his, raise it, and put it to her breast –

'I am not a child!'

– as he pulls his hand away; there is a minute's undignified tumble, rolling on hard, gritty metal; and then she gets her hand to where she intended:

'Is *that* how you respond to a sister?'

Hainzell, now reaching to her, is astonished: she rolls away and stands up, hair tangling across her face; stands and backs away, as he (with some physical difficulty) moves towards her.

'I thought you wanted –' He, almost laughing, almost crying: 'Just when I began to think of you as a woman, not seeing you for years, you're different, not a child –'

Sanzia kneels down, a few yards away; her legs are shaking. One of her own rough-skinned hands moves to lie on her breast, feeling the erect nipple through the cloth; and then moves down to rest at the junction of her thighs, as if unconsciously protecting the ache that is there.

'I don't want – it would be like bribery; as if I tried to make you stay here –'

'Don't whine!' He is breathless with anger: anger at being made ridiculous, at being rejected, at having his – charity? – despised. And resentful, as a boy is resentful; and turns aside to arrange himself in his clothes, swearing in frustration. 'And isn't this the same – I can't have you unless I stay, isn't that it?'

'No!' A whine of despair. And then Sanzia takes a breath, looking at him clearly and coldly for a time, while the sea-fog condenses and pearls in her hair. At last she sighs and her taut shoulders relax; she sits back, laying her hands flat on her thighs.

'It shouldn't be something for bargains or contracts,' she says, 'or staying or leaving. . . . You're not who *I* remember you to be, either. Does it matter? I want you, I want no other; that doesn't mean on no terms –'

Hainzell, more sulkily than seems possible for a man of his age, says, 'I'm cold.'

She grins at that. He, hearing himself, smiles reluctantly. Not long after that, they sit together again in the shelter of the wall.

Moved with no thought of the future, it is Sanzia who reaches across to take his hand, and clasp it in both of hers. She sits with her knees raised, resting her arms on them; resting her mouth against the skin of his hand, that is fine-textured and cool. Thinking *This moment, now, no future and no past, only now.*

He reaches across her with his free hand, fumbling in her pocket so that she (surprised) giggles; it is when she realizes that he is trying to get the Tarot dice that she snorts, breaks into giggles that would have been controllable had Hainzell not, in a voice of completely bewildered irritation, said 'What's the matter *now*?' and then she laughs so long and so violently that she breaks off in a fit of coughing; takes one look at his lined and puzzled face, tries to say something, and laughs again until she has to hug her ribs against the pain of it.

Hainzell, looking down at the dice in his hand (seeing *The World-Tree*, *Plague*, and *The Triune Goddess*), shakes his head. And then grins like a boy.

'Sorry,' he says.

'What did you – think you –'

Seeing her threaten laughter again, Hainzell says, 'Some kind of guidance, a reading, a. . . . I wanted something else to make up my mind for me. I've had too many years of making my own decisions. I'm tired.'

Sanzia lets go of his hand and moves to embrace him: sisterly. And, her eyes fixed on his, reaches down to unfasten the buckle of his clothing where he is (still, or again) hard; trying to read in his face his reaction, his flesh warm in her palm, her muscles loosening with want.

He pulls her to him, reaching to her; there is a confused few minutes of cold hands and squeals and helpless laughter (he who has not laughed for so many years); a few minutes in which she can think of the ridiculousness of elbows and knees and one convulsive moment that is never passion but always a cramp in the hip-joint (laughter again) and then they are unshelled, hot flesh in the fog-ridden air, joined and co-joined and half-controlled – pulling clothes round them in a warm nest – and most uncontrolled: Tarot dice forgotten except as small and sharp obstructions under incestuous bodies.

She wakes alone.

Before dawn, she comes to the Edge, and waits while the Heartland's radiance makes the east grow bright.

Pale snow-light illumines the city. The towers, gables, cupolas, battlements, arches and spires are limned with white. Shadows fall towards her: cobalt-blue. She leans her bare arms on the roof-rail and feels the iron bite. Below her, myriad rows of windows set into the building's cliff-face burn orange-gold. A chill wind blows out of the east. Her bare feet are too numb now to feel the cold. She grins, sniffing back tears, and beats her blue-purple fingers together. They clap loud in the silence.

She leaves off looking at the city (all its filth and poverty hidden from this height) and crosses the snow on the flat roof, where other feet have trodden before her, while she slept. And comes to the rust-orange rail that is all the barrier now between herself and the Edge.

The sheer side of the building falls away at her feet, red bricks blackened with aeons of neglect, windowless, obscure, spidered across with great vines and creepers.

Below the building – she must strain to see down so far – the brick ends and the solid rock begins. Rock as black as iron, faceted, terraced, creviced, split. Some ledges are grown over with what she at first takes to be moss, but then as her sight lengthens sees to be giant pines, firs, sequoias.

Down in the dark gold-dusted air, clouds gather and thicken.

Then a rift appears in the clouds far below her, and she sees down through it the fingernail-patches of green, the bright thread of a river that becomes spray and a last rainbow where it pours over the farthest Edge . . .

Down to the darkness where stars shine.

Just once, she thinks of following him; of letting her snow-tracks end here, as his do. She lifts her head. She sees the light behind the sky and hears the depths singing, tastes snow and fire in her mouth – and grips the rail tightly enough to dapple her hands with rust and blood.

Defeat is bitter in her mouth.

Time passes.

Travelling, she is aware at one point that her hands, stiff in the cold air, are liver-spotted, the skin pinched with age.

Sanzia returns from the Edge, alone, limping because the soles of her feet are blackened and swollen with cold-bite, the pain just on this side of what she can bear.

Midwinter lies on the city now, with more than a vengeance, with a black-ice hatred that matches her heart and mind.

I had him, I held him; his breath was warm and moist on my skin; I felt his heart beating in the circle of my arms that I could barely make enclose him, and now that warmth is gone forever, and this is selfish pain: *I don't care, I hurt!*

In her mind, the voice of Luce (long dead now) asks her 'Where is the comfort that you had from the ordered patterns of the universe, that dance of symbols, that endlessly-returning spiral: the Thirty Faces of the Arcana Dice?'

She walks across a great square. The paving-stones are vast, and between their irregular joints creep up small tendrils of black weed. Frost is stark on the stone. Somewhere there are voices, somewhere there are people doing whatever it is warm breathing people do in this black-ice stasis of the heart.

Sanzia walks across the paving-stones and the sky above her head is that colour between milk-white and blue that comes with midwinter. She stops then, and quite deliberately kneels down on the frost-cracked stone. The melting ice touches the flesh of her shins, cold through cloth; darkens the hem of her jacket. It is not difficult then for her to feel through her pockets for the dice. She must hold all five of them cupped in both her hands or they will spill.

Sanzia's hands are brown, with snow-burns from the Edge; and on them blue veins stand up like worms and serpents. Dirt is grimed into the skin so deeply that now they will never be washed clean, and they are (are they?) an old woman's hands, though her face framed in that metallic hair still seems young.

She casts the dice, or lets them fall.

The Weaver. Flight. The Rose. Death. And – *The Triune Goddess.*

Sanzia turns her face up to the sky. It is noon, and the sun is a white disc, no more brilliant (or no less) than her hair. *The Sun* is also a card. And the dice are a weight in her hand, an irregular weight: *These are loaded dice, they cannot fall differently* –

Her breath is white in the air, the stone a bitter cold under her flesh. She casts again:

The Weaver. Death. The Phoenix. The Phoenix – again; and again *The Phoenix.*

Thirty die-faces, thirty Arcana cards, no way for double and triune images to fall.

Her eyes fill with water that is momentarily hot on her cheeks, and then as it runs becomes ice cold and burning. *The Rose* gone, gone with *Flight*: that Icarus-love of the Edge that is stronger than whatever they had between them, not-brother and not-sister.

And the stone is numbingly cold now, and the voices louder, approaching. In the middle of the square is a mausoleum, and steps, and on them stumps of rusted metal that might have been bars, a lock, a cage. There are no high walls of the White Rose's Church, the name of the Bridgebuilder is forgotten.

She casts again those heavy cubes of bone that she, long ago, so carefully drilled and weighted with lead:

The Phoenix. The Weaver. The Phoenix. The Phoenix. The Phoenix.

And now that finely-etched skull is gone, with the periwinkle-blue flowers inset into its empty eye-sockets, as blue as the eyes of Luce in the long-ago. Sanzia is afraid to cast again, cast with loaded single-image dice that should not be able to fall against the grain of this world. Afraid that the spider-*Weaver* should go and all five dice show a white bird consumed in the fire of its own making.

She casts again, bent in concentration over the flagstones, idly brushing away fronds of black weed that the frost had killed . . .

And it is there that they find her.

There is a man wheeling a cart that steams with its load of hot food, small coins scattered in his tin; with him is a boy. After them comes a woman dressed in blue, and after her a woman who cradles a bundle of her work-clothes under her arm (you will notice that things have changed in the time that has passed, a change that has very little to do with Sanzia or Hainzell or Luce; though it has not changed as much as either the men or the women think. And if the time has come for that, perhaps the time has also come to award the crowd names):

Foxfield, resting the cart on its supports for a moment, looks uncertainly at the woman who kneels (it is an unfamiliar posture these days). He turns to the small crowd that has gathered, hoping for some kind of support:

'Is she ill, do you think?'

The woman with work-clothes, Gilfrin, says, 'An old woman like her out in this cold, it's shameful!' at the same time as Foxfield's boy Veitch (who will grow up to have one of the finest minds in the city, but that is much later) exclaims, 'She's too young to be out, she's only a girl –'

After that they stand and watch her for a while, and the wind blows colder, and she sits, nameless, staring at five Tarot dice (but do they show what you expect to see?).

If the dice show *The Phoenix,* one of the citizens of this city, probably the other woman, Tallis, will take her home; take her into warm shelter in the iron tunnels, where braziers glow, where there is food, where she can sleep, where they can watch her to see what she will become –

If the image is *Death* they will remember who she is or was, and see in her face what was once seen on the face of Luce, and I think they will kill her –

If what shows is *The Weaver,* they will abandon her as a politic madwoman or mystic, and the bitterblack winter cold will kill her –

The dice cannot show *The Rose* or *Flight,* these two are not hers to have, they belong with whatever bloody death or lightborn apotheosis he now owns –

But then, there are Thirty cards in the Major Arcana, and once loaded dice have gone wild and random, any of the symbols may fall in that scatter to the frost-bitten stone. As the eyes of these people see an old woman and a girl in the one face (who knows how differently they see each other? Allow them their different vision) so who can tell which may fall: *The Hanged Man* or *The Magus* or *The High Priestess* or *Last Judgement,* cards of sacrifice, of magic, of occult knowledge, and resolution; or perhaps, it may be, that dancing figure that is both Woman and Man, surrounded by symbols of beasts and apotheoses, the card *The World.*

Throw the dice and see.

Ask: you will be answered. Between destruction and transformation is only the space of a breath. I am only bone and inlaid enamel, I can only tell you what story you think I will tell –

And she, rising, looks at the faces that surround her; takes Veitch's hand, with a nod to Foxfield, and – as she begins to speak with Tallis and Gilfrin – they walk away, across the weed-studded square, leaving the dice where they have fallen.

Anukazi's Daughter

'**O**ur information was correct,' Ukurri said, pointing. The ship was just visible now, its prow appeared out of the dawn haze, already in the calm water of the bay. 'Let them come ashore. Attack as soon as the light's good.'

'Prisoners?' Rax asked.

He grinned at her. 'Try to keep one or two alive. They might have things to tell us. These Islanders are weak-willed.'

Low chuckles came from the mounted company that formed Bazuruk's first Order of the Axe.

'Ready yourselves,' he ordered.

Rax knotted the war-horse's reins on the saddle. She breathed deeply, excitement cold in her gut. Her palms were damp. She wiped them on the black surcoat, feeling cold links of mail underneath, and adjusted the buckles on her leg and arm greaves. The shaft of the war-axe was familiar under her hand. The shield hung ready at her side.

The ship nosed close inshore. Sea foam went from grey to white. A cold wind blew. Here great shelves of rock jutted out into the sea, channels worn between them by the waves, so that at low tide a ship could put into what was a natural quay.

There were thirty men – no more – she estimated. Our numbers are equal, then.

'There!' She saw the flash of light from the cliffs at the far end of the bay: a signal-mirror in the hands of the Third Axe, telling them that the other half of the company was in position.

'*Now!*' Ukurri shouted.

Her heels dug into the horse's flanks. For a few strides she was out in the open, ahead of them all. The rocks echoed. Sparks struck from flying hooves. Rax, cold clear through, hefted the great axe. Ukurri and Azu-anuk and Lilazu rode with her, and the rest of the Order behind, but she spurred forward and out-distanced them all.

The war-mount cleared a channel where crimson weed hung delicate and fragile in clear water. She heard cries, shouts; she saw the men half ashore from the ship and heard the thunder of the riders from the far end of the bay. She rose up in the saddle – sweating, cold as death under her mail, excitement drying her lips – and caught a spear-thrust on her shield. She struck. The great blade sheared up under the man's helmet. The jaw, ear, half the skull ripping away.

Another struck at her, jabbing with a barbed spear. Her blow, which seemed only to brush him, spilled a crimson trail.

On the backstroke she put the axe's spike through another man's eye socket and left him screaming. The horse reared, came down, crushing with iron hooves. Smooth rock became treacherous, slick with blood. The sun hit her eyes. Her face was wet, and her black surcoat had turned rust-coloured with blood – not hers. An Islander fled. She leaned dangerously far out of the saddle to slice through his leather jerkin and left him face down on the rock. She smelled burning and heard flames crackle. A dozen of the Order were at the ship. The pitch that caulked its seams burned fiercely. A man screamed. She saw Ukurri strike, hurling the man back into the blaze. Flames were invisible in the sunlight; only the shimmering air betrayed them.

'Bazuruk!' She heard the war call behind her.

She wheeled, lifted the axe – it was heavy, and her arm was stiff – and saw Lilazu fighting on one of the narrow rock spurs. His horse shifted uneasily. It was no help now to be mounted. Two Islanders had him pinned against the water's edge.

Her thrown hand-axe took one in the back. Rax struck with

the flat of the axe, sending the other man full-length into the shallow pool. Lilazu acknowledged Rax's aid with a raised hand, guiding his horse delicately onto solid rock, then galloping off toward the last knot of fighting.

Rax leaned down from the saddle, using the spike of the axe to hook the stunned man ashore.

The crackling of the flames was loud. Surf beat on the rocks. Gulls cried. The air smelled of dank weed, of burning, of blood. Rax's hands were red, her arms streaked with blood that dried and cracked. She hauled the Islander over her saddle, clicking to the weary horse, and rode over to where Ukurri watched the burning ship. The early sun was already hot. A warming relaxation spread through her. If she had not been exhausted, she would have sung.

'Rax Keshanu!' Ukurri slapped her leg and pulled the Islander down from her saddle. 'A live one . . . and not half-killed. Good! That's four.'

She was grinning amiably at nothing in particular: she recognized the after-battle euphoria. 'Shall I bring him with me?' she asked.

Ukurri hesitated. Rax's light mood faded.

'Do you think I'm stupid enough to let him escape?'

'Women have soft hearts,' Ukurri said and then laughed as Rax held up her bloody hands. 'But not in the Order of the Axe, no – though we've only you to judge by. Bring him with us to the Tower, then.'

The others were rifling the dead, leaving the bodies unburied on the rocks. If the stink offended any of the nearby settlements, they'd send a burial party. If not, enemy bones would bleach in the cove, and the storm tides would carry them home to Shabelit and the Hundred Isles.

At their first camp, she tended the unconscious Islander's head wound. He was young, no more than twenty, she judged: Ukurri's age, ten summers younger than Rax. He had pale skin, red-brown hair, and green eyes in a face marred by plague-scars.

She felt an indefinable pang: not of desire or pity, but somehow familiar. If I'd seen him, I couldn't have killed him, she realized. Anukazi! What's the matter with me?

She had fought before, taken prisoners for ransom; none had ever disturbed her the way this Islander boy did.

The Order headed north, resting in the heat of noon, crossing the humid, insect-ridden flats of the Shantar marshes. Rax guarded the Islander closely. After the first day his rage and grief – displayed beyond what a Bazuruki considered proper – subsided into quiet. She thought that meant loss of spirit until she caught him cutting himself and the other survivors free with a stolen knife. After that she watched him constantly.

'I didn't think he had the wits to try it,' she admitted to Ukurri, as they rode on north.

'You served on the barbarian frontier, the Crystal Mountains. They're cunning in the cold south,' he said. 'The Islanders are the worst of all. That one's a Vanathri – you can tell by the cropped hair. The others are mercenaries, from the Cold Lands, I'd guess.'

Rax shrugged. 'It's not our concern. They'll discover the truth in the Tower.'

That night she took a water flask for the Islander. He regarded her with disgust.

'Bazuruki killer,' he said.

She pulled off her helmet, letting the coarse black hair fall free. She grinned, feral, content.

'Yes,' she said, 'I am a woman and a warrior.'

She realized that he wasn't shocked or even surprised. That sent her back to Ukurri with oblique questions, and he told her that in the Hundred Isles a woman was barred from no profession, not even that of warrior.

On the third day they rode through rice fields to the river estuary and came to the city.

'That's Anukazi?' The Islander rode beside her on a remount, bound securely. 'A great city, Rax . . .'

'Wherever you heard my name, keep it out of your mouth.' She almost regretted her harshness. Her curiosity was stirred. 'Why did you come here – one ship's company against all Bazuruk?'

'You have my freemate there.' His voice was rough. 'I would have fought my way to the city – but I used mercenaries. It is no surprise that I was betrayed.'

The Order rode down the brick-paved way that led to the

South Gate. Ox-carts drew aside. Insects whirred in the dust-clouds. The heat made Rax thirsty. As the shadow of Anukazi's squat square buildings fell across her, she became aware that her joy at returning was less than usual.

'You have women-warriors in your islands, then, Vanathri?'

'If you can recognize a Vanathri, you know we don't bind ourselves with useless laws.' His body tensed as they rode down the wide streets. 'Though it seems your laws aren't as strict as I'd heard.'

'You don't think so?' Her bitterness was never far below the surface. Her long fight to be accepted in an Order had been successful, but the struggle robbed her of half her satisfaction. At last she said, 'I've spent most of my life in the northern mountains. All I know of the Archipelago is rumours.'

'That can be remedied.'

He was talking to keep his fears at bay, she guessed. He didn't look at her. She studied his familiar features. What does he see when he looks at me? Rax wondered.

She listened while he spoke of the Shabelit Archipelago, which began in the sandbars off Bazuruk's coast and ended as far south as the Cold Lands. He talked about the Hundred Isles, where life was trade and where half a hundred petty lordlings engaged their private quarrels, with no Tower to bind them into one nation. . . .

'Rax,' Ukurri called, as they entered the Tower walls, 'take that one down to the cells with the mercenaries before you go off duty.'

She acknowledged his order curtly. While the rest of the Order dismounted at the stables, she made her way with the prisoners to the dungeons. The underground shadow was cool.

'You've got another Islander in here,' she told the jailer, keeping charge of the Vanathri man. 'Put them in together. They might talk.'

Brick walls were scarred with nitre. Pitch-torches flared, blackening the ceiling. The jailer searched down the entry scroll.

'Three-five-six,' he announced. 'Let him sweat. They won't get to him for a while.'

'Why not?'

'A conspiracy was discovered against the Firsts of the Orders.' He glanced fearfully at her. 'The guards are interrogating everyone in the Tower and executing traitors.'

'Anukazi save the Tower from harm,' Rax said, and the man echoed her fervently. 'Give me the keys, I'll take this one down for you.'

Shadows leapt as they descended the long stairways. Rax held the torch high, searching for the right cell.

'I'll send a physician to look at you.'

'No.' He was hostile.

'You're young,' she said, 'but you're not stupid. If you've no friends, you won't live long here, Vanathri. These cells are plague-pits.'

'I'll do without Bazuruk's help.'

She fitted the key in the lock, thrust the torch in a wall-socket, and pulled the heavy door open. There was only one other Islander listed – a Shabelitan – so this must be his freemate It would be interesting to see a warrior-woman, Rax thought. thought.

The Islander came into the torchlight, dragging his chain. Rax was disappointed. It was a man: stocky, in his forties, with a lined face and mocking smile. This is the wrong cell, she thought, or the Islander woman's already dead –

'Devenil,' Vanathri said, holding out his bound hands. The other man stepped forward and kissed him on the mouth with a lover's kiss.

'So here you are to rescue me. Again.' The older man smiled tightly. Behind his mockery there was pain. 'Vanathri are impetuous, I know, Kel. But this is stupidity.'

'Did you think I wouldn't come?' Kel Vanathri asked, looking younger than ever.

'Did you come for me or for Shabelit's heir? Vanathri's not a rich island, and if ever I inherit Shabelit – though lord knows my mother may outlive us all – then I can see why you'd want to be Shabelit's freemate.'

'I'd stay with you even if I thought you'd never inherit – or if you weren't heir at all. You should know that by now.'

Cynicism marked Devenil's face, but his voice was tired and uncertain. 'Would you? Yes, I think you would.'

'I should have managed this better.' Anger darkened Kel's eyes. 'I'm a fool, and I've paid for it. I've lost a mercenary company and my freedom. But a chance will come. We're not dead yet.'

Rax crept away from the spy-hole, leaving the torch to burn itself out.

I should report it.

Lost in thought, Rax made her way to the Axe Order's building in the Tower complex. Devenil, that was the name: heir of Shabelit of the Hundred Isles. They can't know, or they'd be asking a ransom for him. But they'll know as soon as they start interrogating him, as soon as this purge is over.

Anukazi keep them from me!

She reached her own chambers, a bare brick-walled room divided by rice-paper screens. Through the window she could see across the flat roofs and ziggurats of the city. She pulled the thin linen shutters closed in order to keep flies and a degree of heat out. Then she shed her mail, bathed, and donned a silk robe.

She sat on the pallet. A brush and paper lay on the low table, unfinished calligraphy spidering across the page. She wasn't yet calm enough to write. She called the house slave and ordered rice and herb tea.

The Islanders had reeked of dead meat. So they eat animal flesh, Rax thought with revulsion. The men couple with one another, and the women too, I suppose; and women are warriors, and men – but he's a fighter, that Kel Vanathri.

Seated cross-legged before the carved Keshanu mask that hung on the wall, she gazed at the abstract face and tried to achieve harmony. Patterns of light and shade entered her eyes. Her breathing slowed.

She was free, then, of Rax. She could stand outside herself and see the tall strong-limbed woman whose skin was lined with exposure to wind and sun. With black hair, green eyes, red-brown skin, she was born of hot Keshanu in the Crystal Mountains . . .

But then she thought of Kel Vanathri and Devenil, Shabelit's heir.

She tried to consider them dispassionately. The image that came to her was not Vanathri's but Ukurri's. Of an age with the young Islander, Ukurri was already First Axe of this Order, her commander and sometime bedfriend. And she, a decade older, with experience gained on the barbarian frontier . . .

You'll never be First Axe, a voice said in her mind. No matter how good you are, how many successes you have, they won't give you an Order because the men wouldn't accept you as commander. You're good, better than Ukurri, but you're a woman. woman.

In Vanathri, Kel said, there are women-warriors; and in Zu and Orindol and Shamur, and all the Hundred Isles . . .

She cursed Kel for disturbing her peace of mind.

He's young to end in the Tower. He, she thought, has courage, too; he crossed the sea, which is more than I'd do.

Outside, the gongs sounded for evening prayer. She belted her hand-axe over her robe and put on her sandals, preparing to go down to the main hall.

Keep low, Rax thought. There have been conspiracies and interrogations before. I'm loyal to the Tower. They'll take Anukazi's sons but I don't think they'll take Anukazi's only daughter.

She followed the disciplines of the Tower, attended weapons practice and theory classes and services for the preservation of Anukazi's priests. She knew better than to ask about missing faces or empty places. Finally the atmosphere of tension eased: the purge was – for this time at least – finished.

The dice were kind. Rax found herself on a winning streak for the first time in a long while. She was able to bribe extra rations for the Islanders without touching her own pay. When she heard that the Guard had begun interrogating the mercenaries, she went back to the Tower and paid for an undisturbed time in the cells.

The torch burned bright. Kel had fallen against Devenil while he slept, and the older man sat with his back to the wall, supporting Kel. All the mockery was gone from his worn face.

Rax was noisy with the lock, and when she had the door open, hostile stares greeted her.

'What do you want?' Kel Vanathri demanded.

Rax shook her head. The calmness that was a discipline of the Order deserted her. She couldn't name the influence the Islanders had over her.

'They're starting the questioning soon,' she said.

'Bring me a knife,' Kel said, 'I won't ask more, Bazuruki.'

It was pointless to tell them that one day their rations would be drugged, that they would wake in the upper chambers – in the hands of the Anukazi Guard.

'Say you're only mercenaries, pirates, whatever,' she pleaded. 'As for freemates, for the love of Anukazi himself, keep that quiet!'

'There's no love in your Orders?' Devenil asked skeptically.

'I –' The Order denied love fanatically and practised it covertly. Every Order had its pretty boys, vying for favour and carrying rumours. Looking now at Kel and Devenil, she thought no, it's not the same thing at all.

'What they forgive themselves, they hate in others.'

'Take advice,' Kel Vanathri said, 'stay out of here.'

She knew they had plans to escape, or to invite a quick death. The thought bothered her more than it should. She slammed the door and walked away. In a little while they'd be dead.

They'd be good companions in an Order, she thought. It's a senseless waste . . .

To kill Bazuruk's enemies?

No!

What am I thinking? We're caught between the northern barbarians and these damned islands, which, if they could ever unite, could crush Bazuruk. We can't afford mercy, not even for those two. Ah, Anukazi! Why should *I* care?

Rax couldn't sleep that night. She rose and dressed – in mail, with her war-axe – and went down to the main hall. But even dice-games couldn't ease her spirit.

All the city slept. There were no lights in the squat buildings, no noise from the beast markets, no carts in the street. She went by way of the river wall and entered the Tower as the guards changed shift.

Torches burned low in the guardroom.

'Jailer –' Some instinct held her hand, when she reached to shake him awake. A thin thread of blood ran out from under his head, bowed on the table.

Movement caught her eye, where the torch guttered. The axe slid into her hands. A scuffed noise came from down the passage. She tensed. The jailer had no knife or sword. They would be armed, then.

Softly she said 'Vanathri?'

'Be silent.'

'Devenil.' The strength of her relief was alarming. 'Where's

Kel?'

'Put down your axe!'

She rested the spike on the floor, hands clasping the shaft. 'Now I'll tell you something. You're not the first to kill a jailer and come this far. But can you fight your way out past every guard in Anukazi's Tower?'

'If we have to.' It was Kel Vanathri's voice.

'Wait.' She sensed movement. 'Suppose you were taken out of here by a guard? There are river boats. You might cross the sea to the Hundred Isles.'

'And let you sound the alarm?' Kel said. 'Put down the axe. I can throw a knife as well as any Bazuruki.'

'You're not listening to me, Islander. Take the jailer's uniform.'

They stepped forward into the light. Devenil nodded, watching her with a curious expression. 'We'll lock you in one of the cells, unless you prefer a glorious death – as Bazuruki do, I've heard.'

'And how will you get past the gates? I'll have to speak for you. Trust me,' Rax said. 'Only be quick!'

It was only then that she knew her long career with the Order of the Axe had ended in betrayal.

A fishing boat was moored with sails still raised. The man aboard answered Rax's hail from the dock.'

'Stay back,' she said to the Islanders. The man's head came above the rail, and she drove her knife up under the soft part of his jaw. Blood spilled over her hands. She wrenched the blade loose, feeling it grate against bone, and shoved the body off the side. It sank quickly. She led the Islanders down the stone steps.

'Now, Devenil, Shabelit's heir,' she said, 'take this young fool with you and get out of Bazuruk. The alarm's out, I expect, but the tide's in your favour. Go!'

'They know who brought us out,' Kel Vanathri said. 'You can't stay.'

'But my Order –'

'You should have thought of that.' Devenil gave a sardonic grin. The early sun showed dirt, blood, the traces of long confinement; he looked a good ten years older than his age. His mocking face disturbed and attracted her. She felt he understood motives she herself didn't recognize.

'We owe a debt we'll never pay you,' said Vanathri. His young face looked vulnerable. 'But if you come with us to the Hundred Isles, we'll try.'

From the first moment I saw you, she thought. That lover's kiss between you and Devenil . . . how could I leave you two innocents in the Tower? You remind me of –

Yes. Is it that simple? He'd have been very like you, if he'd lived: my son Tarik.

'I'll come,' Rax said.

The sun burned, and the sea shimmered. The stars hung like a mist of diamonds, and the night wind cut to the bone. Cottonwool fog hugged the coast. The deep swells rolled like hills. They headed south, into ever-colder seas.

Rax lay moaning in the coffin-sized cabin, sweating, heaving with every lurch and dip of the sea. Days passed. Kel and Devenil sailed, fished, fed her fresh water. Once she woke to see them lying together, Kel's pale arm across Devenil's scarred body.

Solitude and loss and sickness frightened her. She slept with the war-axe tight in her grip. No Tower discipline, no skill learned in battle helped her now.

On the tenth day, when they sighted the coast of Dhared, she barely stirred, and at noon, when they passed it and came to Vanathri itself, she was too weak to do more than stare. She saw a green land, chill under a grey sky and lashing rain, where slant-roofed buildings hugged a narrow harbour. They sailed into it and were recognized.

Rax stood on the quay, swaying, seeing Kel and Devenil in each other's arms – in broad daylight, she thought dizzily. Then they pulled her into their embrace. The gathering crowd of Vanathri Islanders cheered, and every bell in the town rang out.

When she was well, they crossed the straits to Shabelit, and there Devenil took her before the Island lords and the head of the Council.

'Lady Sephir,' he said to her, 'here is our rescuer, Rax Keshanu of Bazuruk, axe-warrior of Anukazi's Tower.'

The chamber was full of brightly dressed men and women – and children, she saw, appalled. The air stank of old cooking, new perfumes, and the sea. Rax pulled her stained surcoat over

her mail and kept the axe close to her hand. Shabelitans
jabbered and pointed while Kel Vanathri told what had
happened in Bazuruk.

'We do not welcome Bazuruki,' Sephir said, when she had
heard his story, 'but you have brought my son back to me and
restored Kel to Vanathri. You are welcome, Rax Keshanu, in
all the Hundred Isles!'

The woman, white-haired, had Devenil's face with more
delicate lines. She stood as Rax bowed – the formal acknowledgement of a Bazuruki warrior – and embraced and kissed
her. Rax froze, smelling the scent of a meat-eater.

Amid the general applause, the Lady Sephir pronounced her
an honorary captain of Shabelit. It was then, identifying the
white scars on the old woman's arms as ancient sword-cuts, that
Rax realized she had met her first Shabelit woman-warrior.

Cold spring turned to cool summer. Rax moved into rooms
in Shabelit, a city founded on trade and almost as big as
Anukazi. She lived with Islander customs as much as was possible for her but followed her version of Bazuruk's discipline.
One midsummer day Devenil found her in the practice courts
using the war-axe.

'Come up and talk,' he said, and she joined him on the sea-
fort's wall.

'I see too little of you both lately,' Rax said as she pulled on a
tunic against the Archipelago's cold wind. 'I suppose Kel's back
on Vanathri or another of your damned rocks.'

'Kel offered you a place on his ship,' Devenil said. 'Why
don't you take it?'

'The sea, with that sickness?' she scowled.

A brisk wind blew across the sea-fort, spattering her face
with dampness. She watched the light on the straits.

'If you wanted to come, sickness wouldn't stop you.'

'I'm a soldier,' she said at last. 'You people . . . I didn't
expect anything like the Orders, but you've no standing army
at all. You don't understand. I'm a warrior. It's what I do, and
I do it better than most. You're asking me to drop it and ship
out as some kind of deck hand –'

'A guard. You'd work on the ship, but so do Kel and I. Even
Bazuruki aren't killed by honest work.'

'Damned Islanders,' she said.

Devenil smiled. 'You're not the first person to perform a generous act and regret the consequences.'

'I don't regret what I did!'

In her mind's eye, Rax saw her chambers in the Tower of Anukazi. The cool light, the shade, the fine carving of the Keshanu mask. Ever since I came to the islands, she thought, my mind's been in a fog.

'Let us pay our debt to you,' Devenil said. 'Come with us on the *Luck of Vanathri*, if not for our sake, then for your own.'

'You love him, don't you?' The thought still amazed her.'

'I'll do anything I can for him, including ordering you aboard the *Luck* if it eases his mind. I'm still Shabelit's heir. I can do that.'

I got you out of the Tower, she thought. How much more must I give?

'You don't order me. I'm Bazuruki.'

'Not any more! You have to see that.'

She sighed. Eventually she asked 'When do you sail? I'll come if I can, Devenil, but don't wait for me.'

They waited anyway, but she never came.

'You've got company,' Garad said. 'At least I'd swear it's you he's looking at.'

Rax glanced up from the dice. Sun and windburned from his months at sea, brown hair grown untidy, wrapped against the cold of a Shabelit winter night – Kel Vanathri.

'Stay here,' she said, 'we'll continue our discussion later.'

Garad smiled, shuttling the dice from hand to hand. 'Don't leave. I have your debt-slips –'

She gave him a look that stopped his voice in his throat, then crossed to the doorway.

'Rax!' Kel gripped her hands, then let them fall, puzzled by her lack of response. 'The time it's taken me to find you –'

'Did I ask you to come looking?'

'I came anyway. It's a strange place to find a Bazuruk warrior. With mercenaries.'

'Mercenaries and gamblers are no worse company than traders' sons and lords' heirs with nothing better on their minds than piracy.'

Her message hit home. She sensed that he was on the edge of violence, and she grinned. He studied her closely.

'You're drunk,' he said, amazed.

'Am I? It's a custom we could do with in Bazuruk.'

He frowned. 'Devenil said you'd end in a place like this. I'm sorry he was right.'

'Listen.' Rax laid one long finger on the centre of his chest, leaning closer. The spirit-fumes blocked his meat-eater scent. 'I'm a soldier by profession and choice. I had no quarrel with Bazuruk, except they wouldn't make me First Axe, which I earned. I'll practise my skills where I please. You were glad enough of them in Anukazi.'

'You can't live on old debts.' His anger was under tight control. 'I see you have new ones. I'll leave you to settle them, if you can.'

She waited until he'd left the smoke-filled inn before she went back to the table.

'That's a rich trading house,' Garad said. 'The Vanathri.'

'Shut your lying mouth.' She fell into the seat, draining the mug of spirits.

'Gratitude doesn't last.'

I'm trapped, Rax thought foggily. Money doesn't last, honorary captaincy carries no pay – and I won't beg from Kel or Devenil! How else, in Anukazi's name, can I live? And to sneer at me for being with mercenaries . . .

She missed the act of violence, the revulsion that, in the cold moment before battle, transmuted to recklessness; the empathy that made her imagine each blow, each wound. It was not skill nor craft, but art – an ache and an addiction.

'I can find the people you need.' Garad interrupted her thoughts. 'There are lords in the Cold Lands who'll pay well for a mercenary company, but first you need money to equip them.'

'And pay off my debts.' Rax said, grinning. 'We'll talk. Call to mind three or four men you can trust, and a good lockpick. I've a plan to pay off my debts and get all the gold I need to go to war.'

The house was dark. Rax led them cautiously. Her hand clamped over the mouth of a guard, and her long knife cut his throat. She wiped her hands. Garad came forward with the lock-pick. Their breath was white in the icy air. Rax took another drink from the flask to warm herself.

'It's open.' The lockpick stood back.

Her heel skidded in blood. She cursed and regained her balance. Darkness cloaked them. She led the way to the cellars. Above, the house slept. Rax hummed under her breath.

'It's a fine revenge on Vanathri,' Garad said as his men searched the stacked chests. Silver glinted in the lantern's light.

'It's only a joke,' Rax corrected him. 'Try that one there – yes, and there. Good.'

After a few skirmishes in the Cold Lands, I'll come and pay back what I've taken. I wonder if he'll see the joke? she thought.

The flare of the lanterns took her totally by surprise.

The war-axe slid into her right hand, the throwing-axe into her left. One man yelled. Dazzled, she struck by instinct. Garad heaved up a chest and threw it at the advancing men. She let fly with the throwing-axe, heard a scream as it found a target. Garad screeched –

New lights from five or six bright lanterns blinded her. Something struck a paralysing blow to her arm. The men, out of her striking reach, held crossbows. Fear sobered her. Even mail could not stop the crossbow bolts pointing at her breast.

A familiar voice shouted, and no one fired.

Garad bubbled out his life at her feet. The lockpick breathed harshly in the sudden silence. Her other men, and several guards, lay dead. Kel Vanathri stood at the head of the steps, in night robes, carrying an unsheathed sword.

He cried out.

Devenil slumped against the wall. Blood matted his hair and soaked his shirt; his flesh was laid open, and white bone showed in the redness. The throwing axe's blade was buried under his ribs. He was dead.

'He was always a light sleeper.' Kel sounded stunned. 'He said he'd see what the disturbance was. By the time I could follow –'

'I'm sorry,' Rax said. 'I liked Devenil.'

'I loved him!' Kel's agony flared. 'He was the best. The Island will never see another like him. That you could kill him . . .'

'His rescuer in Bazuruk is his killer in Shabelit,' Rax said, rubbing her face wearily. Chains clinked. 'He'd appreciate the irony.'

It was less complex in Bazuruk, she thought. That is what comes of charity. I'd never have hurt him if I'd seen who it was – Devenil.

'You're nothing more than a butcher. I thought you were different because of what you did in Anukazi, but you're just another Bazuruki killer.'

'Of course I'm Bazuruki.' She was bewildered. 'I was born in Keshanu. I spent ten years defending the borders of the Crystal Mountains. What else would I be?'

It took time for the anger to leave him. Almost to himself, he said, 'That's the tragedy. I know you have compassion, but it doesn't matter, does it? The Bazuruki training is what matters.'

'I am what I am,' Rax said, 'and so are you. And so was he. We can't change.'

'I can't believe that.' He stood, pacing the cell. The guard looked in and went away again. They wouldn't stop him from visiting his own justice on her, she guessed. Not on Shabelit, Sephir's island. She knew how a mother felt for a dead son.

'What will you do?'

'Nothing. You will answer to the law for theft, murder, Devenil.'

'Not a cell. Not caged. You owe me that.'

'I owe you nothing!' Leaving, he stopped. 'He – loved you, Devenil did, for fighting to be what you were. He would have given you a lord's inheritance if you'd asked. You wee his friend.'

She watched him with Bazuruki eyes, Rax Keshanu, Anukazi's daughter.

'Tarik – Kel, I mean –'

'Better we'd died in Bazuruk.'

'I'm a long way from home,' Rax said. 'I'm tired, Kel.'

'I won't cage you,' he said from the doorway. 'But I won't let them free you, not after what you've done. If you leave, there's only one other way from here.'

'Yes,' she agreed.

After a time, she knew he had left.

She stood looking down through fine rain into the prison courtyard, where soon they would raise a block, and Rax Keshanu would for the last time behold the clean stroke of an axe.

A Sun in the Attic

The Archivist sits in a high room, among preserved (and precisely disabled) relics; sorting through notes, depositions, eye-witness accounts, and memoirs.

Outside the window, the city of Tekne is bright under southern polar light. The room is not guarded. There is not the necessity.

In the somewhat archaic and formal style proper to history scrolls, the Archivist writes: In the Year of Our Lady, Seventeen Hundred and Ninety-Six –

Then she pauses, laying down the gull's-quill pen, staring out of the window.

Beyond the quiet waters of the harbour, the slanted sails of the barbarian fleets have drawn perceptibly nearer.

The Archivist turns back to her material.

Tell it as it happened, she thought. Even if it is not in a single voice, nor that voice your own. Tell it while there is still time for such things . . .

An airship nosed slowly down towards the port's flat-roofed buildings. Beyond the harbour arm, the distant sea was white and choppy. Tekne's pale streets sprawled under the brilliant Pacific sun.

103

'It *may* be a false alarm.' Roslin Mathury leaned on the rim of the airship-car, protesting ·defensively. 'You know what Del's like, once he's in his workshops.'

'That's why you've brought us back from the farm estates a month before harvest, I suppose?'

Roslin busied herself with straightening the lace ruffles at her cuffs and collar. Without meeting Gilvaris Mathury's gaze, she said, 'Very well, I admit it, I'm anxious.'

The airship sank down over the Mathury roofs, the sun striking highlights from its dull silver bulk. The crew tossed mooring ropes, and house servants ran to secure them.

'I should have made him come to the country with us!' Roslin said.

'No one ever made Del do what he didn't want to,' Gilvaris observed. 'I should know. He's my brother.'

'He's my husband!'

'And mine, also.'

'When I married you, it wasn't to be told the obvious,' Roslin said, equally acidly; gaining some comfort from the familiarity of their bickering. 'Well, husband, shall we go down?'

The mooring gangway being secured, they disembarked onto the roof of the Mathury town house. The airship cast free, rising with slow deliberation. Its shadow fell across them as it went, and Roslin was momentarily chilled. She saw, as she looked past it, the crescent bulk of Daymoon, blotting out a vast arc in the western sky.

'*Se* Roslin, *Se* Gilvaris.' The house-keeper bowed. 'We're glad to have you back safely –'

Roslin cut the small elderly man off in mid-speech. 'Tell me, what's so bad that you couldn't put it in a message to us?'

'The *Se* Del Mathury worked while you were gone,' the shaven-headed servant said. 'He made some discovery, or thought that he did; he had us bring food to his workrooms, and never left. I think he slept there.'

Roslin nodded impatiently. 'And?'

'He saw visitors,' the housekeeper continued, 'admitting them privately; and received messages. Three weeks ago we brought his morning meal to the workrooms. He was gone, *Se* Roslin. We've seen and heard nothing from him since.'

Light sparkled from glass tubes and flasks and retorts, from coiled copper tubing and cogwheels. A half-assembled orrery gleamed.

Gilvaris turned, pacing the length of the workroom. Boards creaked under his tread. Sunlit dust drifted down from the glass dome-roof, and the swift shadows of seabirds darkened it with their passing. Their distant cries were mournful.

'He might have forgotten to leave word,' Roslin offered.

'Do you really think so?'

The caustic tone moved her to look closely at Gilvaris. Unlike his younger brother in almost everything: tall and dark where Del was fair, secretive where Del was open, slow where Del was erratically brilliant.

'No,' she said, 'I don't really think so. Where *is* he? Is he still in Tekne, even? He could be anywhere in Asaria!'

Gilvaris absently picked up a few bronze cogs and oddly-shaped smooth pieces of glass, shuffling them from hand to hand. 'I'll try Tekne Oldport. That's where he commonly gets his supplies. And I'll ask at the university. Also, it might be wise to discover who his visitors were.'

Roslin dug her hands deep into her greatcoat pockets, feeling the comforting solidness of her pistols. 'Damn, when I see him –'

'If he didn't go willingly? House Mathury has enemies.'

Her dark eyes widened. 'So we do . . .'

'Now wait. That's *not* what I meant. I know House Mathury and House Rooke are rivals in trade, but –'

Roslin came over to him, took his hand. 'Trust me.'

'You shouldn't see Arianne.' Gilvaris put an emphasis on the first word.

'Should I not?'

'You don't have the temperament for it.'

'And you do, I suppose?'

Gilvaris raised an eyebrow. 'I have been told that I resemble my aunt closely.'

Roslin bit back a sharp answer. 'Don't quarrel. You go to the Oldport, I'll ask questions elsewhere. We can't waste time. I'll never forgive myself if Del gets hurt because we weren't here when he needed us.'

A summer wind blew cold through the streets. Roslin walked

down to the wider avenues of new Tekne, under the tree-ferns that lined the pavements. Sun gilded the white façades of the city houses. Daymoon was westering, its umber-and-white face blotting out a third of the sky.

She stopped to let a roadcar pass; the engine hissing steam, pulling its fuel car of kelp and a dozen trailers.

House Mathury has enemies, she thought grimly, approaching the wide steps that led up to one of the larger houses. She passed under the archway and entered the courtyard beyond. Servants showed her into the house. As she expected (but was none the less impatient) they kept her waiting for some time.

'*Se* Roslin.'

She turned from pacing the hall. '*Se* Arianne.'

Arianne Rooke, being a generation older than her, still affected the intricately braided wig, the face-powder and high-heeled boots of that fashion. Her eyes were bright, lively in her lined face; and they gave nothing away.

'It is a pleasure, *Se* Roslin. You should visit us more often.'

Her smile never faltered as she ushered Roslin through into a high narrow room. The walls were lined with bookshelves. It smelled faintly musty: the unmistakable scent of parchment and old bindings.

'House Mathury has, after all, connections here.'

'Connections? Yes,' Roslin said bluntly, refusing her offer of wine and a chair, 'you could almost say I'm here on a family visit.'

'I don't quite understand.'

She looked the woman up and down. Arianne was small and dark and, despite her age, agile. Roslin didn't trust her. She was head of House Rooke; she was also Del and Gilvaris's mother's sister.

'Where's Del?' Roslin demanded.

'*Se* Roslin, I don't —'

'Don't take me for a fool,' she said. 'Our houses have fought for . . . but he's one of your own blood! What have you done to him?'

Arianne Rooke seated herself somewhat carefully in a wing-armed chair. Resting her elbows on it, she steepled her fingers and regarded Roslin benignly over the top of them.

'Now let me see what I can gather from this. Your husband Del Mathury is missing? Not your husband Gilvaris too, I trust? No. It would never do to lose two of them.'

Roslin said something unpardonably vulgar under her breath.

'And for some reason,' Arianne continued, 'you imagine that *I* am responsible? Come, there are far more probable reasons; you as a wife should understand this.'

Such delicate insinuations did nothing for Roslin's temper. 'I'm not as stupid as you think!'

'That would be difficult,' Arianne agreed.

'I ought to call you out,' Roslin said, savagely, regretting that her pistols must be left with the servants.

'My dear, you're a notable duellist, and I have a regard for my own skin that only increases with age. So I fear I must decline.'

Roslin, aware of how much Rooke was enjoying herself, thought: Gil would have done this better.

'You're trying to tell me you don't know anything about what's happened to Del.'

'I can but try.' Arianne spread her hands deprecatingly. 'Would that I did. Would that I could help.'

That hypocrisy finished it.

'You listen to me, Arianne. I mean to find Del. And I will. And if you've had anything to do with this, I'll take my evidence before the Port Council, I'll bring House Rooke down about your ears, my friend. Or,' she finished, blustering, 'I may just kill you.'

'Isn't melodrama attractive?' Arianne Rooke observed. 'I'm sure you can find your own way out.'

She could not know that, when she had gone, Arianne Rooke chuckled a little. Then, sobering, took up pen and parchment to write an order for the immediate and secret meeting of the Port Tekne Council.

'Anything?' Gilvaris asked.

'No. She made me lose my temper, so naturally I didn't learn anything. Except that I shouldn't lose my temper. You have any better luck?'

'Not so far.' He sat back on one of the benches. They haunted the workrooms, he and Roslin. 'He could be held somewhere. Now we're back here, we may get a demand for money.'

Roslin looked round the darkening room. It was the short Asarian twilight: Daymoon had already set.

'Maybe . . . It doesn't look like there was a struggle here, does it?'

Gilvaris shook his head. 'It seems to me that there's equipment missing. I wouldn't know for sure – but it could be so.'

She knew he rarely admitted ignorance. Part of the reason for that was a life spent struggling in the effortless wake of a brilliant younger brother; if Del had not loved him so devotedly, Gilvaris's life might have been bitter.

Del, she thought. We're not whole without him.

'What I'm saying is, it's possible he packed and left. He's clever enough to do it without the servants knowing, if he thought it necessary.'

'You think he left us?' Roslin said, incredulous. 'Damn, you're as bad as Arianne Rooke.'

'I don't think he left *us*, specifically,' Gilvaris said, unruffled. 'I think he left. Those visitors he had: some were tradesmen, and some were from the harbour. But at least one was from the Port Council. They're no friends of Mathury. I think Del's in hiding.'

Roslin considered it. 'Why?'

Gil shrugged. 'Haven't I always said, one day he'll discover something that'll get him into trouble?'

'It's amazing,' Roslin said, as they dismounted from the roadcar on the Oldport quay. 'I always saw Del as a loner, shut away in those rooms. He knows more people than I do.'

'He kept in touch with a lot of colleagues from the university,' Gilvaris said.

The wet morning was closing to a rain-splattered noon. They had seen and spoken with, so far, a maker of airship frames, a glassblower, a metalsmith, a windvane repairer, a clockmaker (this being a woman Roslin disliked instantly, knowing that she had been a frequent visitor to House Rooke before Roslin had), as well as printers of news-sheets, and at least four sellers and importers of old books. All knew Del professionally and personally. None knew where he was now.

'He was on to something. When he shuts himself up and works like that . . .' Roslin shook her head. Gilvaris linked his arm in hers and they walked.

'Metal and glassware. His most recent orders.'

'Meaning?' Roslin queried.

'I wish I knew.'

A harbour ship chugged past, and the smell of steam and hot metal came to Roslin through the damp air. Viscid water slapped at the quay steps. Out in the deeper anchorages, up-coast ships spread flexible canvas shells. Steamships wouldn't risk leaving Asaria's canals for the cold storm-ridden seas. Down-coast krill-ships were arriving from the southern icefields.

'If he was that desperate, he wouldn't take one of our ships,' Gilvaris forestalled her. 'I've made enquiries, there's one more chance. A barbarian ship.'

Roslin looked where it was moored by the quay, saw low sharp lines, great jutting triangular sails. And thought of Del: intense, impractical, obsessed.

'Would he go? Without a word to us?'

'He would, if he thought that staying would put us in danger.'

Roslin blinked. 'I – damn, I can't think like that!'

'There's plenty who can.'

After a moment Roslin put her free hand in her pocket, gripping the butt of the duelling pistol. They went forward to hail the barbarian ship.

'I have seen no one,' the barbarian insisted, in passable Asarian.

He was a tall man, taller even than Gilvaris, with pale yellow skin and bright, braided golden hair. His robes were silk, and from his belt were slung paired metal blades. Roslin recalled that rumour said barbarians fought with these long knives, like servants.

No one? she thought. He's lying.

'Perhaps I can speak to your captain. Will she see me?'

He said, 'I am captain here.'

'Oh.' Roslin sensed rather than saw Gil's amusement. Momentarily at a loss, she glanced round the bare cabin. Cushions surrounded low tables. The table from which the barbarian had risen was covered with parchments and thin ink-brushes. Seizing on this, she commented, 'Skilful work. What do you write?'

'Of my travels.'

Roslin studied the script. A scant number of repeated symbols were inscribed from right to left across the page, instead of from top to bottom.

Partly gaining time, partly curious, she asked, 'What do you say about us?'

He smiled. 'That the southern polar continent of our legends is no legend. That Asaria is a land in which women head the family; that women here take many husbands – where I come from, men take many wives. And that otherwise the strong oppress the weak, the rich oppress the poor; knaves and fools outnumber wise and honest men; and that the machines of peace are very apt to become the engines of war. In short, that Asaria differs very little from any other continent of the globe.'

' "Engines of war"?' Roslin queried.

'Why, ma'am, consider this: you have your cars not pulled by beasts of burden, what strong and tireless transport they might make for cannon! And your kite-gliders, they would let you know of the enemies' advance long before he sees you. You have ships that need not wait on wind or tide. You have ships of the air. Consider, there is not a city wall that could stand against you!'

Gilvaris Mathury, a little satirically, said, 'Ah, but you see, cities in Asaria have no walls.'

The barbarian inclined his head. 'Indeed, I have studied your Asarian philosophy: it's alternative is to put walls around the mind.'

Roslin ignored that. 'In your history, sir, say also that in Asaria women love their husbands, and men love their brothers –'

'Man,' said Gilvaris, 'do you think *we'd* harm him?'

'Let us say,' the barbarian said carefully, 'that *if* there were such a man, and *if* he were due to arrive here, you would have but to wait until he came to the ship. But say also, that you may not be the only ones he is hiding from, and that – if you are seen waiting – you will not be the only ones to find him.'

Seabirds roosting under the eaves of the Oldport houses cried throughout the night. Roslin lay awake. Gil's arms round her were some comfort, but she missed the complementary warmth of Del.

Lovers: husbands: brothers. It was not in her nature, as it was not in Asarian custom, to compare. Two so different: Del with the obsessed disregard of the world that first attracted her, Gilvaris who had spoken of marriage with House Mathury (and only in that moment had it crystallized, to be without either of them was unendurable).

So she had spoken to her mother, head of House Mathury, and little help did she have from a woman whose three husbands had been acquired at different times from all over Asaria. Roslin, nevertheless, married the brothers. And a season later was, by virtue of the plague, left sole survivor and heir of Mathury, which served to bind them closer than was common.

Beside Gilvaris, aware of his quiet breathing, she knew he did not sleep. They lay awake and silent until Daymoon rose.

'Are we right to be here?' Roslin sat on the edge of the bed, lacing up her linen shirt. She could see from their high window the steps of Oldport South Hill, the fishing boats at the quay. 'Can we trust a barbarian?'

'It's all we can do. Can *he* trust us, that's what he'll ask.' Gilvaris's voice was muffled as he pulled on his coat. Adjusting the mirror until the polished basalt oval gave back his reflection, he flicked the lace ruffles into place. 'It could take time to get a message . . . *Quiet!*'

For once he moved faster than Roslin. She barely caught the sound of footsteps on the stairs, and he was by the door, pistol raised. There was a sharp repeated knock.

Roslin grinned, relaxing. 'That's the landlord. Breakfast, I'd guess, and not Arianne Rooke's cut-throats.'

Without releasing the pistol, Gilvaris pulled the door open, surprising the visitor with his hand raised again to knock.

It was Del Mathury.

'It's no good yelling at me!' Del protested. 'I didn't want to be found. I wouldn't be here now, if the barbarian hadn't said it was the only way to stop you turning all Tekne upside down.'

'What the –'

Roslin's temper cooled. She felt the sting of tears behind her eyes.

'What did you think we'd feel like?' she demanded. 'Damn, you might have been dead for all we knew!'

'You knew I'd be all right.' His open face clouded slightly. 'Didn't you? You didn't think I'd . . . it was a matter of staying out of sight until the ship sailed. I was going to send a message to you both then, so that you could join me on board.'

Roslin sighed, sat down on the chair-arm, and put her arm round him. Gilvaris positioned himself protectively behind Del.

It's like Del not to see the obvious. But you knew that when you married him, she reminded herself.

'Del, love, why would we want to go on a barbarian ship? And for that matter, go where?'

'Somewhere I can work without the Port Council bothering me.'

'You're the brilliant one,' Gil said. 'Tell us why we've got to leave, not Port Tekne, not the up-country farms, but all Asaria?'

'Don't be angry with me, Gil.'

'I'm not.'

Roslin had a sudden vision of them as children: the elder brother eternally trailed by, and eternally protective of, the younger. She wondered if either of them coveted the other's relationship with her as she coveted their brotherhood before they ever knew her.

'It was made very clear to me,' Del said, 'when I talked to people, that what I was doing wasn't liked. I don't know why. I don't expect it matters . . . Gil, Ros, I missed you when you weren't here. You'd better come and see what I've been working on.'

Del led them high up among the old deserted houses of the South Hill, below the derelict fort. Roslin was sweating long before they reached the ultimate flight of steps. She saw, across the five-mile span of Tekne, North Hill push out like a fist into the sea, and the kite-gliders and airships anchored on its crest. Inland from the Tekne the country went down into flat haze, broken only by the vanes of wind- and watermills.

'We should have stayed on the estate,' Roslin grumbled. 'You and your machines – Gil's conspiracies – I don't like any of it.'

Del, who was perfectly familiar with that complaint, only grinned. He took them up to the top floors of a derelict mansion that jutted out over the streets below. The walls ran with damp, and clusters of blue and purple fungi grew on the stairs. A continuous thin sound broke the quiet: the sifting of old plaster and stone dust in decay. Roslin smelt musty ages there. The sound of the wind died, and with it the shrieks of birds.

At the very top of the house, in an attic with a shattered dome-roof, Del had set up his makeshift workshop. Half of it was in crates, ready to go aboard the barbarian ship; but Roslin could only concentrate on the massive structure of metal and glass that all but filled the room.

'Look at this.' Del picked up a brass cylinder. Roslin turned it over in her hands, then gave it to an equally puzzled Gilvaris. Del snatched it back impatiently, and manipulated some of the wheels jutting from it. 'No. Like this.'

Dubious, Roslin copied him, holding it to her eye. The metal was cold against her skin. Her lashes brushed the polished surface of the glass. She felt Del take her shoulders and turn her towards the window. She saw a white blur, felt swoopingly dizzy; then as her long sight adjusted she made out houses, streets, tree-ferns . . . And lowered it, and the side of North Hill sprang back five miles into the distance.

Roslin turned the tube in her hands. It was blocked at both ends by glass, one piece of which slid up and down a track inside the tube, adjusted by cogwheels.

Del took it away from her and rubbed her fingermarks off the glass.

'It's a pretty toy,' Gilvaris observed, making the same test, 'but as to people's concern, I confess I don't understand that.'

'The principle can be applied to other things. It's producing the lenses that's most difficult; they have to be ground.'

Roslin, gazing at the arrangement of tubes, prisms, lenses and mirrors that towered over their heads, began to make sense of it.

'Hellfire! I bet you can see as far as the barbarian lands,' she said.

'Further than that –' Del stopped. Gilvaris held up a hand for silence. 'What is it?'

Roslin listened. There was something you couldn't mistake about the tread of armed troops. She moved to look down the stairwell.

She said, 'It's Arianne Rooke.'

'One would suppose we were followed.' Gilvaris leaned over her shoulder.

Roslin saw the first shadow of confusion on Del's face.

'You led them to me,' he said.

'Looks like we did.' There was movement below in the shadowed stairwell. Deliberately she drew the pistol from her greatcoat pocket, cocked it, aimed and fired.

The report half deafened her. A great mass of plaster flaked off the far wall and spattered down the stairs. The scramble of running feet came to an abrupt halt. Roslin handed the pistol back to Gilvaris to reload. She leaned her elbows cautiously on the rail and called down: 'Come up, Arianne. But come up alone – or I'll blow your damned head off.'

Arianne Rooke gazed up at the spidering mass of tubes and mirrors and lenses. The late-morning sun struck highlights and reflections from them. Roslin watched her lined, plump face. Her heels clicked as she walked across the floorboards, circling the scope; and she at last came to rest standing with hands clasped on her silver-topped cane. Her braided wig was slightly askew; exertion had left runnels in the dark powder that creased her skin.

'I have thirty men downstairs,' she said without turning to look at anyone there. 'This must be destroyed, of course.'

'You –'

Roslin gripped Del's arm, and he subsided.

Arianne Rooke turned, regarding Gilvaris with some distaste. There was a distinct resemblance between aunt and this one of her nephews. Roslin wondered if that meant Gil would, when he reached that age, be like Arianne. It was an unpleasant thought. And then she wondered if they would – any of them – live to reach Arianne Rooke's age.

'You,' Arianne said, 'I thought you, at least, had some intelligence, Gilvaris.'

'This rivalry between Rooke and Mathury is becoming a little . . .' Gilvaris reflected, '. . . excessive, isn't it?'

The older woman inclined her head. 'Think that, if you will.'

'This won't give you any trade advantage,' Del said, bemused. 'Or is it that you can't bear Mathury to have something Rooke doesn't?'

Roslin caught Gil's eye, and saw him nod.

'Arianne,' she said, 'do you know a woman called Carlin Orme? She's one of my husband's colleagues. She has a printing press. You may know her better as editor of the Port Tekne news-sheet.'

Rooke frowned, but didn't respond.

'I spoke with Carlin Orme last night,' Roslin said. 'And with a number of other news-sheet editors. I thought, in fact, that it would be a good idea if someone other than Arianne Rooke followed us here. They'll be interested to see what my husband Del has discovered. And to know that House Rooke is here with thirty armed men.'

'My dear,' Arianne said, 'never tell me that was your idea?'

'Well, no. Gil's the subtle one. I'd settle for something more straightforward. And permanent.'

The last chimes of noon died on the air.

'Call off your people,' Rooke said, 'and I'll do the same. Quick, now.'

Roslin said, 'I ought to give them something, *Se* Arianne, if I can't give them the treachery of House Rooke. Why shouldn't Tekne know about this?'

The woman looked round at all three of the Mathury. Roslin waited for the outcome of the gamble.

We have to win here, in Tekne, she thought, glancing fondly at Del. Because that ship's a dream – there's nowhere to go.

'Oh, you children!' Arianne Rooke swore explosively. 'You haven't the least idea of . . . Do you know that I can call on the Port Council to silence you? Yes, and silence Carlin Orme and her like, too, if I need. *Se* Roslin, I don't want to have to do that. Your husbands were Rooke before they were Mathury. But I will if I have to!'

'Port Council?' Gilvaris demanded.

For answer, Arianne Rooke drew from under her coat what even they must instantly recognize as being the Great Seal of the Port Tekne Council.

We underestimated you, Roslin thought.

'What *is* all this?' she demanded.

'Delay Carlin Orme.' Rooke reached out with her cane to tilt one of the great framed lenses. 'I'll tell you – no, I'll show you. I'll show you without any of us having to leave this room.'

Arianne Rooke stepped back from the scope, which she had most carefully adjusted. She handled it a sight too familiarly for Roslin Mathury's peace of mind.

'I want you to look through this – *without* upsetting it.' She arrested Roslin's hand. Her fingers were cool, almost chill. 'Each of you. And while you're doing that, I want you to listen to me.'

'So talk.' Roslin, hands clasped behind her back, bent to the eyepiece – and forgot all about listening to Arianne Rooke.

It took a moment for her eyes to focus. One side of her field of vision was starred with the sun's glare, and there was the deep purple-blue of Asaria's summer sky. And . . .

She gazed through the scope at the surface of Daymoon.

All her life it had been familiar, the sister-world that dwarfed the sun in the sky. Now she saw lands, seas, icecaps. The webwork of dry rivers, the arid ochre land; and white cotton that specked the world under it with the minute moving shadows of clouds.

A bright metallic spark travelled across her vision, high over the deserts of Daymoon, a sharp, unnatural shape that fell into shadow as it entered the crescent's darkside. Roslin went cold. Another speck followed. Now she became adept at picking them out, their mechanically perfect flight (and thought, without reason, of Del's workshop and the half-repaired orrery).

'But –' she straightened, blinking. 'Then it's true, the legends are *true* –'

'No,' Rooke said. 'Not now. Now there is nothing there. In all the archives of the Port Council, we have no record of any life. Look at what you do *not* see: patterns, lines, edges. No fields. No canals. No cities.'

'But I saw . . .'

'What you see are machines. Del Mathury, you will most readily comprehend that.'

'I thought as much,' Del admitted, unsurprised.

'Tell me country tales, servants' tales,' Arianne invited Roslin. 'What is there on Daymoon?'

Roslin recalled shadows and firelight, and how tall the world is to a small child.

'Daymoon's a fine world. The people live in crystal houses, and their lanterns burn for ever. They build towers as tall as the sky, and fly faster than any airship ever made. Their carriages outrun the speed of the sun. Each woman there is richer than a *ser* of the Port Council, each man also. They cross the seas and span the land, and no disease touches them.'

Abandoning the child's ritual, still bemused, she said, 'So I was told, when very young. Servants believe it still, and think to go there when they die.'

'Which is well, since few of us can be *ser* here in Asaria,' Gilvaris commented acidly, straightening from the scope. 'Is that what you'd hide, that they've no paradise waiting? That Daymoon is a lie?'

'Daymoon is true. *Was* true,' Rooke corrected herself. 'And you see what is left. To put it most simply: I wish to keep us from that road, the road they followed to destruction. Del Mathury, worlds have been destroyed by those like you.'

Roslin stared blankly. Gilvaris, glancing at Del, thought, No, you're not the first. How many years has the Port Council studied, to be so knowledgeable? And how many years have they kept it secret?

'I have often thought, in all of *that* –' Arianne Rooke's gesture took in light-years, infinity, '– that there must be worlds enough besides us and Daymoon. A million repeated worlds, differing only in small details. No sister-world, perhaps, or no southern Pacific continent, no Asaria or perhaps a barbarian empire of the north, or – many things.'

Suddenly practical, she turned to Del. 'If you must work, then work *with* the Council.'

Del laughed. '"Must" work? If no one made anything new, we'd never change.'

'I should not be ashamed to stay as we are now.'

'No, I dare say *you* wouldn't.' Del was caustic.

Roslin said, 'We'd better work out something to tell Carlin Orme.'

There was some argument, Roslin hardly attended. She was watching Arianne Rooke, who stood there with one hand on her cane, and the other tucked into her waistcoat pocket, for all the world like a Fairday shyster.

'I'll talk to Orme,' Gilvaris announced, cutting off further discussion. 'Del, you'd better send word to the barbarian ship.'

Roslin quietly moved aside, to stand near Rooke.

'"Machines"?' she said.

'On Daymoon, they mock the dead race that made them. Is that what you'd have over Asaria?'

She heard unaccustomed seriousness in Rooke's voice.

'Do you think you can undiscover things?' Roslin asked. 'Silence every Del Mathury yet unborn? You're mad!'

'I'm not mad. But I do have visions.' Arianne Rooke laid a dark hand on the scope. 'I believe there is a choice at some point. Perhaps now: an age of reason. And then an age of passionate unreason, ending as you have seen . . . There are scars of war on Daymoon. No, I don't seek to take away the machines, so much as the desire to use them so poorly.'

Roslin said, 'I don't understand you.'

Del, as he went past them, said, 'Arianne Rooke, who gave you the right to play God?'

As close to pain as Roslin had ever seen her, the woman said, 'Nobody.'

Silent for a moment, Roslin watched through the attic doorway as her younger husband went to speak with one of Rooke's armed men.

'How long have you been watching us?'

'Some years. The rivalry between Rooke and Mathury hasn't made it any easier, I'll admit. And for that reason – that you're less likely to believe me – I've taken the rather extraordinary measure of summoning the Port Council to full session. They can confirm what I say.'

After a perfectly-timed pause, she added, 'We shall have to do something for young Mathury.'

'For House Mathury,' Roslin corrected, at last on sure ground. 'Shall we say, a seat on the Council? Gil would be good at that. You see, if Del's going to work with the Council, I think he needs someone there to look out for his interests.'

Arianne Rooke chuckled. 'You bargain well.'

'And you flatter a little, bribe a lot, and hold force as a last card.'

'Which is only to say, my dear, that I'm a politician.'

Roslin squinted up through the broken roof at the sky. An airship glided soundlessly overhead.

'I don't understand what's been happening here.' She met Rooke's gaze. 'I'm missing something. Some chance I ought to take, some question I ought to ask.'

Motionless, watchful, Arianne Rooke gave the conversation more attention than an outsider might think it warranted, and thought to herself, Can this woman, who (let us be honest) is not altogether *bright*, can she come close to a Del Mathury's curiosity? Because if she can . . .

Rooke said, 'And shall I tell you more, *Se* Roslin?'

A silence fell. The sunlight sparked from brass, mirror, lens. And in the pause, it became apparent that Roslin Mathury could not summon so irresponsible a curiosity; did not desire, or see the need for it.

'No,' she said, smiling. 'Leave me to run the Mathury estates without your interference. That's all I want. Now do you think we should go and bring a little order out of this chaos?'

Rooke thought, I spoke with a barbarian once, what did he say? 'Putting a wall around the mind . . .'

The Archivist pauses.

That last sentence, true in its way, fails to suggest the whole truth. She carefully erases it.

Outside, bells ring gladly, and pennant ribbons uncoil on the breeze. She blinks away images three generations dead. Sees Tekne, now little changed. Fewer airships, fewer steamcars (but there are always servants to do the work). The only significant change is that there are barbarians in the streets.

But really, one shouldn't call them that. Not with the ser *-Lords of all four continents here to celebrate the centennial of the* Pax Asaria. *And what better to encourage them in Asarian philosophy than a dramatic reading? she thinks, smiling at her own vanity.*

Even if such turning points in history are largely guesswork . . .

In haste to join the carnival, the Archivist inscribes her final lines:

In haste to join the carnival, the Archivist inscribes her final lines:

Arianne Rooke, alone and last to leave, adjusted one of the free lenses to catch the sunlight through the broken roof. She walked unhurriedly away. Where the sun focused, a thin wisp of smoke coiled acridly up from the wooden attic floor.

A Shadow Under the Sea

'Look!' Ellis shouted. 'It's happening again – now!'

Spurlock took the ancient spyglass from her, training it on the sea. Light blinded her, images blurred: then she focused on the distant fishing boat.

'I see nothing.'

'Wait – there!'

The seawind whipped around them where they stood on the beacon hill. Under the cliffs, the tide beat against Orindol's coast. A calm summer day, nothing to trouble a ship's crew – particularly a crew from the Hundred Isles.

'There's nothing we can do, lady,' Ellis of Orindol said bitterly. 'Even if we had another ship out there, what could they do against *that?*'

Distant, soundless: Spurlock saw the tragedy. The fishing boat (every minute detail clear, down to the nets spilling silver on her decks, the barefoot running sailors) heeled over and shipped water. Waves broke, spray flew. The boat was tangled in a great bed of floating weed . . .

'Clingweed?'

'I wouldn't bring you all the way from Shabelit for that, lady.'

The boat turned broadside to the wind, shipping water, foundering. Spurlock saw the crew running this way and that in panic, saw the soundless gouts of spray where they threw themselves overboard, and the weed-mass moved –

Moved lazily, opened a mouth of darkness.

Timbers floated on the water. Nothing else of the ship remained. The water swirled, then quietened, where the last man had been swimming desperately for the beach.

A great mass slid into the depths, out of sight of the spyglass, down into the hidden darkness. Spurlock lowered the glass, blinking at the suddenly-removed world. She was cold.

'That outsizes my largest ships,' she said.

'It's taken five boats in the last month,' Ellis said. 'Each time the crews were – killed. Only a coaster escaped – perhaps because the beast had fed, I don't know – to bring us the news. We didn't believe. Now it comes to our very shore. Lady, you must help us.'

Gulls cried, soaring in the middle air between beacon hill and the roofs of Orindol. Spurlock looked down on peaked roofs, tiled and slanting, bowed with age. The early light sent the gull's shadows darting across clapboard walls. Down on the beach, men and women were clustered round the net-drying sheds, talking in the shade of the tall tarred buildings. Fishing-boats were drawn up on the shingle. The fishmarket was closed for lack of business, and there too the Orindol islanders stood talking. The bright sea was empty.

You cannot have the Hundred Isles forbidden the sea, Spurlock thought, chilled. All the Shabelit Archipelago has trade for its life-blood.

'You're First in Council,' Ellis urged, 'you're lady of Shabelit itself. Help us!'

'That's nothing to send spears against. It would take a warship down as easily as a fishing boat. I won't send Shabelit's galleys.'

Ellis looked hopelessly at her. 'I know. I knew before I came to Shabelit. We can't kill it. But what am I to say to my people?'

What am I to say to mine? Spurlock thought, with a certain grim humour. How long will I be First in Council if I go away wringing my hands and crying defeat? More to the point, how long will the Peace of Shabelit last when the Hundred Isles hear of it?

The younger woman said, 'In the old time, they made sacrifices to the Kraken. That will begin again, now it has returned.'

'The Kraken is a myth. That's a sea-beast, nothing more. Listen to me,' Spurlock linked arms with the young islander, leading her down the track toward the village, 'the first thing you must do is leave poisoned bait. Float out a raft with rotten carcasses on it; let it take that for a guts-ache. If that doesn't discourage it, we'll think again.'

She left Ellis and the Orindol islanders working and went back aboard the warship. She dismissed all except her aide.

'Well, lady?' Dinu asked. 'Will you call the Council to Shabelit?'

'Too long a delay. They'd have to come from all the Hundred Isles. It's all stopgap measures! Sit down,' she said, knowing that his wound from the long-past Bazuruk campaign still troubled him. 'You're a south-islander. Tell me all the legends you know about the Kraken. I have to think quickly.'

'We've lived well under the Peace of Shabelit,' Ellis said. Rain had darkened her fair hair, her plain tunic and britches. The *Wind's Eye* rocked gently on the swell. 'But if we can't fish, or trade . . . that's when the fighting begins. Durinsir, Merari, Gileshta, Orindol; we're none of us wealthy islands. Lady, if your warships should be penned up in Shabelit –'

'Let's not anticipate. I've no wish to see the old days back. Island against island . . .' Spurlock shook her head. She wondered if Ellis were old enough to have fought in the last wars, the wars that Spurlock had led to bring about the Peace. 'The poison failed?'

'Perhaps it is no ordinary beast.'

In the silence, the summer rain was loud; and under it they heard – as you hear anywhere in the Shabelit Archipelago – the beating of the sea.

'Then it will take no ordinary means to defeat it. In my judgment, no other weapon but sorcery. I will leave you my Second, Dinu Vanathri; he will direct you to feed carcasses to the beast, so that it leaves your ships.'

'We haven't enough to feed a Kraken's hunger!'

'For a while,' Spurlock said. 'I am going south, to the Cold Lands.'

Ellis shivered. 'Lady, I do not know who has the greater peril; we who stay, or you who go to – that land.'

'They have powers. We must turn some weapon against the beast.'

The Orindol woman bowed respectfully. 'I wish you safe voyaging, lady. And I beg you; be as swift as you may. For all our sakes.'

The First in Council should have been received with great honour in the Cold Lands cities, anywhere from Sakashu to Tulkys. Instead, Spurlock took the *Wind's Eye* down past Goldenrock and the Spice Isles, avoiding the populous regions of the Cold Lands, and came within the month to a narrow fiord far down the southern coast.

She left the ship moored there, taking none of her guards when she went ashore.

The valley grass was lush, rising to meet the blue-black forest that seamlessly covered each dip and hollow of the foothills. Above the tree-line, naked rock rose up to the snow. Sharp and cold, glittering white against a sky so dark a blue as to be almost purple: mountains. The wind blew damp.

How long since I went alone into wild country? Too long, she answered herself. A First in Council gains enemies.

She strode on, still a little uncertain of the solid ground after the shifting deck of the *Wind's Eye.* Herds grazed on the lower pastures, and the herders had pitched their skin tents by the river. They sent her on into the hills, towards the mountains and the pass that led eventually to great Tulkys. There, by a spring, she found a stone hut; beehive-shaped, a thin grey trail coiling from the smokehold. *Maresh-kuzor*: the shaman's house.

Spurlock hesitated. Many years had passed since she came to Tulkys, or crossed the pass, or visited the valley.

'Ash!' she called.

When the sound had died, the skin curtain of the hut was pulled back and a woman came out. She wore a skin tunic and leggings. Animal teeth hung on thongs round her neck and were bound into her braided gray hair. As she approached,

Spurlock caught the smell of animal fat.

'You look well,' she said.

The shaman woman gazed at her. It was oddly disconcerting. Partly it was that her pale eyes, under the broad forehead, were set wide apart; she stared bird-like first from one eye, then the other. Partly it was her indefinable aura of power.

'I know why you are here,' she said. 'The far-sight brought me a vision of you. Come in, my sister. Talk if you will. I warn you now: I will not leave the mountains. I will not come to the islands.'

Spurlock nodded. 'Yes. We need to talk.'

The years were treating Ash well, Spurlock thought. Apart from the gray hair, you wouldn't guess that she – a handful of years older than Spurlock – must be close on her fiftieth winter.

'I have an armed company on the ship,' Spurlock said confidently. 'I could have come here with them. Or, with a little more time, those in Tulkys would have commanded you to my aid. I won't tell you how Shabelit will reward you, because what would that mean to you? I can't bribe or force you. All I can do is come here and ask. Ash, the islands need your help.'

The high air was cold. Pale sun gleamed through the hut's entrance. They sat facing each other over the fire-pit. Spurlock leaned back against the rough wall, shifted her scabbarded blade.

'I can't help you. This beast –'

'This beast,' Spurlock said, 'is the Kraken.'

Ash was quiet. At last she said, 'Away from this land, my powers are small. If other shamans were with me . . . but none will leave; and they are too widely scattered to be found quickly.'

'If you need help, I'm of your blood.' Spurlock moved as the setting sun shone in her face. 'Will you have it known in Tulkys that you're half-islander?'

'Will you have it known in Shabelit that you are half blood of the Cold Lands?' Ash's gaze was steady. 'I cannot speak untruth. You know that.'

Spurlock scratched through her cropped hair and sighed. 'Ash, I don't like to say this, but . . . I looked after you when we were children, when we thought you were – before we knew it was the shaman-power.'

'And you will say I owe you a debt – you, First of Shabelit?'

Taken by surprise, Spurlock laughed. 'No. No, I don't think I'll try and persuade you of that.'

Ash smiled, losing twenty years. For the first time, there was the old warmth between them.

'Your way isn't my way,' Spurlock admitted, 'and I have to say I like most things that go with being First of Shabelit. I've earned them. But peace is a fragile thing. You're not stupid, you can see what will happen if I'm beaten here. Every minor lord between here and the Bazuruk coast will be grabbing whatever he or she can get. Then I've to fight all the last battles over again – and I'm not as young as I was.'

'And then,' Ash said softly, 'there is the beast.'

Spurlock nodded mutely.

'Wait,' Ash said. 'I'll see what I see.'

Spurlock settled herself in the smoky interior of the hut. Ash went out to the forest, returning some time later with her hands full of small scarlet fungis. She let the skin curtain fall, cutting them off from light and air. She fed the fire, chewing on the fungi, fed it until the stones in the fire-pit glowed white.

In the hot darkness, Spurlock edged back against the stone wall. She was sweating heavily; the palms of her hands were slick. She thought, What am I bringing back to Orindol?

Ash took up a wooden bucket and threw water on the stones. A sheet of steam hissed up. Spurlock's nails dug bloody imprints in her palms. Her lungs were seared, her eyes wept.

In the long darkness, Ash cried out.

Air was cold on her skin. She blinked, dazzled by early sunlight, and saw above treetops the floating crests of mountains. The stones under her were cold and hard.

My old bones don't like this, she thought as she stood and stiffly brushed herself down.

'Ah.' Ash came out of the hut. Briefly she laid her hand on Spurlock's forehead. 'You have returned, good. Do you remember anything of your time in the Otherworld?'

Spurlock adjusted the laces of her chainmail, and her sword-belt, before she answered.

'I'm a soldier, not a shaman.'

Ash nodded. 'I will remind you, as I was with you. This I learned from the Otherworld. Your Kraken is one of those elementals that cannot be killed – she is Water. You can no more slay her than you can prevent the tides.'

Spurlock was surprised by a sudden total and overwhelming terror. She gasped as if it was actual pain. When it ebbed, she saw Ash nod.

'Yes. That is the other thing. You islanders depend on the sea. Your children walk decks before they touch land. Yet you suffer foul winds, rocks, treacherous currents, storms . . . she is your special fear, the Kraken; the shadow-soul of the sea itself.'

More incredulous than offended, Spurlock said, 'You're calling me a coward.'

'You come from Shabelit and see the beast . . . you could have sent word by your Second, I know Dinu Vanathri, but no; you board the *Wind's Eye* and sail from Orindol as fast as the winds will take you.'

'I had to speak with you,' Spurlock protested angrily.

'It will be the same for any islander. She is your fear.'

'If you're telling me you won't help us –'

'I didn't say that.' Ash regarded her sadly. 'I will need your help, sister; but even the sea can be contained. It will not be easy. It may fail. But I will come with you to Orindol.'

Spurlock studied the charts, and they sailed back up the Archipelago by a route that kept them away from deep water. Ash insisted they stop at Goldenrock, where they took on bales of the weed the islanders call *dekany*. She sat cross-legged on the deck, stumpy fingers knotting a five-stranded web. The *Wind's Eye* sailed, the web grew, and before midsummer's day passed they anchored off Orindol. Ellis and Dinu were there to greet her.

'It's taken ships as far north as Shabelit itself,' Dinu said, limping up the shingle beside her. 'We thought we'd lost it to Bazuruk's coast, then it was sighted off Sephir, and a few days ago here at Orindol again. Half the Council's here.'

'And in a panic, I'd lay bets.'

'You'd win, lady.' He glanced behind, where the shaman

woman was being ferried ashore by Spurlock's guard. 'Is that
. . . can she help us?'

Spurlock avoided the question. 'Ellis, I want all the animal
carcasses you can find and spare, on the nearest islands too, as
well as Orindol. Dump them where the current will take them
out toward the Western Ocean. I want that beast fed.'

'We'll do it,' Ellis said.

We must be close to it, Ash had said. You must help me,
sister.

Spurlock refused to acknowledge her fear. 'When you've
done that,' she said, 'find me a small boat – one that can be
crewed by two.'

Her legs felt loose behind the knees, and her stomach
churned. It was a long time since she'd sailed a boat, and she
was clumsy. This isn't nerves before battle, she thought,
remembering the dry-mouthed excitement that changes to
exultation. This is fear.

The boat slid down a hill of water. Waves smacked the bows,
and spray shot into the air. Sunlight refracted rainbows. As
they came into deeper water the swells calmed. Orindol slid
east away from them.

Ash sat with her back to the coffin-sized cabin, checking the
knots. Stones weighted the net. It was smaller than even an
Orindol fishing-boat's net.

'You must cast it,' she said. 'I will chant the protection on
us. If I fail in that, then it will take us.'

Spurlock was lashing the tiller. 'You haven't seen it. It's the
Kraken! That net wouldn't hold a rock-devil or dire-shark,
never mind . . . ah, what's the use.'

Ash smiled.

'You might as well hope to net Orindol itself.'

'Then why are you here? the shaman woman asked.

'Those credulous fools on the Council would tell you I won't
send someone else to do what I wouldn't do myself – and it's
good for me they think that. I won't tell them we're sisters. But
believe me, if you didn't need blood kin to help you, I'd be
ashore with those others, cheering you on.' Spurlock recovered
confidence when she heard Ash laugh. 'Stand away. We don't
need the sail now; we'll drift.'

She lashed the sail tight. She went to the side. The ship was so low in the water, she could have dipped her hand in it. The sun shone down, picking out grains of silt. Clear water for a few feet, then murkiness; gold, gold-green, dark. She strained her eyes, searching for movement. A shoal of minute fish darted past, sparking briefly in the sun.

Behind her, Ash breathed in sharply. *'Arak-sha u elish tu –'*

The chant continued urgently. In the depths there was movement. A dark sliding: rising to the edge of vision.

Spurlock saw brown scales crusted with barnacles, clotted with weed; brown scales edged with black. Plate-scales the size of a man's body. Sliding past under them, endless. She stared down into the clear water, searching.

There was no end. To either side the scaled body glided by, a scant few feet under the surface. Seeing it from the beacon hill, one had no idea of its size. Its shadow darkened the sea as far as she could see. The boat was a wood chip floating above it. Crusted flesh gliding under them, bulking in the depths. The boat so fragile, so easily shouldered off into the water –

She was on her knees, her hands knotted on the rail. They were out of sight of Orindol, of any of the islands. There was only the empty circle of the horizon, the tossing boat, and the monstrous body of the Kraken under them. She saw it curve; they spun like a chip in the whirlpool of its turning.

One of the carcass-loaded rafts drifted ahead of them. Spurlock saw the darkness rise. It broke the surface, curving above them, a sliding hoop of flesh that streamed water. The pale underside was puckered with rosettes of suckers. Gently, scarcely seeming to brush it, the loop of muscle closed over the raft. Wood creaked, split with a sound like gunshots. The raft broke up.

'. . . *anu-elish geir u turaksha ke –*'

Ash's voice rose higher. The weights of the net rolled against Spurlock. Her hands locked on the rail. A lurch of the boat nearly jerked her arms from her shoulders, Spray flooded them. A wave burst over the side. Salt water burned her mouth and lungs. She choked.

'– *shansa ke anu* – Spurlock! – *anu keshta kerasha –*'

Ash clung with both hands to the edge of the cabin, chanting, her face twisted with concentration. The coiled net spilled across the deck. Spurlock saw it. She should move, cast it.

The dark behind her eyes was speckled red. She flattened herself against the deck, clinging to ropes, to the mast, to anything. Nails broke, rope-burn scarred her arms. Wood was rough under her cheek.

'– *kazarak u elish-nar* –'

The begging appeal in Ash's voice forced her eyes open. A hill of flesh reared up against the sky. Crusted with weed; white foam spuming down, slicing –

Ash let go the ship, swept and cast the net. The sheer effort halted the chant. She stumbled with the words, missed the rhythm.

The deck slammed against Spurlock's head. She tasted blood. Her eyes clamped shut. She clung to the rail. Under her the world shifted on its foundations. Ash screamed.

The beast came.

Wavelets slapped the side of the boat. All else was silent. The heat of the sun dried her and left salt caked and cracking on her skin. Her hands bore the raw imprint of rope. She stood, slipped down on hands and knees, shaking so violently that she couldn't get up again.

The sea was calm. Snagged on the prow of the boat, the *dekany* weed net was full, stretching with the weight of its catch. Darkness coiled and thrashed in the meshes. At sight of that transformation, she made a dry, unrecognizable sound. It was laughter, relief at being alive, at having survived.

Ash lay cramped between the mast and the cabin. Blood soaked the soft skin tunic, now ragged. Shoulder, ribs, hip and leg were torn with bloody disc-imprints.

Spurlock crawled across to her. The woman was breathing shallowly.

It's over, Spurlock thought. Hoist the sail and go home. Go home and tell them when Spurlock of Shabelit, First in Council, fought the Kraken – she fell down and cried like a newborn brat. Tell them that, Lady of the Hundred Isles.

She lowered her head and shut her eyes, hot with shame and despair at this final failure, where success was most needed. All the hard years between a beggar-brat's childhood in Tulkys and the High Council of Shabelit fell away as if they had never been, as if she had never fought her way up, never imposed peace on the Hundred Isles.

Ash's pulse was irregular. The blood pulsed slower now, soaking the deck. Quick attention might save her. If they reached Orindol. . . .

If I'd awakened a little later.

Spurlock cursed, driving the thought from her mind. It returned. Sister she might be, liar she could never be: Ash would say, when anyone asked her, precisely what had happened here in the Western Ocean. And they would ask. And they would spread the story from one end of the Archipelago to the other: Spurlock has turned coward. The peace is ended. Each island turning against the other.

Spurlock saw very clearly what would happen to the First in Council who had betrayed them.

Ash's eyes opened, sought her face.

'I may be corrupt,' Spurlock said, 'but I'm the best chance the islands have. What about Ellis and Orindol? They won't care about the truth. All they want is to live in peace.'

The shaman woman tried to speak and choked. A thin line of blood ran out of her mouth and down her neck.

'I didn't work all those years,' Spurlock said, 'to give up what I have now.'

She sat by the mast, leaning back against the lashed-down sail, and waited.

It was Dinu Vanathri who found her. The celebrations in the great palace at Shabelit were in their third day and showed no sign of slackening. Spurlock was being hailed as the greatest hero since Bran Double-Axe. He found her in the inner court-yard where fountains tumble into a marble pool deep as a well.

'Lady?'

She was looking into the water. A lean aging woman, court clothes uncomfortable on her as battle-gear never was; a sandy-haired woman with a lined face, and the first hints of age in her movements. Dinu stood beside her.

In the black depths, scales glinted. He saw a coiling far down in the water, glimpses of the Kraken seen as if through the wrong end of a spyglass. He thought of it as he'd seen it off Orindol, and his skin crawled.

'The delegation from the Cold Lands is here,' he said. 'They would like to take the body of the shaman woman back to Tulkys. The lords of the Council say she should be buried here, since it was she who aided you, and so aided us too.'

'She was a brave woman,' Spurlock said. 'We will set up her image in the Great Hall. Let them take her. She loved Tulkys. It's fitting she should lie there.'

'She was your friend.' Dinu absently ground his knuckle into his aching hip and shifted his stance. 'It's a bad thing when friends die.'

'I wouldn't be where I am without her.'

Down in the shadows, the Kraken stilled.

'Come on.' Spurlock said and clapped him cheerfully on the shoulder. 'Let's go back to the celebrations. It's what Ash would want us to do, isn't it?'

The Pits Beneath the World

A wind stirs the blue grass of the Great Plains. The flat land stretches out to the perfect circle of the horizon. There is not a rock or tree to break the monotony. Seventeen moons burn in a lilac sky. A blue-giant sun is setting, its white dwarf companion star hangs in the evening sky.

The small figure stands waist-deep in the grass. She aches from running bent over in a crouch. Now she straightens, biting back a gasp at the pain.

Shrill chittering and whistling noises come from the distance. Seen!

Up until today she's been sorry that she's small for her age. Now she's glad. Only a small human could lie concealed in the Plains grass. She edges away and crawls on, hands and knees stained blue by the grass sap.

Behind her, the whistling of the Talinorian hunting party begins again.

There is no doubt: she is their quarry.

When did it go wrong? Pel Graham wondered. The Talinorians are our friends. What happened?

She was hurt and bewildered as well as afraid.

It had all been fine until two days ago . . .

★

132

There! — the Talinorian whistled. — The *chelanthi!* —

Pel peered ahead between its sheaf of stalked eyes. Far out across the Great Plain, grass rippled where no wind blew.

'Hold on!' called Pel's mother, riding high astride the glittering carapace of another Talinorian, Baltenezeril-lashamara.

With a clatter of shell the Talinorian hunting party edged down the side of the cliff. Pel clung as Dalasurieth-rissanihil lurched under her, body-suckers clutching the rock as they moved down the almost vertical surface. The long segmented body rippled.

'Faster!' she yelled, and then remembering that the human voice had too low a frequency for the Talinorian's sensors, tapped the message out on the alien's eye-carapace. The stalked eyes retreated briefly under the hard shell. Pel had learned to interpret this as amusement.

Now they went more slowly. The Talinorians were better suited to rocky cliffs and scarps. Only for the traditional *chelanthi* hunts did they venture down onto grassland.

Pel waved to her mother, and to the other members of the Earth scientific expedition honoured to ride in the Talinorian hunt. It was a time of relaxation. They must have finished negotiating, Pel thought, not very interested. She didn't want to leave Talinor yet.

The wind blew her hair in her eyes. She turned her head, seeing the rocky 'coast' behind them. Clusters of rock rose starkly out of the flat grassland. It was impossible to think of them as anything but islands, jutting out of a grass ocean. On the rocking-gaited Talinorian, Pel felt like a ship at sea. Hunting the beasts of the ocean, the *chelanthi.*

– We're falling behind –

The other unburdened Talinorians were faster. Dalasurieth-rissanhil slowed still further.

The 'islands' they had left were small, and in a natural condition. They were covered with bush-berry-trees, the purple fruit hanging down in long strings; and with the *cureuk* flowers that folded up when touched. Mothbirds flew only in this hour between the blue sun's rising and the white sun's following, when they again roosted. A multitude of singing insects nested in the crevices of the rock, and the nights were bright with luminous starflies. It was different from Talinor-Prime, Pel thought, where the expedition had set down the shuttle.

– They have made a kill –

– Where? –

Pel stared ahead over Dalasurieth-rissanihil's carapace, but saw nothing in detail. If she admitted the truth she preferred riding to hunting, and wasn't sorry to miss the end.

A wisp of smoke coiled up ahead.

– Dala', look! –

– Stray laser-beam. Don't they realize what a grass fire might do?' –

Dalasurieth-rissanihil sounded, so far as she could tell, furious.

– I thought you had to use spears? –

– Tradition demands it. The leader will have something to say to them back at Prime! –

Pel saw the Talinorians put the fire out before it could spread. Others carried the scaly *chelanthi* slung across their patterned carapaces, held in place by their forked scorpion-tails. Clusters of thin jointed arms waved excitedly.

– Will you stay for the hunt tomorrow? –

– I have to go home. It's my – The click and whistle language failed her. – It's a party. The northern team should be back. And besides, it's my . . . –

She couldn't find a word for 'birthday', and struggled to make it clear. Dalasurieth-rissanihil rattled its forked tail.

– So you will have been alive eleven seasons of your home world? That is a long time to be adult. I had thought you younger –

Privately she laughed. Aliens were often stupid about the most obvious things. Except, she thought, I don't suppose it *is* obvious to them; not even an eleventh birthday . . .

– How old are you, Dala'? –

– I have been adult three seasons –

Pel couldn't be bothered to translate that into Earth-stand-ard years. She knew it wasn't long.

– Yes, but how long ago were you born? I mean, I'm not adult. Not exactly. I don't come of age until I'm fourteen –

– You are not adult? –

– No, not yet; I told you. Oh, you don't understand –

★

They were turning back towards the islands and Talinor-Prime. Dalasurieth-rissanihil was unusually silent on the way back across the plain, and she wondered if she had offended him.

Talinor-Prime. An 'island' in a grassland 'ocean', but this island was a continent. Big enough to take a flyer three days to cross it. A rock plateau a few metres higher than the surrounding plain, and with a totally different ecology – as Pel's xenobiologist mother was very prone to telling her. More important from Pel's point of view, Talinor-Prime held the city and the starship landing-field.

It was noon before they arrived. The two suns – blue Alpha and white Beta – blazed together in the sky. Pel had a black and a purple shadow following her on the carved rock walkway.

'Ready for the party tomorrow?' her mother asked.

'You bet. Are the others back yet?'

'Not yet. I'm expecting them to call in soon.'

The long arthropod bodies of the Talinorians glided past them on low trollies. Some preferred the powered walkways that riddled the rock of Prime. They were too low for an adult human to enter without stooping, but Pel was small enough to stand upright in them.

They turned down another walkway and saw the starfield between the wasp-nest dwellings of the Talinorians. Pel looked through the view-grills as they walked. She liked the inside of the 'nests', with their powered valve-doors and beam-operated equipment. Talinorian manipulative limbs weren't strong, but they were good at delicate work. Their great love was glass, which their formulae made stronger than anywhere else in the galaxy. Sculptured, woven in filaments, blown into spheres and cubes and octagons, the ornaments glittered in the light of the two suns; and Talinor-Prime chimed as the wind blew.

'Pel!'

Pel ran on from staring through a view-grill. She caught up as they began to walk across the vast expanse of the starfield. The blue-grey rock was hot underfoot.

'Tell me,' her mother said, 'what do you and Dala' talk about?'

'Oh . . . things.' Pel shrugged.

'I'm sorry in a way that there are no other kids with this expedition. I always wonder if it's fair to bring you on these trips. But since there are just the two of us . . .'

Pel made a rude noise. 'Try and stop me coming with you,' she invited. 'Anyway, it's training – for the future.'

Her mother laughed.

The starfield was on a long spit of 'island' jutting out into the grassland. At that time there were no other ships there. Pel looked at the squat dirty shuttle with affection. It would be great to have the other half of the team back with the ship.

I wonder if they brought me any presents? she thought; and didn't answer when her mother asked her what she was grinning at.

Blue Alpha's dawn light stretched her shadow far behind her on the rocks. The morning smelled clean, spicy. A cool wind blew out of the south. Pel scrambled down the long spit towards the edge of the grassland. Mothbirds beat their fragile wings round her, bright against the amethyst sky.

She could just have waited on the shuttle. But Pel preferred to keep watch in the open, and wait for the ship's return.

Something whirred past her ear.

She swatted at it automatically. Glancing round, she saw some Talinorians on the slope above her, and recognized one of them as Dalasurieth-rissanihil.

A shadow flicked her face.

The spear clattered on the rock beside her.

Pel sprang up. The red line of a laser kicked the rock into molten steam. While she watched, Dalasurieth-rissanihil raised the gun and took aim again.

She took a flying leap off the rocks, running as fast as she could through the grass. It slowed her, but she managed to reach the cover of a rock overhang.

Another party of Talinorians waited beyond it.

She swerved out into the open, running like a hare. Arms and legs pumping, lungs burning; she fell into a stride that took her far out into the blue grassland.

It dawned on her as she fell into the scant cover that the grass afforded, far from Talinor-Prime, that those first shots had not been meant to kill. Only to start her running. Only to force her out into the grass ocean, where killing might take place honourably with glass-tipped hunting spears.

She put her head down, gripped her knees, and tried to stop shaking. When the first panic subsided, bewilderment remained. Then it hardened into a cold determination.

Pel Graham looked back to the distant cliffs of Prime. She thought, Somehow I'll get back. I'll make them pay. Somehow I'll find out . . . Dalasurieth-rissanihil – *why?*

She heard the hunting party in the distance.

Evening found her still further away, driven out of sight of Prime. The islands were specks on the horizon. If it had not been for the gentle ridges and undulations of the ground here, she would have been spotted long ago. Now she clung to cover under an alien sky. The grassland went from aquamarine to azure to indigo as Beta set.

The expedition will come looking, Pel thought. I only have to stay free until the shuttle flies over and finds me. I bet they're already on their way –

The grass rustled.

Pel flopped down on her stomach. A blunt muzzle pushed along through the reed-bladed grass. A *chelanthi.* Its low flexible body was covered in mirror-scales, camouflaging it. She saw tiny eye-clusters almost hidden under the muzzle. The actual mouth was further back, between the front pairs of legs. As she watched, it began to crop the grass.

Aren't they meat-eaters? Pel wondered.

A scaly hide brushed her arm. She shot back, biting off a yell. The *chelanthi* raised its muzzle, eye-stalks wavering reproachfully. Pel stifled laughter. It scuttled off past the first *chelanthi.* She followed it.

The ridge concealed a dip beyond. The hollow was pitted with holes, among which many *chelanthi* were grazing. They seemed harmless. They probably were . . .

Another *chelanthi* emerged from one of the pits. They must burrow deep, Pel thought. How else would they hide from the Talinorians?

A long whistle sounded through the gathering twilight. She thought, what if the hunters have heat-seeking equipment? That'll show up human body-heat miles off when it's dark . . .

Pel Graham grinned. It was a crazy idea she had. Good, but crazy; still, she might be a little crazy herself by now. There was every excuse for it.

The *chelanthi* did not object when Pel crept into one of the pits beside them. It was dry, earth trodden down hard, and surprisingly roomy. She lay sheltered among their warm scaly bodies, hidden from anything on the grassland above.

The blue sun set in an ocean-coloured sky. The few stars of the galaxy's rim burned in lonely splendour. The moons rose, all seventeen of Talinor's satellites. Sometimes their varying orbits made them appear in clusters, but now they hung in a string of crescents. Pel Graham slept fitfully in the warm night. The Talinorian hunting party passed five miles to the west.

Morning came chill. Disturbed out of one pit when the *chelanthi* went to graze, Pel crawled into another. It had only one occupant. This *chelanthi* made a racheting noise like a broken clock and nipped at her hand. Pel backed out in an undignified scramble.

She watched. The *chelanthi* was busy at the mouth of that pit. It appeared to be stringing a substance from glands under its body. The stubby forepaws gripped the pit's mouth, and Pel saw that it was beginning to weave a web over it.

She listened, but heard no sound of the hunt.

I'm safe here. At least I'm hidden. But I have to get back to Prime. I have to warn them!

The day wore on. Pel was extremely bored by the *chelanthi*. True, they did her no harm. They did nothing except crop the grass. The webbed pit remained closed, and she was not sure if the *chelanthi* inside were sleeping, hibernating, or dead. Hourly the mass of its hidden body became more shapeless.

Unless the Talinorians stumbled across her, the *chelanthi* would hide her. They camouflaged her against long-distance night sensors, and in the day radiation from the two suns made long-distance sensing impossible.

It was not until then that it occurred to her; if she was hidden from Talinorian sensors, she must also be hidden from those of the Earth expedition.

The second evening came. The blue giant Alpha eclipsed the white dwarf Beta as the suns set. Pel was hungrier than she had ever thought it possible to be. Thirst made her drink the water that collected on the flat-bladed grass, and hope that it didn't carry infection.

She was even more determined to get back to Talinor-Prime. It was think of that, or panic, and she didn't dare panic.

The *chelanthi* gave up grazing and headed for the pits.

Pel thought about the webbed pit, she hadn't looked at it in a while. She walked over to it.

As she watched, the webbing over the pit's entrance twitched. It bulged as if something beneath it were trying to get out. Pel stepped back rapidly.

The webbing reared up and split. Something sharp, grey, and glistening protruded. It twitched again, slitting the web still further. A multitude of thin many-jointed and hard-shelled limbs followed, gripping the sides of the pit. A carapace emerged. Under it, clustered eye-stalks waved. The body heaved itself up onto the grass, segment by armoured segment, disclosing the suckers on the underside. The patterned shell gleamed. Last to leave the pit was the forked scorpion-tail.

Pel stared.

The young Talinorian looked round at the grass-eating *chelanthi*, at Pel Graham who stood frozen with astonishment, and clicked and whistled softly. As it scuttled off it said – Don't you know that there are some things it's better for you not to see? –

It changes everything! Pel thought.

The grass was harsh under her hands and knees. She followed the line of a low ridge. The pits and the broken web were far behind her. She knew that the new-born Talinorian would betray her to the hunting party as soon as it found them.

White Beta rose, and the plains flooded with colour. A little warmth came back to Pel as she moved.

It spoke. It was a *chelanthi*, and it – changed.

It had looked very like Dalasurieth-rissanihil, who was only three seasons 'adult'.

Shrilly in the distance came the whistle of the hunters. Abandoning the *chelanthi*, she had abandoned safety.

I will get back to Prime! she told herself.

She saw something flash in the morning sky like a thrown coin.

'Hey! Hey, shuttle!'

They'll never hear me, never see me, never sense me . . . . If there was any way I could mark myself out . . .

Fire would have been best, but she had no way to set the grass lands on fire. And then she remembered the *chelanthi* hunt.

Deliberately Pel stood up and ran to the crown of the ridge. She waved both arms over her head, semaphoring wildly.

The shrilling of the hunters was louder, much louder.

As fleet as fear could make her, she ran. A laser-beam licked redly out to her left, and even through her exhaustion she had time for a grin of triumph.

A line of grass burst into crackling fire. The shuttle's course veered wildly. It began to descend.

Pel could hardly breathe. The world was going red and black round her. But she staggered over the ramp a hundred yards ahead of her pursuers and fell into her mother's arms.

The Talinorian hunting party dwindled below.

'*That* took some sorting out. You mustn't blame them,' Pel's mother turned away from the computer console. 'It's not uncommon in nature to have a larval stage, after all. Even on Earth, moths and butterflies . . . And until they change they're quite unintelligent. Just animals, really.'

'Did you tell them?' Pel asked. 'About – children?'

Outside the shuttle's viewport, Talinor-Prime sparkled in the light of two suns. The wind ruffled the grasslands.

'It's a great step forward in understanding each other.' She put her hand on Pel's shoulder. 'You see, when you said you weren't adult –'

'They thought it was all right to hunt me down?'

'Don't be bitter. Worlds are different places.' She turned her back. 'If they'd hurt *you* . . .'

Pel knew what that note in her mother's voice meant. Lightly she said, 'I'm all right.'

'I know you are, love.'

But you don't understand, she thought. Dalasurieth-rissani-hil was my friend . . .

'Were you afraid? Oh, that's a stupid question . . . it was a brave thing you did, Pel.'

'Will they stop the hunting?'

'You don't have to be afraid. Not now it's been made clear to everyone.'

'No.' Pel shook her head impatiently. 'The *chelanthi* hunting. Will you stop that?'

'You know we can't interfere on alien worlds.' Her mother sat down at the console. 'You get some rest. I'm going to pilot us in.'

The door irised shut. Back in the main body of the shuttle, Pel stared out of the port. Hunger, exhaustion; she has been told that these will pass.

Two suns cast the descending shuttle's double shadow on the landing-field. She remembers the endless grassland like a great sea. She remembers Talinor-Prime jutting up in headlands and cliffs and peaks. And she remembers the pits beneath the world, and the *chelanthi* as they nuzzled at her in their sleep.

She sits down and hides her face in her hands.

Pel Graham is thinking of the other children.

The Knot Garden

'I don't know why you're so *afraid* of them,' the ex-Scholar-Soldier Valentine protested. 'They'll only be the watchers of the Invisible College, keeping an eye on us.'

She lay on her stomach on the grass and watched him work. Her shaved-off hair was growing back cinnamon-coloured, but still plentifully flecked with white. The short fur made a child of her.

'You're filthy,' she added, throwing a ball of binding-twine at him, 'go and *wash!*'

The Lord-Architect Casaubon straightened up with an effort. All the fat rolls of flesh on his heavy bones settled earthward, answering to gravity. He wiped sweat from his chins, leaving smears of dirt there.

'If it's the pox-rotted Invisible College, they would have contacted *you*,' he said.

'Oh, see you, they maybe would not. . . . And if trouble's coming, I'll handle it!'

Sun sank like treacle onto the Miracle Garden. Sweat made vast dark patches on the Lord-Architect Casaubon's shirt, at the neck and in between his flesh-padded shoulderblades. Yellow light drenched the grass, the neat topiary arches, the marble statues from which fountain-waters sang. It made the earth in which he sank his hands warm to the touch.

'They do fright me,' the Lord-Architect admitted. 'Watchers.'

Bags of vari-coloured sand leaned haphazardly together on the lawn. Casaubon stood in a bare octagon enclosed by miniature hedges, with dirty sandalled feet planted apart, tipping out the contents of a sand-bag in a stream. His fat features creased in concentration. As he moved smoothly, he poured out the red sand in curious patterns, figures, sigils, and knots.

'You'll be surprised when you see what I can do –'

He interrupted, 'I want something to drink.'

The skin crinkled around fox-tawny eyes as she grinned. 'Maybe.'

'Dammit, girl –!'

Her gaze went beyond him. 'Here's the Chancellor. You'll have to stop. I'll get you a drink, you baby, wait for me!'

Casaubon straightened up, watching the shaven-headed woman covertly as she limped towards the summerhouse, and the stone bottles left there in the cool. She was only just beginning to recover her strength.

He turned. The white marble facades of the City rose beyond the golden hedges, and the dapper figure of the Chancellor approached from that direction. The Lord-Architect Casaubon wiped his hands on his once-white shirt.

'Chancellor Parry,' he said. 'Have you discovered it yet? Who are they?'

The woman was younger than Casaubon: thirty-five to his forty. Tabitha Parry was debonair, dressed sleekly in blue satin coat and breeches, and as she looked at the Lord-Architect she fastidiously adjusted the clean white ruffles at her wrists.

'That's something strange,' the woman said. 'Lord-Architect, I can find no "they". Only rumours –'

'Oh, Hell's great yellow teeth! What do I keep a Chancellor for? I could have told you myself there were rumours. I want to know who these people *are!*'

Parry reluctantly offered a white cotton-gloved hand. He gripped it as he heaved himself over the low hedge onto the lawn, and nodded thanks. She examined her mud-stained glove dispiritedly. Valentine called a greeting to the Chancellor from the summerhouse.

A shudder went across Casaubon's skin, like a horse

troubled with flies. He dismissed it.

'How is she, your Lady Valentine?' Tabitha Parry enquired.

'Well enough. Not one in ten recover from the plague, and not one in fifty so well as she.' Casaubon's blue eyes were troubled with an old, averted grief. Then he admitted, 'She's well enough, finally, to be bored with necessary resting; as a consequence, my life becomes a hell . . .'

'She itches to take up the sword and scroll again.'

Casaubon grunted. 'I'd call in the Scholar-Soldiers myself, if I didn't know them to be the visible branch of the Invisible College, and *she* swears these slinking renegades come from them.'

'Unsubstantiated –'

'Oh, by the Great Architect's Symmetrical Anus!'

Chancellor Parry persisted: 'Merely unsubstantiated rumours of some several unregistered watchers –'

The earth twitched.

Casaubon staggered, lost his balance, sprawled forward on the dry grass, and knocked all the breath from his vast bulk. Tabitha Parry yelped with shock. The dazzling sunlight blinked, once, and then again. Casaubon dragged himself up onto hands and knees, ham-limbs weighing him down, and gasped in the suddenly static-filled air.

Valentine sprinted across the lawn towards him calling, ''Quake!'

She cleared the low hedge of the knot-garden at a run, bare feet scuffing the sand patterns, silhouetted against the umber and ochre earth.

Suddenly it seemed that she swerved. To Casaubon, it was as if she set her feet on one of the curving sand-lines and ran along it. He caught one glimpse of that fox-narrow face, determined and intent. Then with a twist of her shoulder, and a flick of sand as her heel skidded, she leaped to the side, and faded into the bright air.

A scatter of sand pattered down.

Tabitha Parry covered her mouth with gloved hands.

'*Valentine!*' The roar hurt Casaubon's throat.

He stared at the knot-garden. Then he scrambled heavily to his feet and stared around. But the expanse of golden lawn remained empty.

His inner eye kept the image of a tawny-haired woman

fading; fading like a lithograph exposed to the light.

'Valentine!'

No footstep, no echo of her voice.

He staggered forward, crossing and re-crossing the knot garden, fat arms outstretched as if he might sweep her into them, until at last he tripped on the hedge-border and fell to his knees.

Chancellor Parry patted his shoulder ineffectively while the noble Lord-Architect Casaubon wept, as noisily as a child.

The wood panelling on the study wall had grown warm in the sun. Casaubon continued to sit and stare at it. From time to time he scratched as his copper-red hair, inspected the scurf under his fingernails, and then went back to staring at the wall.

Chancellor Parry coughed, discreetly.

'Noble Lord. . . .'

'It's a pox-ridden trick and I can't see how they did it!'

Tabitha Parry blinked at his vehemence. Casaubon leaned back in his chair. He grabbed another bottle in his pudgy hand, knocked off the neck against the table's edge with practised ease, and drank, and belched. When he slammed the bottle back down a spurt of wine leaped up, soaking his green satin sleeve.

'It's been two *days!*'

Parry smoothed one white-gloved hand with the other, and shot her cuffs nervously. 'She's nowhere in the City. I've searched. I'm sure. As to the lower city, I can't claim to be so certain, but . . . no demands for ransom. Noble Lord, I'm sorry; I swear.'

Casaubon drank from the bottle again. Then he put it down, gripped Tabitha Parry's sleeve with a wet hand, and shook her bracingly. His breath reeked. The Chancellor winced, not quite able to pull away.

'Come with me,' he said. 'Come with me.'

Parry recovered her arm, and trod delicately down the corridors of the Belvedere in the Lord-Architect's wake. Casaubon whistled absently through his teeth. He missed a step, once, and staggered.

'Find me one of these "unsubstantiated" watchers,' he said without looking back at the Chancellor.

'No more available than the Lady Valentine, I fear.'

'She'll survive. She's alive.' Casaubon paused, and spat on

the tesselated marble floor. 'She was a Scholar-Soldier before she was an Architect-Lord's Lady – Parry!'

One broad hand shot out and pinned her against the panelled wall. Tabitha Parry pawed ineffectively at her crumpled lace, and the fat, strong hand of the Lord-Architect.

'Don't ever speak to me as if she were lost, Great Architect rot your soul!'

'*Sir –*'

He released the Chancellor and lurched on down the corridor. Parry tugged her ruffle and coat straight, and followed.

Casaubon led her into a small room, where sunlight through the leaded glass windows shone on a bare floor, and a plain wooden table, and on the table, an artifact of metal and glass and wire. Small lights burned like rubies in the heart of it.

'See that?'

The Lord-Architect's warm, alcohol-laden breath hit Tabitha Parry full in the face.

'See that? Janou gave us that. Told me, if ever it stopped transmitting, the Invisible College would come to see why. Well then.'

Casaubon glanced round the room. Nothing presented itself to him. He moved to the table, bent, and wrapped his arms around the artifact's metal casing. Parry watched strain tighten all the muscles buried in his fat. Then he lifted the mechanism, halted for a second, raised it, and flung it down on the marble floor.

It shattered with a stink of sulphur.

Parry stepped back, waving her hand before her nose. When she was certain it would do nothing, she came to look at the smashed mess of metal. The ruby-lights were gone.

'Want to talk to the Invisible College!' the Lord-Architect said pugnaciously. Having squatted down to stare at his handiwork, he now slid down into a sitting position and leaned back against the wall. Before Tabitha Parry could quite collect her thoughts and speak, he began to snore.

'How long will it take the Invisible College to get here?'

The Chancellor realized she was talking to herself.

'Or . . . are they here already?'

Water lapped at the very window-sills of the clapboard

houses in the city's River-quarter. The wheels of the cart kicked up spokes of spray, although they went at a slow pace, and the oxen lowed in protest.

'The road's blocked up ahead,' Feliche called back.

Janou sat on top of the loaded cart. She had her heels up, resting on an old leather pack; and across her lap was a plain-scabbarded sword. When Feliche spoke, she shifted round and scrambled on hands and knees across the tarpaulin bundles, to fall on her stomach and stare ahead. The sword jabbed uncomfortably into her belly.

Ahead, the lane went downhill. The floodwaters swirled in and out of windows and doorways. A chair floated past. Some houses had only rooftrees visible, some reared above the flood. All the upper windows were hung with drying blankets and shirts, and children leaned out dangerously and shrieked as they saw the painted carts.

Janou sat round and stood up. She balanced precariously, barefoot, and gave out with a piercing whistle.

'We'll have to go back – go around! Back up!'

Heads turned on the other wagons. Water, rising up the spiral-painted spokes, lapped at the stars daubed in silver, blue, and emerald on the wagon-sides; and the riders clinging there waved acknowledgement to the girl. A woman in a cape, clinging to the bars of the animal-cage, let go and splashed down into breast-high water, and waded towards the oxen. Two men followed.

While the awkward business of backing and turning the other oxen was underway, Janou slid down to sit beside Feliche. The clouds were breaking. Sunlight shone onto the floodwaters, making the road ahead an unbearable white mirror. A rank smell of fish and rotting vegetables steamed in the air.

Feliche said, 'Well, Scholar-Soldier?'

Janou kicked bare heels against the footboard. Flecks of paint from the old wood starred her skin blue and crimson. She scratched at her cropped spiky hair. 'Call this a disguise? If there's anyone in the City who hasn't seen us this time tomorrow, take my sword and call me witless!'

'The lower city, but not the *City*,' the big man emphasized. 'And in any case, my love, where better to hide than where everybody's looking? Didn't the Invisible College teach you anything?'

'They taught me to stay low, and keep out of the company of seditious anarchists,' Janou said pointedly.

'It's true I have my own business here.'

Feliche tugged his wide-brimmed hat down, so that she saw only his red-brown beard, and a curl or two of his hair. A crimson feather was buckled to his hatband. Shirt and breeches were plain, but he had taken up the travelling fair's habits and wore an orange sash round his waist, and gilded spurs on his high boots.

He said, 'We've got enough material disseminated. I believe the local groups will begin action soon.'

Janou stood up. 'You can back the cart now – I don't think we should wait until we've seen Valentine tomorrow. Let's move today.'

'Are you not anxious to see her, after a year?'

One bare foot went up onto the backboard, and she rested her arms on her knee, and between calling directions to reverse the cart in the flooded street, said, 'I know what Valentine meant when she said a Scholar-Soldier has no friends. Before I come out of hiding, I have to know why we were called here. The College has enemies.'

A voice from below said, 'The Invisible College also has allies.'

'Hell's great gap-toothed gaping maw!' Janou muttered. She leaned precariously off the footboard. 'See you, master, I've not the slightest idea to what you refer.'

Below, a boat wallowed among the refuse of the flood. A man sat in it, dark hands folded. He wore a baggy white tunic and trousers. It was difficult to guess his age: something between thirty and sixty.

Janou met blue eyes made brilliant by his brown skin.

'We're setting up in the market square if you want to see the show.'

Light reflected up from the water. It cast rippling shadows of brightness on the man's face. When Feliche glanced across at Janou, he saw that the girl was frowning. The tip of her scabbard scraped across the headboard as she moved.

'On your way, master,' Feliche rumbled.

Without gripping the sides of the skiff, or even putting down one brown hand, the man stood up in the boat.

It seemed to Feliche as if the mist that the sun called up from the floodwaters muffled sound. The noise of grunting oxen and yelling riders faded. It all became background for the small, dark man who stood in the boat, regardless of the rushing waters, and did not seem even to have to balance. The boat was as steady as dry land.

The man held up his hands, open and empty, to Janou.

'Master-Captain, I mean nothing but peace.'

Feliche was about to protest, but the girl flopped down on her stomach on the cart and reached for the man's hand, turning it over, studying something that had sparked sunlight.

'That's one of the rings mentioned in *Ghâya*. Oh, say you, I meant no offence! What brings one of you to the City?'

Bewildered, Feliche said, 'You trust him?'

Both of them ignored the big man.

'Well?' Janou persisted.

'They have already taken your colleague Valentine,' the brown-skinned man said. 'I thought it might be as well if they failed to take you. I come with that warning. And, it might be, if the Invisible College will accept it, an offer of help.'

Janou asked, 'What is it we face here?'

'My name is Al-Iskandariya,' he said, 'and I will tell you.'

They came from diverse places, each one alone. Some lost, some lame, some full of knowledge; dark and twisted from what had happened to them on the way.

But the stars were turning, returning to their ancient configuration.

And as the constellations returned, so did they, the Circle drawing together again, not one of its long-dead members lost to this new life and ancient purpose.

They met secret from all the world.

And as the Circle joined again, their power grew.

'But, rot you,' Casaubon said, 'all I need to know is whether she can be alive or not!'

His voice echoed in the vast Library. Some of the students raised their heads, saw the Lord-Architect, and went back to their scrolls and parchments. A final echo whispered off distant stacks, and the blue-and-gold constellations painted on the interior of the dome.

'What's so difficult? You're versed in those Arts, more than any man I know. Tell me if I can hope or not!'

Scaris, the Librarian, blinked watery eyes. 'Noble Lord, I don't know. Nothing like this has ever happened before in the City.'

'Not the City,' Tabitha Parry (in unaware echo) said, 'but, perhaps, the lower city?'

'Oh, see you, that's good! That's it!' Casaubon's meaty hand smacked her on the back. The Chancellor staggered.

'*Sir,*' she protested.

The Lord-Architect seemed to sag where he stood, all the weight of flesh pulling him earthward. There were new wine-stains on his green satin coat, and his shirt was rimmed with black; a stench of unwashed linen came from him. He looked at Parry, rubbing a hand through his slick copper-red hair.

'I'll have the man or woman who robs me of hope into the oubliettes beneath the Belvedere, so fast –'

Scaris interrupted.

'Noble Lord, has it occurred to you to think this might be voluntary on the Lady Valentine's part?'

'Oh, what!'

'No, hear me out.' Scaris collected his thoughts. It was hot in the Library, and he pushed sweat-soaked white hair out of his eyes, and adjusted the neck of his black satin robe. Age made him wish for somewhere to sit down; caution, thinking of what he was about to say, made him wish himself younger and faster.

'Think about it,' he said, slightly breathless. 'You still do not know, I think, where she was born. You know she was a Scholar-Soldier, which means (we now find) she was *aide* to the supposed Invisible College. Into what grey areas of Art that may have taken her . . . well. She had mercenaries for close friends, and agitators, and –'

Casaubon said, 'True, you were my Chancellor before Parry here. That doesn't give you licence to slander.'

The old man threw up his blue-veined hands.

'I should have said this before! She was nothing but a mendicant lecturer before she came here and enspelled you. She had no fortune, no beauty, and not enough wit to – and you were three times her age!'

Chancellor Parry stepped in front of Casaubon as he lumbered forward.

'*That woman saved your life!*' Casaubon roared.

'It isn't myself I'm concerned with!' Scaris pushed the dapper Chancellor out of the way, and glared up at Casaubon. 'This is the only opportunity I've had in a year to say this. The girl was young, and lively, and she loved the sword and the scroll; and yet she gave it up to be your Lady? It was *obvious* she would do this – choose a way to leave you that absolves her of blame. Why would she stay with you?'

Tabitha Parry glanced from the breathless old man, his rheumy eyes brilliant with anger, to the Lord-Architect. Casaubon's ham-like hands were clenched into fists. There was something terrible in the deliberation with which he relaxed them.

He said mildly, 'You could ask why, since Valentine was the most cross-tempered and curst woman I've ever met, *I* stayed with her? Truth, I don't know. We laughed at one and the same things. Scaris, you would say none of this if you'd seen her face when – when it happened.'

'I don't doubt she could *feign* well enough.'

Tabitha Parry smoothed her embroidered lapels into place, and continued the gesture easily into taking the Lord-Architect's arm as he stepped forward. For a second it was as if she had taken hold of a rolling ox-cart.

'One of my clerks.' She pointed with one white-gloved hand. '*Lord Casaubon!*'

The clerk's boots clicked across the floor as he approached. Tabitha Parry beckoned him across to her, glad beyond words for the interruption, and then gaped as he was pushed aside by the two people who trod at his heels.

The first was a slight, dark man. Parry thought him unremarkable until she caught his gaze, and felt a literal physical jolt at the intensity of his blue eyes. The second, energetically kicking out the trailing hem of her robe as she walked, was a young woman.

'Lord-Architect or not, you'll get no help here!' The Librarian turned his back on Casaubon and limped off across the wide floor.

'Whoreson ungrateful bastard!' Casaubon yelled at Scaris's departing back. He swung round, ungainly. His copper hair was disordered, and his skin flushed red. His chins shook with anger. 'What do *you* want?'

Al-Iskandariya, in quiet amusement, said, 'I came to tell the noble Lord-Architect there is a power abroad in his City. It has begun to act. If you wish to know how, noble Lord, I suggest . . .'

'Janou!'

Casaubon's loud yelp made Chancellor Parry jump. The fat man lumbered across the marble floor and enfolded the second person in a cushioning embrace.

'Oh, see you, do you want me suffocated? Put me down!'

'Where's Valentine? Is she with you?'

'If I knew what happened to Valentine, I wouldn't be coming to *you*.' The girl shook out the folds of her long, black gown, and adjusted the straps of her backpack. She looked up from this, and made the somewhat embarrassed admission: 'See you, I didn't mean that as it sounded.'

A laugh growled in Casaubon's chest. He looked at the dark man. 'Who's this? Another of your beggarly College?'

With something between asperity and wounded dignity, the man said, 'I am Al-Iskandariya of the Brotherhood. The stars have led me across half the world, to this place. Noble Lord, if you want to know why, then come outside, and look at your city!'

A clot of dung, thrown accurately and hard, smacked into the back of Casaubon's head. Someone laughed. The noble Lord-Architect dragged out a large dirty kerchief and wiped at the rolls of fat at his neck.

'I don't like to disappoint you,' he said to Al-Iskandariya, 'but the Architect-Lords have *never* been popular in the lower city. Dissent hardly counts as a supernatural omen!'

Chancellor Parry picked her way along the lane beside Casaubon. Her nose wrinkled in helpless disgust. Here, the floodwaters had recently receded, leaving a thin skin of slime over the cobbles. Steam went up in the hot sun. There was a stink from fishheads in the gutter, and ordure. Many windows were marked with a smear of silver paint.

Al-Iskandariya said, 'There are a group of people coming to
the City, or it may be that they are here now. Either they have
a power, or they are proxies for people who have. You will not
find them easily. But we may see signs of their power growing.'

'You'll see,' Janou said. 'You'll see. This way. Down here.'

The sight of satin coats in the lower city attracted a crowd.
Thin urchins hung lovingly at Tabitha Parry's heels, holding
up filthy hands for pennies. Her gloved hand went automatically to the pocket of her blue satin coat, and found that her
purse was already missing. She muttered something obscene,
and then blushed in case she should have been heard.

'I always said we should have burned this lot to the ground,'
Casaubon rumbled. 'House this rabble up in the City, clean
'em, give 'em honest work, they'd be far better off.'

'You're a whoreson ignorant pig,' Janou said. Before the
noble Lord-Architect could reply she led them into the market
square.

'There,' Al-Iskandariya pointed.

The Lord-Architect stared. He had a supreme unconscious-
ness that he also was an object of regard, that the men and
women in the marketplace stopped their business to gape at
Lord-Architect, Chancellor, and two strangers. The noble
Lord-Architect only looked where the dark man pointed, at a
canvas-covered structure set up against the corner of Blind
Lane and Bone Alley.

'It's a fortune-teller's booth,' Casaubon said blankly. 'You
dragged me down into the lower city, on the hottest day in the
year, to see a charlatan fortune-teller?'

'Wait,' Al-Iskandariya said. 'Watch. See the pattern.'

The sun shone on the marketplace. Wet straw, trodden
underfoot, steamed. To begin with there was no pattern, only
people. There might have been fewer children squatting under
the edges of stalls, playing, or sitting up on the rails of beast-
pens; fewer men and women in conversational knots outside
each of the three inns.

Fully half the stalls were bare.

The weatherbeaten wood, marked with a slash of silver,
spoke *plague*. There was a shrillness about the customers at
remaining stalls, where they argued or bought or talked while
they waited for purchases to be boxed. People moved quickly:

carters driving oxen carelessly down the gaps between the tables. A scorching yellow sky hung over the gables, beneath it were arguments.

Gradually Casaubon began to see the others. Two drunken rapier-wielding boys attempting a show-duel for pennies and falling over each other. Bundles against the walls that might be sleeping men, or dead.

A woman with black-grimed skin and ratty hair shoved a few blown wild roses into Chancellor Parry's face, mumbling something, other hand outstretched. Parry sidestepped her. There were two small, silent children clinging to the woman's dress.

Strangers soon ceased to be a novelty. Only the occasional glance was spared now for the satin-coated.

'If it's sedition being spread under cover of a debased Art, that's not new,' Chancellor Parry protested.

'Oh, what! You think these people have to be *told* when they should complain?' Janou glared up at Parry. She jerked her thin shoulders, hitching up her gown, and scowled. 'You don't even know the River-quarter's flooded — you can't see what's in front of you!'

A man came out of the fortune-teller's canvas booth. He was fair, bearded, young. He stood for a moment, blinking, and it seemed to the Lord-Architect Casaubon that the man stared over the roofs of the leaning tenements, towards that dream of white marble that is the City.

A sense of strain made itself felt in the air. Casaubon felt his skin twitch.

He grunted, opened his mouth to say that he recognized this, that they should run, flee, and then he bent and retched. He spat on the filthy straw.

He saw the fairhaired man take a step forward and fade. Fade into the air, as dust sifted down. Fade: with a look not of surprise but of recognition on his face.

A child ran off, crying.

Casaubon wiped his mouth on his wine-stained sleeve. No man or woman turned to see what had happened. And, now he looked, it seemed that no one in the market-place willingly turned towards Blind Lane or Bone Alley. As if there was a conspiracy against seeing the canvas booth . . .

The woman selling wild roses met Casaubon's eyes. She had something in her hand, some small object that she caressed with her grimy thumb. She smiled. It was an odd, self-conscious smile; it had regret in it, and a rueful admission. She stepped away from her flower-stall. Her two silent toddlers wandered away, hand-in-hand.

He was not surprised when she, also, merged into the air and vanished. It seemed as sweetly natural as a bird flying to its nest.

'Pox rot it! It's no more *natural* than the plague –'

Al-Iskandariya's voice at his ear said, 'But for a moment you felt it was.'

In a voice of concern and paternal outrage, Casaubon said, 'They're taking my people!'

Janou leaned up against the side of the inn, standing on one leg, kicking a bare heel against the lath-and-plaster wall.

'Oh, that's horse-dung! Nobody's being *taken*. They're going because they want to. Because the lower city's a plague-ridden slum. Because they'd rather take the unknown than stay here!'

The Lord-Architect looked round the marketplace and counted the number of empty stalls.

'They go of their own wish,' Al-Iskandariya said, 'or, most of them do. But the Brotherhood is not certain that where they go is where they wish to go. I have tracked this across continents. Noble Lord, it could empty cities.'

The fat man did not reply. He stared at the dirty canvas booth that stood in the marketplace.

'Perhaps she did leave me,' Casaubon said; and, in a lower tone, 'Perhaps I am not the man that she would choose to stay with.'

Janou shifted off the wall, and swiped him across the arm with a swift hand. 'Dolt!'

'Does it matter?' he asked. 'I am not such a fool, to think because she means so much to me, it has any other importance.'

Al-Iskandariya's sapphire eyes sought Casaubon's face.

'Lord-Architect, the first thing the Circle did, before they acted openly, was to rid themselves of the Scholar-Soldier Valentine. *That* tells me she is important.'

The air quivered.

Tabitha Parry jumped. She felt as if some appallingly loud

noise had just ceased to sound. When she looked at the Lord-Architect and the dark man, their faces showed something of the same disquiet.

The crop-haired girl shivered, and thumbed the strap of her backpack; scabbarded sword bound in with scrolls and parchments.

Parry said, 'Noble Lord –'

The air sung like struck glass, shattered, just for a second.

A large drop of dark red blood fell onto the straw at Tabitha Parry's feet.

'– And stay out!'

Casaubon hurled a pewter pot for emphasis. It smacked into the closing door, behind the landlord's departing back.

Janou picked at her slightly-snaggled teeth with the quill end of a duck feather. '*Someone* has to go into that fortune-teller's booth. I'll go.'

Al-Iskandariya, who had not eaten, remained standing at the window, looking out into the square. The abandoned market stalls now outnumbered the occupied ones.

'That, or one of the dozen others.' He shrugged. 'There will be a hundred before the week is out.'

Sun tumbled into the inn's main room through leaded panes.

Tabitha Parry shook out a white silk kerchief and placed it on the inn bench, before sitting down carefully, with her knees pressed together. She fiddled with her hair, tied formally at the nape of her neck.

'Here.' The Lord-Architect pushed the pewter ale jug across to his Chancellor. 'You look as if you need it.'

Casaubon sat in a stout-armed chair. He wore a brown satin coat, with deep cuffs and pockets, unbuttoned; and his belly hung out and rested on his spread thighs. As Tabitha Parry watched, the Lord-Architect dug in one pocket and produced a rat, which he sat on his wide white-breeched thigh, and proceeded to feed scraps of cooked duck from his fingers. The rat was a dirty yellow, with spiky fur, mad red eyes, and a bald and scaly tail.

After the blood-fall, perhaps nothing could have retrieved Parry's scattered wits but this. She watched, fascinated and appalled, as the rat sat on its haunches and took titbits from its master. It had enough, finally, and scuttled up Casaubon's mountainous belly, and vanished into an inside coat pocket, with a last flash of carious fangs.

The Lord-Architect, not pausing to wipe his hands, dug into the pan for another slice of meat. He chewed thoughtfully, licked grease from his fingers, and then, through a fine spray of food-fragments, said, 'Now that I've seen others go, I'm convinced Valentine's alive.'

'If I might,' Al-Iskandariya began. Janou interrupted him: 'We don't know what it is she knows.'

'Her friends —' Casaubon frowned. 'Master-Captain, that hurdy-gurdy man that we knew last year, Feliche, was it?'

Janou said, 'Who?'

'It may be something she learned while she was a wanderer, before she came to the City, that made them choose first to be rid of her?' Tabitha Parry made the suggestion with diffidence.

Al-Iskandariya said, 'I —'

'She'd never have kept it quiet!' Janou crossed her heels, and rested them up on her pack on the bench. 'She was the most braggart Master-Captain we had!'

Casaubon frowned. Janou waved an airy hand:

'Valentine could never have taken to the *covert* side of the College. She could never keep her mouth shut about how wonderful she was. And she was good. Best for fighting, and for finding out your causes, first and secondary ... If she discovered anything, she'd have let everybody know!'

The Lord-Architect pushed himself up out of the chair. The wood groaned. Yellow sunlight stained his dirty shirt, shot copper lights from his hair. 'The other possibility is that she was not taken, that she chose to go.'

Chancellor Parry looked up from smoothing her blue satin knee-breeches, and her compulsive search for blood-marks. 'Noble Lord, she wanted to shine in your eyes. She would have told you anything to her credit. And ... her illness may have made her think, for the first time, of the future.'

Then she smiled, slightly. 'Valentine would give me advice, being new, on how not to offend ex-Chancellor Scaris's faction. It was well-meant; I thought well of her for it.'

'Didn't need it, did you?' Casaubon grunted.

'She had a good heart, noble Lord.'

Al-Iskandariya said, 'If her illness were near-mortal, that would make her sensitive to occult influences. I, myself –'

'I'll go after her,' the Lord-Architect announced.

The dark man said, 'Noble Lord –'

'Whatever the reason for her kidnapping,' Tabitha Parry put in, 'would it not be better if we first knew something about those supposedly responsible? This "Circle"?'

'*That is what I am trying to tell you!*'

Casaubon looked at Al-Iskandariya with great kindness and said, 'Please. Proceed.'

Sounds came in through the inn-door, now ajar; the shrill voices of the diners in the next room and the drinkers out in the yard; the bellowing of oxen, and the squealing of pigs in market pens. Smells of stale cooking lingered. The dark man clasped his hands, and looked down at them as if they (or his rings) were a source of strength.

'The mathematico-magical treatise *Ghâya* speaks of those whose powers derive from the star-daemons,' he said. 'I believe the Circle to be of that nature.'

He raised his head. The sapphire eyes met Casaubon's.

'I do not know who they are. Or what they are. Lord-Architect, listen to me. Whatever they are now, they *were* alive, last, six-and-twenty thousand years ago. It was they who brought the Sardicinien Empire down. The *Ghâya* speaks of them. There are covert references in the *Hieroglyphika*. It was they who made dust from the City of Bright Waters.'

Now they were silent, even Janou. Chancellor Parry began obsessively to smooth down every crease in her knee-breeches. The Lord-Architect nodded for Al-Iskandariya to continue.

'The Brotherhood of which I am one is old. The Invisible College knows us. To us, the infallible signs by which to recognize the Circle were passed down – how wandering stars return at last to certain constellations, and the sun rises in ill-fated Houses, and the Great Conjunction comes. That Great Conjunction will occur soon now. We must find the Circle before the Circle is complete, and they can call on all their power. Find them, and we will find the Art of compelling the star-daemons to serve us –'

Janou sat up. 'Oh, see you, what happened to how you'd

save the City? You just want their knowledge!'

'No, no, no.' Al-Iskandariya shook his head. 'But if we have
not their Art, we have nothing to fight them with. They will
corrupt the City. Until it pleases the City to serve them.'

Casaubon snorted. 'Not after last year! Master Al-Iskandariya,
I am still an Architect-Lord. This City is laid out according
to the principles of harmony and hierarchy. My Miracle
Garden is a microcosm of the great cosmic harmony. There's
nowhere for Corruption to gain a foothold.'

'We also study the stars,' Chancellor Parry said quietly.

'*But I tell you –*'

Casaubon interrupted Al-Iskandariya for the last time. 'The
answer in all cases is my Valentine. Find her, find what she
does or doesn't know; find out, so, what the future holds for
the City. Parry, I'll leave you to alert the City Councillors. I
myself will go after Master-Captain Valentine.'

Pewter pots scattered from the table as he pushed past. He
strode from the inn, out into the plague-hot marketplace, head-
ing for the fortune-tellers's booth.

The hot darkness of the canvas booth is empty, no one is there. A
ricketty table occupies the space, covered with a dirty grey cloth,
and on it a scatter of gemstones: carved in minute detail with the
faces of old gods, the symbols of decans, and the hieroglyphics of a
language long forgotten.
Amber, tiger's-eye, black pearl, and diamond.
Beautiful enough to attract the eye, and the hand.

Casaubon thrust under the flap and into the tent. A rip in
the canvas let a hot fragment of sun in.

By that gold light he saw the stones. An agate with an intaglio of a man carrying a cornsheaf and leading a bull. A black
pearl layered to the silhouette of a barbaric city gate. A carnel-
ian with twin androgynes carved on it. Carved with a glyptic
Art lost long ago.

'Master-Captain!' He would not touch these for his life.

On the last stone, a striped gold tiger's eye, was carved
a fox-faced woman, hardly more than a child, the face
Valentine's.

'Noble Lord!'

They staggered in after him: Al-Iskandariya running, Janou tripping over the hem of her black robe. The young Scholar-Soldier cannoned into the back of Tabitha Parry, who fell forward onto the straw floor of the booth.

'*Don't touch that –*'

'It's her face!' Casaubon seized and held up the carved tiger's-eye stone.

There was an ominous creak. Janou recovered her balance and looked up. Over their heads, the canvas of the tent was sagging.

'We'd better leave!'

The Chancellor knelt up and pointed at Janou. Janou couldn't make out what brought fear to the woman's white face. She grabbed Parry's arm and pulled her towards the exit.

A sharp *crack!* and one corner of the tent came down. As if some great weight pressed on it – Janou picked up her skirts and followed the Chancellor out through the booth's loose flap. Her feet burned with pain. White light dazzled her. Another *crack!* and then she turned to see the old canvas shred and fall in on itself under a weight of white.

Under snow.

Janou spat, 'Casaubon, you great fool –!'

Tabitha Parry pointed again at clouds of frosty breath issuing from the girl's mouth.

They stood in the great City square, knee deep in snow.

It stretched away from them, acres of unbroken whiteness, merging with the distant marble facades so that Tabitha Parry was uncertain whether she saw a city of stone or ice. She looked across to the Belvedere, and then to where steps went up to the Miracle Garden. All the same: all transmuted to winter.

'How . . .?'

The shadows of buildings cast on the snow were lilac, almost purple. The sky burned deep blue. Air snagged in Janou's throat, cold and electric, and the sun on the snow hurt her eyes. There was a scent on the wind of nothing ever encountered before.

'He's still in there!' Tabitha Parry swung round and began to tug at the heavy folds of the collapsed canvas. Janou scrambled to help her.

It was not until some minutes later that it became apparent: neither the Lord-Architect nor Al-Iskandariya were trapped under the fallen tent. There was nothing but snow. They were not there.

'What *is* this place?' Tabitha Parry whispered.

A slow, rhythmic sound echoed. Far off, but heard clearly across the winter City. Something in its timbre and slowness made Parry uncomfortable.

Thin particles began to appear. They didn't fall from the sky. Silver metallic flakes appeared in mid-air, dusting the crusted snow. The snow-dunes shimmered, edged with a purple light. Janou felt the icy wind again blow in her face. This time it cut deep, and smelled of wild roses.

'Wait!' She swung her pack off her back, and fell to her knees beside it in the crusted snow. Blowing on her fingers, she ripped open the leather flap, strewed scrolls out of her way, and flipped up the top of a metal box.

The crop-haired girl paused, held up a hand, muttered something, and made a sequence of signs, tracing geometries on the cold air. A faint purple luminosity clung to her fingers. She reached down into the box and began to tap.

Tabitha Parry leaned closer. She saw ruby-lights in the heart of the machine. The girl was tapping out a sequence, pausing, repeating it, waiting again for an answer.

'The College?' Parry asked.

Janou continued to code into the transmitter for long minutes. When she peered in at the tracer-light, she swore.

'Whoreson stupid object! Great gaping Hell's *teeth!*'

Janou picked the backpack up by its straps and swung it, two-handed. It curved in a short arc and smacked into the stone wall of the nearest palace facade. Metal smashed.

'Whore! Pimp! Bawd! *Stupid!*'

Red-faced, she glared at Tabitha Parry.

'Whoreson College told me it would work anywhere!'

Tabitha Parry shivered.

'It appears that this is . . . not the lower city.' She stared at the girl suddenly. 'You're not wearing *shoes*.'

Janou scratched at her fluffgold hair. She picked up one foot and studied the sole, that was still black with the warm mud of the lower city. Her skin was beginning to redden with cold.

'Here.' Tabitha Parry pulled off a buckled shoe. She unrolled her thick stocking and passed it to the girl, put her shoe back on her bare foot, and repeated the process.

As she was pulling on the woollen stockings, Janou paused, reached up to her backstrap, and pulled free a scabbarded sword.

'The winged watchers!'

Parry raised her head.

A chasm gaped across the square.

Bemused, she stared at the raw gash of earth and rock. The marble paving was split in a jagged line that ran between them and the steps of the Miracle Garden. There were other gulfs, further off. She sniffed back ice-tears, and caught a scent from the depths. Something rank, with roses. Parry sank to her knees in the snow.

'I thought – it was a *building* –'

Tabitha Parry, melted snow soaking the knees of her breeches, craned her neck.

The winged watcher crouched at the chasm, front paws on the edge of emptiness. The leonine body shone a dazzling blue-black against the snow. It rose up like a cliff, twenty feet high: paw, shoulder, massive bull-neck and bearded human face . . . and the blue-black pinions, closed against its flanks, rose at their tips thirty feet above the snow in the square.

Janou's hand closed on Parry's shoulder, painfully.

'That . . .'

The winged watcher crouched, barbed tail wrapped round its hindquarters. Its beard hung in tight shiny coils. Its hair, tight-curled, was held back by a basalt fillet. Tabitha Parry stared at its sensual, full lips; at the tip-tilted, closed eyes. Shining blue and ebony under the sun.

'It's a statue,' she said. She did not know, until she gasped air, that she had stopped breathing. 'Look. There's snow on its back. It's *stone.*'

Their breath smoked on the cold air.

Janou leaned against the kneeling Chancellor, and stood on one leg to brush snow off her makeshift stocking. She seemed to be sorting images in her head.

'They're the Lords of the Shining Paths,' she said. 'So *that's* Al-Iskandariya's star-daemons. Turd! Won't I have words with the College when I get back!'

Tabitha Parry heard a soft sound . . . It came again: a distant, implosive noise.

Snow sliding and hitting ice.

She looked at Janou. The girl whisked her sword from its scabbard.

The woman pushed her dishevelled hair back into its clasp with gloved filthy hands, and stared across the chasm. She pointed, mutely. Janou followed the direction of her finger.

The winged watcher opened stone eyelids and fixed them with a yellow gaze.

The winter city sang.

As if every stone vibrated to the frost working inward to its heart, every marble statue and step and balustrade; as if each ice-spear hanging from palace facades chimed; as if the automata in the distant Miracle Garden began to strike; as if the sky itself thrummed with electricity.

The winged watcher lifted its front paws from the lip of the chasm. The remaining snow slid from its back and wings.

It drew back, muscles bunching in the massive shoulders, wing-tips rising. Its hindquarters rose from the snow. The barbed tail flicked once. Then in one movement the winged watcher sprang upwards. Black wings darkened the sky.

The ground shook with its landing, on their side of the chasm. Janou fell to the snow. She clutched the Chancellor, who stared, open-mouthed.

The watcher settled, couchant, folding blue-black pinions down its flanks. The curling blue-black beard touched massive paws. Snow settled. It shifted a hind paw, leaving a mark that an ox-cart would have vanished into, and the full, closed lips curved. A glint of citrine light showed under the eyelids.

Chancellor and Master-Captain pressed close together. They stared up at that vast face. Janou felt a feather of warm breath touch her skin.

Parry whispered, 'Did – is that what's responsible for us being here?'

'Being lured here? Oh, what else!'

Chancellor Tabitha Parry stood. She kicked snow aside as she walked forward, and stopped after a few yards.

'*Send us back!*'

Parry's voice sounded shrill in her ears.

There was a bass rumble that shook snow off the palace roofs. Particles of air began to tingle and glow and dazzle in Janou's vision. She turned her head and spat into the feathery snow. A shadow cut the bright sunlight, and it was suddenly arctic cold.

Janou trudged back to her broken pack, saying over her shoulder, 'It can't hurt us. Not materially. Not yet.'

The Chancellor stared up at the crouching bulk between her and the sun.

'This wants our City?'

A thin sound grew out of nowhere. It sang into loudness, ceased; and the marble paving under the snow split with a *crack*! The chasm gaped another foot. Loose earth tumbled down into the gulf. Parry heard no sound of it landing.

The winged watcher opened yellow eyes, and the curving full lips parted. The rumbling sound modulated into a higher tone. There were separate, distinct sounds in it.

Janou kicked her way through the snow, sword resting back on her shoulder. She was shivering in the thin black robe, but she walked with a swagger, and her eyes were bright. 'Oh, see you, I know that language!'

'Then ask it: where's Master-Captain Valentine? Ask it: where are the lower city people?' Tabitha Parry stripped off soaking gloves and blew on cold-mottled fingers. 'Ask it: how do we get home?'

Janou drew a deep breath, and forced it out again in a chthonic, guttural chant.

The winged watcher stretched a paw. It bent one elbow, raked; claws as long as a human being was tall pulled ice into splinters. As it rose on all four paws, it stretched its wings. Black pinions rustled over their heads; then folded.

The bass tone boomed.

As the winged watcher moved in feline strides over the snow, Janou said:

'That means, *follow*.'

There had been nothing there before, but it was there now, almost daring them to deny it: an unmortared stone bridge that arced up over the chasm. Janou ran to its foot, and then hesitated as she stared down into the gulf.

The winged watcher paced past the Belvedere, across the square, across that great expanse, to the marble steps that led up to the heart of the City: the newly-constructed Miracle Garden. Its shadow darkened the snow, with a stain that remained for some seconds after it had passed.

Ahead, voices rang out joyfully across the snow.

Casaubon thrashed free of the entangling tent-folds. An oblong of light appeared. The Lord-Architect staggered through it, and yelped as he cracked his head on the stone lintel. He touched his hair, and looked at his red-stained fingers in injured affront. Then he licked his fingers.

'Janou? Parry, rot your guts –'

A green and gold light shimmered.

'Noble Lord. Speak softly: there may be strange inhabitants of this plane.' Al-Iskandariya brushed tendrils of green from his baggy sleeves, and trod down spear-bladed grass.

Gold sun slanted through a tangle of vines, creepers, and fern-trees. It was impossible to see the sky. Pink flowers grew knee high. When Casaubon glanced over his shoulder, he saw a stone pyramid, some twelve feet high. Set into one triangular side was a dark oblong: a doorway.

He took his other hand out of his pocket and opened it. The carved tiger's-eye glinted. The intaglio face was still that of Valentine.

Casaubon reached inside his coat, drew out a metal flask, twisted the top off, and drank. The alcohol caught in his throat. He coughed, sniffed back tears, and offered the flask to Al-Iskandariya. The small man refused. The rat peered out of Casaubon's coat, twitched its whiskers, and vanished back into his inner pocket.

'Is this where she went?'

Al-Iskandariya frow..ied, studying the hieroglyphs cut into the pyramid's sides. He glanced inside the doorway, shrugged; and then looked up at Casaubon. 'For each of certain Lords of the Shining Paths – the Power of Strife and Abundance; the Power of the Night of Time; the Power of the Wild Land; the Power of the Throne of Lights and Dominions – for each, there is a realm mirroring our earth. Whether Lady Valentine came to this realm, or another . . .'

'Pox rot your guts! don't you *know*? What use is your "Brotherhood" if you can't answer a simple question!'

'Hardly simple.' Al-Iskandariya bristled.

The moist heat made the Lord-Architect sweat. There were scents on the air that seemed incongruous – dry air and frost?

Casaubon began now to pick out shapes under the covering ivy, vines, and flowering creepers. Here, a pointed gable; there, a glint of light off window-glass. A vine spiralled up and hung clumps of grapes, not from a fallen tree, but from the jutting shaft of an ox-cart. They stood at the bottom of a well, the sides formed by decaying walls, so thickly grown over that the lath-and-plaster could not be seen.

Abandoned, grown over, lost: but still just recognisable as River-quarter.

Casaubon reached into his coat for his flask, and took a deep swallow. He choked, wiped streaming nostrils, leaving a trail on his satin sleeve, and sniffed. 'If Valentine's here, I know where she'll be. The Miracle Garden.'

Fern-trees and vines tangled in baroque complexity.

'Here,' said the noble Lord-Architect Casaubon, 'I *know* you. I had you on trial for sedition in the Moon-hall last year!'

The woman looked up lazily from where she lay in her vine-hammock, a child curled under each arm. She paused in feeding the younger one milk. Light fell green and gold on her emaciated features.

'We were promised freedom from the Architect-Lords – !' She lifted her pointed chin and grunted: a guttural, choking call. Then she looked back at Casaubon, and with the air of one waiting, said, 'I hope he takes you to a world where you fry!'

Al-Iskandariya peered around the Lord-Architect's massive shoulder. ' "He"?'

The woman chuckled. The hammock-bower smelt of milk, and nectarines. She stretched one bruised calf and ankle, turned her face up to the shaded forest heat, and smiled. The baby made small sounds of pleasure. The woman opened eyes that were darkest blue, staring directly at Casaubon.

'Noble Lord, have you been down to those dungeons lately, that you're so proud of? Have you ever spent a night in those oubliettes? Where it's too cramped to lie, and too short to stand, and too cold to sleep? Have you? No – of course not. Noble Lord, you condemned me to *weeks* of that. I was carrying Gillan here at the time. If I don't greatly care what becomes of you, don't be surprised.'

Al-Iskandariya wiped at the sweat that poured down his face. He squinted, trying to see what lay ahead of the woman. Through the crushed grass and fungi underfoot, he began to feel a rhythmic, slow vibration.

'Lord Casaubon, we should leave. There is something approaching that my Art warns me –'

Casaubon waved a meaty hand dismissively. His eyes almost vanished into his cheeks as he screwed up his face in concentration.

'Barbary Axtell,' he remembered. 'You had a printing press.'

Axtell said, 'Yes.'

The Lord-Architect tugged at the black-stained neck of his shirt. The arms and back of his brown satin coat were soaked with sweat, and he had tugged his carefully-tied ruffle open. Sweat glinted in the copper hairs on his chest.

'Oh, see you, how could you expect to print what you did and be allowed to get away with it! You'd have had all River-quarter up in arms!'

'*Yes. Rightly so.*' She shut her eyes. The lids were shaded lilac, sepia. 'But now I've to care for Gillan and Romiley. They're safe here. Someone else will have to carry on the fight. Noble Lord, there were scum and petty tyrants that we scorned to use against you – remember that, now we're gone.'

A skein of flower-vines snapped and fell from a fern tree.

Al-Iskandariya seized the Lord-Architect's coat sleeve and pulled him onwards. Casaubon stumbled as he went. He looked back over his shoulder at the woman, opened his mouth as if to make some reply, and then closed it again, and plunged on through the vegetation beside Al-Iskandariya.

They had struggled perhaps five yards when they came to an open space.

A dozen or so people were eating a feast, spread out in the vine-cloaked ruins of a brick dome – green and gold light fell on them, their laughter echoing. The Lord-Architect recognized most of them from the jails. He paid them no attention.

The domed building was different in all else but its contours
. . . his Belvedere. He turned to point this mirror-image out to
Al-Iskandariya.

The dark man hit his own temple with the flat of his hand. 'I
am a fool! An ignorant fool. There was nothing to say that any
member of the Circle had to be human!'

Casaubon scowled. 'Oh, what?'

'Noble Lord, here is what made that woman promises.'

Casaubon looked. Where the square should be, that here
was golden grass and thick tree ferns, a basalt statue stood.
The light slid down its carved flanks like honey, shining on
massive wings, and curled beard, and open yellow eyes. The
ground shook to its tread. A great cloud of bees rose up and
swarmed joyously round its glistening ringlets, with a hum that
deafened Casaubon.

The dark man moved to stand in front of Casaubon.

'O Thou, greatest among the Great, Thou whose name is
written in the ragged stars, Thou who hast for Thy province all
fruitfulness, all strength, all sweetness; O Thou for whom the
silt-rivers flood their blessing to the fields, Thou of majesty and
power –'

The Lord-Architect saw how his pale blue eyes glittered.

'O Thou to Whom of old my prayers have been addressed,
Thou journey and destination; O Thou Who Standeth at the
crossroads; Thou Who art my desire and my joy and my
subject of praise; hear Thy servant and forbear to take that life
which we owe Thee!'

Tree ferns tumbled, lashed aside. The swarms of bees rose
up into the gold air like mica-flakes. One paw lifted. It came
down, crushing tree ferns and vines. The full lips opened a
fraction. Casaubon scented something, a warm breath that had
a ripe tang in it, like carrion left in the midday heat.

'Great Architect! Is *that* what she was calling?' Casaubon
jerked his head, indicating the woman they had left in the
hammock.

A young man stood and left the feast. He held up honey-
sticky hands. The great winged being halted, one forepaw
raised, and the stone-crowned head bowed until the yellow eyes
perceived the small figure before it.

The air shimmered and sang.

It was as if the young man became invisible to the feasters; they turned away, laughing; and suddenly the temperature soared so that sweat sprang out on the Lord-Architect's face, and he saw Al-Iskandariya's intense gaze falter as the winged watcher reared up and back, wings furling out, knocking aside vines and flowers, to rustle closed again about itself and the young man.

The air sang like cracked glass. A drop of blood fell to the rich grass.

Its wings unfurled. It was alone.

Al-Iskandariya gripped Casaubon's arm. 'It is a star-daemon, a *power*, it has a Name visible in the celestial sphere these six-and-twenty thousand years! Lord Casaubon, *this* is what makes promises to your citizens and lures them onto this plane. Think what we might do now! If we compel it with incantations and diagrams –'

'Compel my great hairy black arsehole! Let these pox-rotted fools stay and be prey to it,' Casaubon advised. 'I'm going to get to the Garden if it kills both of us.'

A few minutes later, red-faced, panting in the forest heat and still running, the Lord-Architect realized that they could not begin to outdistance the winged watcher's slow pacing.

Al-Iskandariya gasped, 'It is – herding us – where it wants us to go.'

'The Lords of the Shining Paths,' Tabitha Parry said, her eyes screwed up against the brilliance of sun on snow. She shook her head. 'The Lord of Winter . . . is there a Summer Lord, too, and a Moon Lord, and an Ocean Lord, as history says?'

'Wouldn't be at all surprised,' Janou grunted.

Voices shouted, louder now, as Janou and Chancellor Parry picked a way up the ice-covered steps.

Before them, the winged watcher paced on.

The Miracle Garden lay under a cover of white. Snow choked the sundials, froze up the fountains, silenced the automata. mata.

A young man and a woman ran past, kicking up scuffs of snow with their bare feet as casually as if it were grass-cuttings. One tagged the other; they collapsed, laughing and rolling in the snow. The girl's eyes were purple-dark with malnutrition. The boy was thin, and the flower-scabs of the plague dotted his face. They were laughing too hard now to run.

'You!' Tabitha Parry snapped. Neither looked at her.

Two women and a child sat by a snow-cloaked sundial. They were cramming their mouths with fruit, fruit as transparent as glass; that when Janou bent to touch it, was cold and ice. The women fed each other quarters of ice-apples and ice-tangerines. One gave the baby an ice-cherry.

Parry shivered.

'Can't you almost hear it?' she appealed to Janou.

An old woman played a pipe. Her mean, thin face transformed, she played music they could only guess at.

Janou's foot tapped on the snow, seeking that silent rhythm and failing. She moved to stand directly in front of the old woman, and was rewarded with a halt in the silent music and an absent-minded smile.

'Don't speak to them,' Parry begged. 'We might . . . join them?'

Janou grabbed the Chancellor's arm and tucked it under her own. 'Not us! It'll have different lures for us. See you, we'll follow it, and plan according to what we see.'

Men broke off from drinking when the winged watcher padded towards them. They took up a kind of running game, with snow-vines and snow-flowers, that ended when they threw the vines over the winged watcher's back in pale festoons. Laughing, they desisted. The watcher shook blue-black wings, and paced on, snow-crowned.

When the men looked at the Chancellor, their gaze never altered.

The winged watcher led them past topiary mazes, marble pools and waterfalls thick with ice. Janou began to limp. She halted with Tabitha Parry at the top of a small rise.

Below, the Garden stretched on forever. White, blue-shadowed, filled with dancers whose feet never printed the snow. Crowds moved there in silent festival. There were men and women marked with plague-flower who now harvested cold fruit, and ate ice as if it dripped all the honey of summer.

'They don't feel the cold.' Janou sheathed her sword, and slapped her mottled hands together as if they were a badge of humanity. 'Do we try to bring them back?'

The Chancellor looked at her in complete incomprehension. 'Of course! They're our citizens.'

The winged watcher led them on, down the far side of the slope. Tabitha Parry recognized the place. Here, a snow-covered hedge rimmed an octagon of ground. The patterns of the knot garden showed silver on white, in ice on the snow.

This knot garden was complete. Its pattern wove in, out, under, through . . .

A bird fluttered past Janou's face. She swatted at it automatically, and then gaped when she founded herself with it clasped in her hand.

Tabitha Parry took it from the amazed girl's fingers. Light wood, carved into fluted feathers, and inside a ticking mechanism of gut and watchsprings. She raised it, let it go. It fluttered up into the frosty azure sky.

The winged watcher stepped forward.

Its vast bulk could not have been contained in the space of the knot garden: still, it seemed that the great paws trod the silver pattern, until with a flick of a wingtip and a skirl of ice, the winged watcher walked out of the world.

Janou caught her skirt up with one hand. The other held her unsheathed sword. She kicked one wool-stockinged heel against the ice, and jumped the low hedge into the knot garden.

She called back, '– a gateway between *their* planes of existence –', and was gone.

Tabitha Parry gazed around the snow-shrouded Miracle Garden. The dapper woman's face was red with exertion; her blue satin was ice- and sweat-stained. She gazed, tempted, at those who trod the ice and never felt it. Then she followed the Master-Captain Janou.

Buildings line the wide, dusty streets. Yellow grit lays heavily piled on triangular pediments, and flat roofs; and on the sides of squat pyramids, into which time has worn cracks and ridges. All the square windows are empty, dark.

Dust skirls on the humid air.

Great buildings, that stand with hieroglyph-covered frontages towering a hundred feet high, now shimmer in the heat-haze. It seems that a radiance clings to lintel and pediment and frieze, honey-coloured and expectant. Dark arches that gaped for long-dead inhabitants now, within their depths, shed sparks of static light.

Now the constellations returning to their ancient positions bring walkers into the streets. By pattern and by patience they return. They spread dark wings in their slow pacing, they turn ancient heavy-lidded eyes to the sun.

Almost unnoticed in the wide streets, four people are reunited.

They followed a winged watcher.

Janou swaggered as she walked the wide street, kicking the hem of her gown out so as not to tread on it. She slicked her hair down, but the heat made it stand up in spiky tufts. Yellow dust crusted on her lips. She grinned at the Lord-Architect.

'Got your flask? I'm thirsty!'

'This won't cure it.' He put a protective hand on the breast of his brown satin coat, that was stained with vegetable green.

Chancellor Parry complained, 'Where's the *real* City?'

The Chancellor seemed unsurprised to see Casaubon and Al-Iskandariya. Casaubon, studying her ravaged face, judged that nothing would affect the woman now, short of an apocalypse.

'And we may get that yet,' he muttered to himself.

The rat scuttled up onto his broad shoulder, and nestled against the rolls of fat at his chin. It fell to washing its spiky yellow fur with a pink tongue. The Lord-Architect gave it his finger to chew.

'We were wrong, I think, to fear a material hurt,' Al-Iskandariya said. His brilliant blue eyes were a little glazed. 'If they were material enough yet to harm us, they would have no hesitation in doing it.'

Janou skipped a step as they walked, to catch up. 'They'll *become* material. The Great Conjunction will happen. Well then. What can we do about stars? Nothing! But there must be something we can do about *them*.'

Casaubon's tree-trunk legs pounded the hard-packed earth of the street. He saw the watcher some hundred yards ahead, where streets intersected. It seemed to be the one from the summer forest.

'They've got their worlds. Why do they have to come

scratching after mine?'

Each street that they passed opened up a perspective view. Lined by vast pyramids, sarcophagi, and mausoleums; carved over with the hieroglyphics of a language aeons dead. The sun glared from a humid yellow sky.

'Even star-daemons can become corrupted, longing for the material plane of existence.' Al-Iskandariya's pace slowed at each inscription that they passed; he spelled out formulae under his breath.

'*Look!*'

Casaubon, who had taken his hand out of his pocket, held it open. The carved tiger's-eye stone rested on his fleshy palm. A purple luminosity edged it. Janou touched a finger to it. A blue-white spark singed her. Light limned the edges of the carved face: Valentine's face.

'Even in this dream-world,' the Lord-Architect demanded, 'could I find something – someone – real?'

Janou lifted one thin shoulder.

'They brought us here. Ask them what they want with us!'

They reached the junction of avenues. The winged watcher paced on, stately and slow, in company with another. This one seemed, if anything, slightly younger: the curved lips fuller and more cruel.

A little way on and, pacing the dusty avenues, came another, sleek and sinuous, whose face was beardless, and whose almond eyes were full of a slow, sweet, lazy wickedness.

'One for each sphere,' Janou said.

They came at last to a Square where great winged watchers lay, barbed tails curled around their flanks, blue-black pinions whispering in the still air. They lay in a vast circle. Between their paws, and facing the great Patriarch of the watchers, a thin, shaven-haired figure sat, cross-legged, studying something that lay on the earth.

Cuneiform clay tablets. Al-Iskandariya took a step forward, as if he ached to run and read them.

But it was Casaubon who cried, 'Valentine!', and lumbered into the circle, between the great haunches and shoulders and forepaws that made him a midget, and without looking at any of the lazy-eyed smiles, seized Valentine in a crushing embrace.

The thin woman stood on her toes to throw her arms about

Casaubon's neck; one foot hooking behind his leg, her face pressed into his shoulder. Janou grinned broadly at Tabitha Parry. Then, getting no response, she looked more closely at the Chancellor's face, and frowned to herself. Parry's eyes were fixed: the shining lenses reflecting nothing but the towering figures of the winged watchers.

'Al-Iskandariya,' she said softly, 'have you any medical skills?'

The dark man started. He took his gaze from Casaubon and Valentine.

'Are you hurt, Master-Captain?'

Janou pulled Tabitha Parry forward. 'See you, what can you do for her?'

While the girl supported her, Al-Iskandariya fixed his intense pale eyes on Parry's face. He murmured under his breath. Janou felt the rock-hardness of the woman's muscles begin to shift.

'*How did you get here?*' the Lord-Architect was demanding.

Valentine scratched at her cropped red hair. She seemed no different from that moment in the knot garden, when she had fled into thin air. She shrugged, and said:

'I saw the way through, and I took it. They teach that a near-mortal illness can give you vision. I'd been having true-dreams for days. I saw that some danger threatened you, and the City. When I saw a chance, I had to jump at it.'

Casaubon dragged out a brown kerchief and dabbed at his forehead and chins.

'*What* chance?'

The thin woman put her hands on her hips, and gazed up at the Lord-Architect. Although she was only two years older than Janou, her hair was growing out white at the temples. She stood there as if the great waiting watchers were no more than cliffs or buildings or statues.

'With the celestial conjunction that was coming up, there was *bound* to be some disaster. I had dreams of ancient ages. Too long ago for the College to know.' She caught sight of Al-Iskandariya, by Tabitha Parry, and casually saluted him. 'Or the Brotherhood. So, if the only way to avert the danger was to know how it was averted *before*, and if that knowledge was on this plane, then obviously when I saw the chance –'

'You shouldn't have done it!' Casaubon was reduced to sounding petulant.

'Why shouldn't I?' Valentine protested. 'There was a danger, I came here –'

'– to confront the watchers of the world in the city where they sleep out the ages,' Al-Iskandariya completed. 'Fool!'

'Oh, see you, they can't hurt you.' The ex-Master-Captain kicked the vast paw that rested in front of her. She grinned up at the idol's wicked smile. 'Takes all their energy now to hold a material form. Janou, I think I have it. You want to check my translation?'

'Show me.'

Valentine knelt by the spike-haired girl to point at cuneiform tablets. The Lord-Architect reached down, grabbed the scruff of her shirt, and pulled her to her feet.

He said, 'You scrofulous, pox-scabbed, dung-brained, irresponsible –!'

Valentine distastefully picked his pudgy hand off her shoulder. She looked at it thoughtfully, and then wrapped it in both of hers, and hugged it to her sharp-ribbed chest. She was still painfully thin.

'You didn't have to come after me,' she said. 'I can handle it.'

The noble Lord-Architect threw down the metal flask that he was holding, stamped it flat, and fetched it a kick that had it skittering off the basalt elbow of the beardless watcher.

'*Women!*'

Janou lay on her belly sorting through clay tablets. She kicked one raised foot against the other, and hummed absently. Her bare sword lay a few yards off, forgotten. She flinched at Casaubon's bellow.

'She *has* got something,' Janou protested. 'Here!'

She rolled over and tossed a clay tablet to Al-Iskandariya. He gasped, all but dropped it, and abruptly sat down on the earth and put it in front of him.

'What is it?' the Lord-Architect snapped. 'Does it help us?'

'Ah.' Valentine scratched her fox-tawny hair. She put her fists in her breeches pockets. 'As to that – you might say, they win, and we win.'

Al-Iskandariya demanded, 'Explain.'

Valentine, slightly pink, said, 'Until the Great Conjunction, more or less all they could do is lure people away – people who might have opposed them for one reason or another, when they broke through and took the City. Agitators, rabble-rousers. Architect-Lords. Chancellors.'

'Master-Captains?' Casaubon suggested pointedly.

'Oh, see you, when all the celestial spheres move into conjunction, what do *you* expect to be able to do about it? The Circle would take the City now, even if you and I had done nothing but sit in the knot garden!' Valentine threw up her dusty hands, gesturing. 'Yes, I was tricked into coming here. Yes, they lured you away after me. But they had to use genuine bait – and I know something now that *they* don't.'

Al-Iskandariya snorted. 'You claim to know how to stop a star-daemon in the fullness of its power?'

The flanks and haunches and wingtips rose up, shining ebony and blue, into the hot yellow sky. Occasionally, heavy lids blinked. The ancient smiles might have been carved in stone.

'It's to do with the influence of the stars. . . .' Valentine flopped down on hands and knees, sorting through clay tablets which she pushed at Al-Iskandariya. 'The fifth Sphere affects the heart, the sixth the limbs, the eighth the brain, the tenth the liver –'

'Yes, yes,' the dark man said.

'A Sphere affecting melancholy; and one for the sanguine of us, and those who are choleric –' Here she grinned at Janou and Casaubon in turn. 'So for each quality of the human, there is a Shining Path of influence from each celestial sphere. But, *non cogunt*, the stars don't *compel* us. And Paracelsus argues that the influence of the Lords of the Shining Paths isn't binding, or even one-sided – ah!'

Valentine seized on one tablet, the surface cracked and flaked.

'You're familiar enough with medico-magical theory, master. To even the humours in a body that suffers ill-health, talismans may be used to draw down the stars' influence.'

'And to draw bodies *into* the celestial spheres?' the Lord-Architect Casaubon tossed the tiger's-eye intaglio to Valentine. She, seeing it, was silenced. He added, 'I am not so ignorant of these matters either. It seems to me that the influence might work both ways!'

Janou jumped up. The front of her black gown was printed with dust, and she shook it vigorously. 'Let's go back. I won't speak of answers. I don't trust these watchers. They could pick it out of your head.'

Casaubon blinked. 'We can go back? So easily?'

'It's near the Great Conjunction.' Valentine nudged a cunei-form clay tablet with her boot. 'I learn fast.'

She squatted down, and drew the pattern of the knot garden in miniature in the dust. It was a different pattern, Casaubon thought.

As he bent forward to study it, the rat slid from his inner pocket, dropped to the earth, picked itself up and sneezed, and trotted, bald tail cocked high, into the dust-drawn pattern. Every yellowish spike of fur bristled. It sprang forward – and faded into the humid air.

They waited, but no blood-drop fell.

Valentine seized Casaubon's hand. Janou sheathed her abandoned sword, linked her arm through Tabitha Parry's, and reached out to the dark man. Al-Iskandariya stepped back, shaking his head.

'It'll work,' Valentine protested.

'It will,' he said. His eyes were on the discarded clay tablets, and not at all on the winged watchers. 'And if I need it, I'll find it, but I wouldn't be part of the Brotherhood if I could pass by an opportunity like this!'

One wing stretched a little, and the sun became shade.

The Lord-Architect Casaubon took Janou's free hand. And then the young Master-Captains dragged him out of the square, and out of the city where watchers wait, and out of the celestial Spheres, and into the world.

Red sand lay across the square, in knotted patterns as Valentine had drawn them.

'We're here!' Tabitha Parry threw her head back, hair flying loose from its clip, and slapped the Lord-Architect's padded shoulder. 'The City!'

Casaubon knelt down, huffing, and snapped his fat fingers. The rat scuttled back across the red sand and up his sleeve, into an inner coat pocket. He grabbed Valentine's hand and got to his feet again.

'How long before they follow us?'

'Hell!' Janou pointed.

Casaubon raised his head, expecting to see the shadow of dark wings.

Late morning sweltered. Wine and blood were splashed on the marble paving of the square, staining it black. A great crowd of people jammed the place, thick as a market-day crowd. But they were not Architect-Lords.

Casaubon kicked a litter of bottles and papers aside, and glared at the men and women who snored drunkenly under the hot sun; at children shrieking and running; at people talking or dancing or sorting through piles of goods.

'What in Hell –'

A sharp cry interrupted him.

'Another whoreson Lord!'

They had meat and drink clasped in their bare, dirty hands: priceless foodstuffs, and bottles from cellars laid down a hundred years past. A woman not far away pointed. She was tall, fair, in her fifties; and wrapped in torn silver-thread draperies. A musket rested back across her shoulder. An emaciated older man beside her yelled and pointed. Heads turned. Gangs of drunken youths began to run across the square.

Tabitha Parry, appalled, cried, 'Where are the Council Lords?'

Valentine grabbed for her sword-hilt; Janou's hand was already over it.

'Are you mad? They'll tear us to pieces!'

A crystal glass arced past Casaubon's head and shattered on the paving. The stench of wine and blood and vomit was strong. Men and women ran towards them. One shrieked Casaubon's name.

Tabitha Parry stepped forward, holding up a peremptory hand, ignoring Janou's grab at the back of her coat. A young man threw himself forward and grabbed Parry's knees, bringing both of them crashing down; and men and women in rags and torn finery piled on top, until the Chancellor was lost from sight.

Casaubon pushed Valentine and Janou behind him, in cover of his bulk. Janou brushed him off and plunged forward into the scrum, bright-eyed, screeching something that made the nearest man leap back; and Valentine struggled first to draw her sword and then to get her breath.

'Hell's red and rotten gullet!' Casaubon snarled. People came running from all directions. The screeching and yelling deafened him. '*Parry*–'

Several men grabbed Casaubon, pinioning his arms.

A hiss of steel: Valentine drew her blade.

'Lay a hand on him and lose it!' the Scholar-Soldier advised as she stepped closer to the Lord-Architect. Four ragged children flung themselves onto her, mobbing her; she struck uselessly with her bare hand.

Casaubon thrust people aside in sheer astonishment. A weight hit his back. As he went down, he saw Janou with one arm around the Chancellor; heard Valentine yell; and then the marble paving cracked across his knees. The noble Lord-Architect batted away fists that struck him.

'Hang him!'

Above, the sun rode up a tawny sky toward the meridian.

Casaubon, brown satin coat filthy and split at the seams, was dragged upright by six of his captors. His copper hair was disordered, there was a bruise under one eye, and his pudgy knuckles were skinned. Hats flew up into the warm air, faces turned to each other, grinning; and a great yell of approval split the morning.

'Make the bastard suffer!'

'*Lynch him!*'

Casaubon fixed first one and then the other of his persistent attackers with an arrogant stare.

'Master Gamaliel!' he greeted one. 'How's the pimping trade? Are you still having to cut your whores to get them to work for you? Or is he feeding them your happy-dust, Mistress Weston?'

He saw Janou staggering beside Valentine in the crowd, Tabitha Parry's arm pulled across her shoulder, holding the battered woman up on her feet. From somewhere a voice yelled:

'*And* the Chancellor!'

'Put her with the other Lords!'

Janou swung around, kicking out the hem of her black

dress.

''Ware the Invisible College –!'

A snarl of contempt answered her, but no one moved to challenge the Scholar-Soldiers.

All the silk banners of the Moon-hall had been dragged out to make cloaks for the people, trodden underfoot and filthy. Silver-thread embroidery and seed-pearl decoration glinted in the sun. Bottles went from hand to hand. The great City square was packed full, people jammed together in the stink of sweat and alcohol and sun.

'We'll hold a *trial!*' a young man yelled.

'Trial?' Casaubon yelped. The men and women who consti-tuted themselves his impromptu jury yelled insults at the Lord-Architect. 'This is frivolous! You expect to try *me?*'

The crowd parted and he saw a group of battered men and women standing with their wrists tied and ankles hobbled, and he recognized the faces and satin coats of the Council of Archi-tect-Lords.

'Is that serious enough for you?' a ragged woman asked.

Under the plague-hot and yellow sky, between the white marble facades of palaces, people stood or sat or stamped or yelled. One or two heaved up cobble-stones to throw. Dust swirled in the hot air. Makeshift galleries had been built up from benches, thrown out of palace windows; and men and women clung to precarious balances on slender mahogany and oak posts.

Casaubon sniffed, and thrust his hands into his deep pockets, and nodded casually to the bruised and filthy assembled Lords.

'See what happens,' he grunted, 'when I leave you alone for five minutes?'

In the centre of the makeshift amphitheatre, backed by the great white marble crest of the Sea Gate, twelve figures stood waiting. Robed in torn, richly-embroidered draperies; scarlet and gold and azure in the noon sunlight. Casaubon could make out nothing of their faces.

The twelfth figure turned to face the Lord-Architect. The nearby people fell silent.

It slid the cloth back from its body.

A sudden stench made the Lord-Architect gag. He gasped, tears running, and leaned forward to vomit; and when he straightened up there was utter silence. Casaubon stared, not wiping his dripping chins.

A ragged, naked figure stood before him.

It had the rotten fragments of skin or cerements still clinging to its bones. It dripped, and stank. White bone shone out through the liquid corruption of its body. Tufts of black hair clung to its skull. It was putrifying, crawling with white grubs that fell from its eye-sockets. And resting around its skeletal neck, the metal sinking into the dead-living flesh, was a collar of iron, from which hung a cuneiform-marked tablet.

All the Lord-Architect Casaubon could think of was what Al-Iskandariya had said: *I do not know who they are. Or what they are. Whatever they are now, they were alive, last, six-and-twenty thousand years ago.*

Lost in the crowd, Valentine's voice came clearly:

'We're too late – the Circle have already come together.'

A man and a woman came forward from the crowd, eyes glittering, lifting the torn length of richly-embroidered scarlet cloth. What had once been a woman or a man lifted its rotting head to receive it as cowl and robe. The stench did not abate.

'*He is not yours to have. He is a sacrifice that will ease the accession to this earth of the Lords of the Shining Paths.*'

A chill went across the square. Some quality of the light altered. Those people nearest – the ones who neither drank nor celebrated nor rioted – murmured, almost with approval, as the edge of the sun's white disc was bitten into. As a solar eclipse began.

'*Hurry. It is almost noon.*'

An anonymous voice protested, 'But he was ours!'

The cowled figure raised its head. '*Bring him.*'

Four of the heavier River-quarter men hustled the Lord-Architect towards the centre of the makeshift amphitheatre.

Most of the crowd – men and women drunk, asleep, love-making, or deep in their own talk – simply did not see. But Casaubon saw an eddy of movement, heard one choked-off scream, and knew that within a few moments he and this abomination would be the focus of noon and the eclipse.

They thrust him, staggering a few paces, towards the circle of Twelve.

'Damn you!' Casaubon yelled. 'You shouldn't even be able

to enter the City! I've spent thirty years constructing orders and harmonies and just proportions –'

'Not in the lower city,' several voices shouted.

He glanced round. Valentine, white with exhaustion, had sunk to one knee, swordpoint resting on the marble paving, supporting herself on the swordhilt. He saw Janou slip away into the mass of people. She didn't return. The Chancellor was being thrust in with the other Architect-Lords.

Casaubon turned belligerently back to the hooded figures. 'Those are my citizens you've been luring off into your private kingdoms, and I want them back – and I want them back *now*.'

One figure spoke, so softly that Casaubon found himself almost bending nearer to hear it.

'We are they who once ruled, in aeons past; we have tarried,' the figure said, 'until the stars returned again. Now will we summon our ancient Masters –'

'Ancient dog-turds,' Casaubon muttered.

The other eleven figures began to cross and re-cross the square before the great Sea Gate. Where they passed, their skeletal feet tracked a pattern in the dust.

The eclipse moved to the full. A white corona sprang out in fire around the ebony disc of the sun, the eye of the sky. The stars of the Great Conjunction began to become visible in the darkened noon sky. Great shapes became implicit in the air; imminent in the shapes of the wind.

'We will give you one chance,' it went on. 'If these try you they will tear you to pieces. We will save you, if you worship us.'

'Worship you?' the Lord-Architect Casaubon said, 'I wouldn't wipe my arse with you!'

'It will not be easy, when our Masters return. They will wreak bloody havoc with their panic terror. Will you have half your citizens crushed, maimed, even killed?'

The figure leaned closer. The air that came off it was chill as a mausoleum.

'It may make the panic a little less dangerous if they see you worship us. It will prepare them. Give your citizens an example, noble Lord. Calm them before they trample each other to death.'

Light crept like honey down the frozen marble breakers of the Sea Gate. Within its Palladian columns the air shivered in a

probability of shapes. Stars burned in the gold-brown sky.
There came the rustle of vast wings.

The Lord-Architect felt silence lapping out into the square
like ripples from a stone. Faces whitened. A dropped bottle
smashed, glass skittering across the marble; and with it rose
voices, protesting, vehement, tense to breaking.

Casaubon took his ham-hands out of his pockets. He spread
his arms in appeal, half-turning to face the people, and raised
his own voice over theirs:

'You can't expect a Lord-Architect to bow down to this
filth!'

'*Thief in satin!*' The old cry came from somewhere high up
on the ricketty, makeshift galleries.

Someone laughed. To the Lord-Architect's strained ears, the
voice was Janou's.

Casaubon scratched at his copper hair, tugged his dirty satin
coat straight, and flung out one arm to the men and women
clinging to the upturned benches.

'My noble citizens, I appeal to you –'

'Now it's *noble!*'

'Get down and beg for your life, *noble* Lord!'

A ripple of laughter went across the galleries. Those people
nearest the Lord-Architect did not smile. One went to speak
urgently with the unrobed figure, and Casaubon saw the
woman point back at him in unmistakable warning, and then
smack her fist emphatically into her palm.

He took a pace towards the crowd, and then made an undignified skip to one side as a lump of dung shied past his head.
The yellowing ruffle at his neck had come untied again. Jeers
sounded louder now: people's attention not on the livid sky or
the Sea Gate, but on the Lord-Architect.

'Would you have me to beg?'

A roar went up. Two or three youths collapsed a lower
bench, and came up laughing from the wreckage; a whole gang
of children in River-quarter's rags began to jump up and down
and jeer. By the Sea Gate, the hooded figures moved in their
minuet, tracing a pattern that was almost complete.

The noble Lord-Architect lumbered round to face the half-
robed skeletal figure. He threw out his fat arms, palms
upturned; and then fell down on his knees, so heavily that the

ground shook. He clasped his hands together. '*Mercy!*'

The men and women nearest to the Sea Gate roared. Crowds were pressing in now, as the news spread. They yelled as they ran, and caught the sides of makeshift benches and galleries, and hauled themselves up to stare at this spectacle.

Casaubon threw himself prostrate in front of the hooded figure, full length, arms outstretched. Keeping his head down, he wriggled awkwardly forward a few inches.

'Mercy!' he yelped, into the cold marble on which his bulk rested; and then hid his face in his pillowy arms. Something solid bounced off his left buttock, and he muttered; and tried to keep the tension out of his prone body.

The woman wrapped in silver draperies yelled, 'Oh, see you, that's our noble Lord-Architect – dignified to the last!'

Casaubon grinned into his muffling arms.

'Let's keep him as a clown –'

The scarlet-robed figure paced forward. In that crepuscular light, it seemed a blackness on the earth, putrid and shifting. It spoke, a hissing sound that cut through the crowd's laughter:

'*Casaubon is condemned to death. You others, and his whore, and his Chancellor, may live and think yourselves fortunate to serve our Masters.*'

The arctic silence chilled. Only the summer wind blew, and it did not warm: it carried the scent of carrion.

'*Execute the Lord Casaubon.*'

It took all of the Lord-Architect Casaubon's willpower to stay prostrate.

The Scholar-Soldier Valentine stood up, at the front edge of the crowd. She glanced round in the strange eclipse-light. Then, she abruptly reversed her grip on her swordhilt, and handed the blade to the man nearest her.

Valentine walked out into the open space before the Sea Gate. Once, she hesitated between step and step. Then the narrow shoulders straightened, and she walked forward to stand beside the prone body of the Lord-Architect, and fix her gaze on the glistening faces of the Circle.

'If you kill him, you'll have to kill me too.'

The men and women on the galleries murmured. One voice yelled approval, was abruptly silenced. Another shouted, 'Kill him then!' There was a confused surge in the space before the

Sea Gate.

A scuffle broke out near the captive Council Lords. A woman kicked and gouged her way out of the crowd and ran forward.

Tabitha Parry, one sleeve missing from her satin coat, hair falling in rat-tails, clenched gloveless fists and planted her feet either side of the prone legs of the Lord-Architect.

'Come on, then!' she yelled, 'come on, then, try it, why don't you!'

The emaciated man with the musket laughed so hard that he fell over. He sat sprawled on the marble, pointing, robbed of speech and breath.

The marble columns and statues of the Sea Gate grew stark, livid white. A sky of brown shadows clustered over it. Thunderously, in the blood, came the beat of wings. The Circle ceased their pacing. They stood in their ragged, bright finery; in the shadow of the eclipse.

At the laughter, one turned a glistening face to the people of the City. Valentine and Tabitha Parry stood, tiny defiant figures at the front of the crowd.

From somewhere far back, a young woman's voice called across the silence.

'Who gave *you* the right to kill him? He's ours!'

'Ours!'

'*It is noon!*'

Casaubon attempted to get to his feet, but his knee bent, suddenly, unable to take any weight, and he sat down again on the marble paving.

Because there was time for nothing else, he reached up and enfolded Valentine's narrow hand in his immense one, and pulled her down beside him. She threw an arm round his neck, the other across his mountain-belly.

Mouth to his ear, she said, 'It may have worked –'

The marble paving-stones of the square shook. A man fell, sprawling across Casaubon's legs, with a girl on top of him, pushing the Lord-Architect over; and the light shifted from brown to yellow to brilliance.

As if they were doors and sockets sliding into place, the interlocking Spheres reach conjunction. All shining paths lead now to the material plane of existence. As carefully, as delicately, as most fragile as if they created spun glass, the Lords of Celestial Power begin to make their selves upon the material Earth.

Sunlight shone out of the Sea Gate.

They came in slow procession, greater here than in their own spheres, towering so high that it was not clear how they passed through the Gate, great wings raised up and blotting the stars from the sky. The vast leonine bodies trod the earth, leaving with each step of hind- and forepaws a deeper imprint. They came, the Lords of the Shining Paths: the Power of the Wild Land, the Power of the Thrones of Light, the Power of the Night of Time . . .

Valentine stared up at vast human faces, at hooded eyes that opened with new appetites, at full lips that slid into lazy, sweet, wicked smiles, to see what they now saw.

'*It is noon!*'

On her knees beside Casaubon, she looked back from that split-second vision. The River-quarter crowd were shouting. Some protested, one fired a musket; children shrieked. Then the front of the crowd surged forward.

'He's ours!'

Valentine put up her hands instinctively, buffeted from side to side. An elbow knocked her, she braced herself, and someone's hand grabbed her arm and hauled her upright. The man, a stranger, grinned. The men and women of the lower city shoved and pushed round Valentine and Tabitha Parry and Casaubon in a tight, protective group.

'*It is noon . . .!*'

'Who gave you the right to tell us what to do?' a woman yelled.

'We had enough of that with the Architect-Lords!'

As if this were the hinge upon which they turned, all things seemed to wait.

Valentine, heart hammering, held fear and awe in effortless check, as if she balanced in some realm where control and abandon were identical. She rested one foot back so that it touched Casaubon, where he lay. 'As above, so below. They influence us, *and we influence them.*'

Tabitha Parry's mouth hung open. She shoved the filthy

hair back from her face as she looked up. In an instant of stricken terror, she backed up against the close-pressed bodies of the city people. One man instinctively gripped her shoulder; a child clung to her ripped coat. Tabitha Parry stared up from amongst their awed, ambiguous, quixotic protection – and then she smiled. Gazing over the heads of the people in the square, Architect-Lords and citizens, only staring up at the Powers as they paced into the world.

She said, in wonder and joy, 'But why didn't I realize –!'

Layers of shadow lifted from the world.

The unstained sun, first crescent, then half, then fully itself, the star-eye of the heavens, spread a hot summer light over the square and the city.

Something cold that had been growing in Valentine's blood winked out like an extinguished fuse. She began to laugh.

Some of the people behind her moved, and Janou reappeared, dragging behind her a bearded man who wore one of River-quarter's green arm-bands. He, with sharp gestures, ordered men and women away from the prostrate Lord-Architect.

Casaubon pushed himself up onto his elbows, and rested his chins in his hands.

Standing in front of the Sea Gate, still wrapped in the stained, foetid remnants of banners, twelve rather ordinary-looking men and women stared at each other in bewilderment. A hot, healing, ocean-scented breath touched them again as it passed.

One of the Lords of the Shining Paths lay, wings furled, massive head lowered, the tip-tilted eyes fixed on a dirty child that sat between its front paws. The child reached up and tugged the curled black ringlets of its beard.

The Lord-Architect Casaubon rolled over with all the grace and gravity of a rhino, and grinned up at the Scholar-Soldier Valentine. 'What would you do without me?'

And slowly, by ones and twos; healed, hidden, and now returning, the refugees of the celestial spheres came walking back through the Sea Gate and into the city.

They are the Lords of the Shining Paths. As they become of earth, Her waters flow back from the tenements and lanes; as they become of earth, His plague and scourge passes from the city; as they become of earth, Their power is a tide moving with Moon and Sun, with Summer and Winter.

They are the Lords of the Shining Paths; they have not the desires and ambitions of men.

All empires fallen, all cities dust that once they knew, they are content now: content to bask under this new sun, in the city of mud and marble, and to watch (with old amusement) the scurrying of humanity about their feet.

Sunlight poured down on the Miracle Garden. Valentine walked with Janou and Feliche, through the holiday crowds.

'The Lord Casaubon may be a little distressed,' Feliche warned. He took off his plumed hat and fanned his face, eyes scanning the crowd. The big man still wore River-quarter's colours, but now in a sash of office.

'Distressed?'

'I couldn't talk them out of throwing him into the Belvedere's dungeons for the night.'

Janou grinned. She had shed pack and sword for the day, and strutted all the lighter for it.

Somewhere a consort of music was playing, something with rebecks and trumpets in it. A spangle-canopied hot air balloon tugged at its moorings. The travelling fair people let a few more passengers climb on, and then released it into the summer sky. Valentine craned her neck to watch it pass over her head.

When she looked down again, dazzled and dizzy, the Lord-Architect Casaubon was standing in front of her.

His hair shone like copper wire, and every freckle was visible on his scrubbed pink skin. He wore white breeches – the top three buttons unbuttoned – and a satin coat of royal blue, embroidered with gold, left open across his ursine bulk. Insouciantly, he tugged the snowy lace at his wrists into place with be-ringed fingers.

'I thought you . . . no, never mind.' Valentine hooked her arm through his.

'Public bath-house,' the Lord-Architect explained, with an expression of distaste. 'The sooner I return to my Belvedere, the happier I'll be.'

As they left the Miracle Garden, they passed by the couchant figures of winged watchers – closed eyelids raised to the sun, sable wings a little stretched, inhaling the material scents of dust and summer. Young men and women particularly, under Janou's age, congregated in the watchers' shadows to argue and drink and debate over the occasional gnomic answer that a Lord of the Shining Paths might give.

'I begin to understand,' Feliche said. 'I think. If there is so intimate a connection between us and the Spheres, that even flesh and blood is affected, it was wittily concluded to suppose that we equally affect *their* nature. But – if you'd not been able to change the temper of the people in the square?'

'Received with terror, they'd have been malevolent, as they were six-and-twenty thousand years ago.' Valentine glanced at Janou for confirmation. 'The clay tablets – what was written there was in a language much too young for the Lords of the Shining Paths to understand. It said, *as they are received, so will their nature be.* From that, I guessed.'

'From that,' the Lord-Architect Casaubon announced, '*I* improvised.'

Janou whooped. 'Oh, see you, as if you know anything about it!'

'A man who is unacquainted with the workings of celestial Spheres could not begin to build a Miracle Garden, which,' Casaubon added, 'you seem to be making remarkably free with.'

'They're public gardens now.' Feliche paused on the marble steps going down into the square, looking back up at the Lord-Architect's massive frame, in gold and blue against the summer clouds. The fat man offered a ringed hand to the Scholar-Soldier Valentine. Janou walked down the marble balustrade, balancing barefoot.

'Given your services to the republic,' Feliche said, 'we thought we might omit your sentence of execution.'

Casaubon's face crimsoned.

'*What* republic?'

'This one,' the Scholar-Soldier Janou advised him. She jumped down from the balustrade into the square.

'This is ludicrous!' Casaubon grunted. 'See you, where's my Chancellor Parry?'

'You mean Senator Parry.'

'*I do not!*' He came to a halt, chins quivering with what Janou took to be outrage. 'Tabitha *Parry's* one of your anarchist council now? Great Architect! what next –'

He stopped, staring at the Belvedere as they came up to that building.

The great doors were flung wide: people walking in unhindered. The palace's many ornamented windows and columned galleries now had mattresses and sheets hanging out over their ledges, airing in the sun.

Casaubon looked up at the patched cloth, bright and faded colours; and heard voices drifting down. Snatches of conversation came from each of the large halls. A sackbut was being played, rather badly, in an upper chamber; and somewhere someone was cooking cabbage.

He sat down heavily on the Belvedere's entrance-steps.

'This is unfair!'

A woman going into the building heard him, and paused to squint at his face. She had rough, reddened hands, and brown hair with violet ribbons threaded through it.

After a moment she approached him, almost curtseyed, and then stopped herself.

'Did it ever occur to you, noble Lord, to wonder who does your washing?'

Casaubon lifted his head and looked at her in bewilderment. 'My *washing?*'

'I do. Did. My name is Tybba,' she said, folding her arms. 'If I'd ever had the price of that coat – even of the *lace* on it – then my Corran would be alive today to see all this.'

Casaubon put one fat hand down, and heaved himself up onto his feet. He opened his mouth to reply, and then said nothing. He took her hand and turned it palm-upwards. As if he could read a past in her rough skin.

Valentine turned away from watching Casaubon when Janou spoke:

'Thought it would be so easy. Giving up the sword and scroll.'

She was looking across at Feliche, and his Senate's sash of office that now replaced the embroidered cloth of the travelling fair.

Valentine looked down at her hands, that had on the right middle finger the callous that comes from holding a pen, and on the left palm the hardened pads of the long-time duellist. 'Yes. So did I.'

'Oh but the road – you miss the road?' Janou smoothed down her spiked hair. 'He actually asked me why Al-Iskandar-iya stayed behind!'

Valentine lifted narrow, bony shoulders in a shrug. 'I know why. *You* know it. But do they?'

Janou had her eyes still on Feliche's bearded face as the big man stooped, seriously, to talk to Tabitha Parry. The dapper woman was neat, now, in ruffled shirt and breeches, with a green sash round her waist. She was pointing at Casaubon, seeming to protest violently something Feliche had said.

'Oh, see you, Valentine, if I go, I'll be back soon enough! Who knows how long these watchers will stay, or what will come of it? They're not *tame*. The City won't do without Scho-lar-Soldiers for long.'

'But she is an Architect-Lord's Lady,' Feliche spoke to Janou as he rejoined them. 'Valentine, you'd better get him out of the City before they forget his part in saving it, and remember the sedition-trials in the Moon-hall.'

'You think he'll go, being Lord here all his life, and the Miracle Garden being here besides?'

Valentine drew a deep breath. The sun was hot on her close-cropped hair, and she felt the shade of the Belvedere welcome on her skin as she walked into it. The Lord-Architect was sitting on the marble steps, outside what had once been his home. She turned to look back across the thronged square, and the white stone under the summer sky.

As if it stood sentinel on the unbroken paving, a Lord of the Shining Paths lay under the carved crest of the Sea Gate.

Casaubon raised his head. 'I spoke to the Lord – the ex-Lord – Lindley, when I went this morning to borrow a shirt and coat. It isn't everyone can lend me clothes . . .'

Valentine sat down on the steps behind him, just able to lean forward and loop her arms around his neck. She made a warn-ing noise in her throat.

'However – to omit detail – he told me something of note.' Casaubon paused. 'I think I've decided to travel.'

He felt her arms tighten slightly round his shoulders but all she said, in a sardonic tone, was, 'That's remarkably wise. Prudent, even.'

The Lord-Architect looked down at his ringed, plump fingers, where tiny copper hairs caught the light.

'Lindley told me there have been *no* new incidences of plague in the city – and that those sick are already recovering. He attributes it to the Lords of the Shining Paths being here, and, who knows, if we and they are so closely connected, that may be so.'

Valentine made a prompting murmur.

Casaubon continued: 'Al-Iskandariya's Brotherhood – they know something of this medical branch of the Art. I had thought . . . you see, these watchers will go, someday, and then the plague may return. If I were to go and learn that branch of the Art to do with healing, the city might have me back – that is, it might be some use my returning here. If,' he said, 'you could bear to travel with me?'

The thin woman vaulted down the steps to stand in front of him. He gazed up at her flushed face, and the greying hair that travelling for the Invisible College had already put at her temples.

'I should not ask –'

'*Travel*, and with us not left a copper penny by this new Senate, and likely they'll be hunting us for jail when they remember who you are, and never mind that it's cold season in two months, and no one between here and the coast to give us refuge, because the Invisible College won't favour an Architect-Lord's Lady, and no idea in the world where to find this Brotherhood? I wouldn't,' Valentine said, 'miss it and you know it!'

Janou heard Casaubon's shout, but by the time she spun round, they were walking decorously across the square towards her: Master-Captain Valentine with hands deep in pockets, and the ex-Lord-Architect reaching up to feed a scrap of something dubious to the white rat that rode his satin shoulder.